"Jenna, some advice?"

She faced him. "Yes, please."

"Keep loving the girls, just the way you are. They'll always remember your love."

Her throat went dry as tears misted in her eyes. "I can do that."

Wyatt reached out to run a finger over her cheek, catching a teardrop. His gaze held hers, dark in the dim light.

"Then you're miles ahead."

The foyer suddenly seemed cramped. The air heated. They stood toe to toe, so close she could feel his warm breath on her skin. His firm fingers circled her arms, drew her closer. He lowered his head, but neither of them made the next move.

Unable to stand the suspense any longer, she stood on tiptoe to brush her lips over his.

D1176955

Dear Reader,

Losing a loved one is always heart wrenching. Losing a child, a much deeper pain.

Wyatt Hamilton thought he lost it all after his son died and his wife left him. Getting through each hopeless day became a major task...until Jenna Monroe comes into his life.

Jenna understands the pain of losing someone close, but also knows hope gives us the strength to carry on with life. Wyatt is drawn to that inner strength, to the promise of hope, and so begins a new chapter for both Jenna and Wyatt.

Of course, the road to love is never easy, but watching two people take a chance on love is exactly why we read romance novels. Overcoming obstacles and shake-ups in our lives is so much better with someone by our side, sharing the load and making the path easier to bear. Hope and love go hand in hand, and I believe that's why we enjoy romance stories.

Once again, I invite you back to Cypress Pointe. There's never a dull moment in this town. Spend a few hours meeting new characters, catching up with old friends and finding new surprises. Thankfully the journey to love is never dull. Enjoy the ride!

Tara Randel

HEARTWARMING

Honeysuckle Bride

—

Tara Randel

H **HARLEQUIN**® HEARTWARMING™

If you purchased this book without a cover you should be aware that this book is stolen property. It was reported as "unsold and destroyed" to the publisher, and neither the author nor the publisher has received any payment for this "stripped book."

Recycling programs
for this product may
not exist in your area.

ISBN-13: 978-0-373-36704-7

Honeysuckle Bride

Copyright © 2014 by Tara Spicer

All rights reserved. Except for use in any review, the reproduction or utilization of this work in whole or in part in any form by any electronic, mechanical or other means, now known or hereinafter invented, including xerography, photocopying and recording, or in any information storage or retrieval system, is forbidden without the written permission of the publisher, Harlequin Enterprises Limited, 225 Duncan Mill Road, Don Mills, Ontario, Canada M3B 3K9.

This is a work of fiction. Names, characters, places and incidents are either the product of the author's imagination or are used fictitiously, and any resemblance to actual persons, living or dead, business establishments, events or locales is entirely coincidental.

This edition published by arrangement with Harlequin Books S.A.

For questions and comments about the quality of this book, please contact us at CustomerService@Harlequin.com.

® and TM are trademarks of Harlequin Enterprises Limited or its corporate affiliates. Trademarks indicated with ® are registered in the United States Patent and Trademark Office, the Canadian Intellectual Property Office and in other countries.

HARLEQUIN®

Printed in U.S.A.

www.Harlequin.com

TARA RANDEL

has enjoyed a lifelong love of books, especially romance, so it came as no surprise when she began writing with the dream of becoming published. Family values, a bit of mystery and, of course, love and romance are her favorite themes, because she believes love is the greatest gift of all. Tara lives on the west coast of Florida, where gorgeous sunsets and beautiful weather inspire the creation of heartwarming stories. This is her third book for Harlequin Heartwarming.

Also by Tara Randel

HARLEQUIN HEARTWARMING

To my dear friend Sheri H. Thanks for the many chats over the years and your support for my books. During the time I needed to lean on you most, you were there. Thanks will never be enough.

CHAPTER ONE

"STAY CLOSE BY," Jenna Monroe called out to her wards frolicking in the ankle-deep surf. Seated on an old beach blanket on the section of dry sand butting up to the water, she had a clear view of the twin girls. Tropical Storm Harry had passed through a few days earlier, leaving the weather unsettled. The forecast today called for patchy sunshine to break through the cloud cover and overall conditions slowly returning to normal.

The two scamps insisted they knew how to swim, but Jenna hadn't lived with the ten-year-olds long enough to trust their credibility. Despite the fact that Jenna had known them since birth, she wasn't up to speed on every detail of their lives. Still, swimming seemed to be big on their favorites list. After three days of unpacking and staying indoors due to rain and gusty wind, the girls had begged to come to the beach. Jenna agreed because they all could use a dose of fresh air. In reality, they needed so much more than that, but for now, the beach would have to do.

Her good friend Nealy Grainger, whom she'd met and worked with in LA, had recently moved back to Florida. Jenna and the girls had needed a change of scenery and at Nealy's suggestion, packed up and made the move from LA to Cypress Pointe. It had been exhausting, mainly because it happened so quickly. Digging her toes in the damp sand, Jenna leaned back on her elbows and took a breath. The first in months, it seemed. One minute she'd been busy filming *Jenna's Cozy Cooking* and making guest appearances as a television chef on various daytime talk shows, the next she'd been listening to the horrible phone call informing her of the death of her best friend, Carrie.

Right on the heels of that devastating news came the reading of the will, when Jenna learned she had custody of the twins since their father had signed away his rights after their birth. Had it only been six months ago? What a whirlwind. She still couldn't get a handle on all the life-changing events. Settling in to this new chapter of her life would take time, but she'd make it work, for Carrie's legacy and the girls' future.

Keeping an eagle eye on Bridget and Abigail, Abby for short, proved a challenge as they darted in and out of the rolling, thigh-high waves. Jenna had always been a stickler for safety, but with custody of two young girls, her untapped maternal instincts materialized daily.

"Aren't you coming in?" Abby yelled as Bridget waved her arm in invitation.

"In a minute," Jenna answered, wiggling her toes in the cool sand.

Giggles resounded over the surf. There hadn't been a free moment since they arrived in town a few days earlier. The cross-country move had been taxing and she took advantage of this rare opportunity to clear her mind. The closest they'd come to the beach was when they'd cruised by the public access before arriving at the rental house. First chore, unpacking, then registering for school. Clothes shopping had been slated next, but was interrupted by the tropical storm, which kept them inside and going stir-crazy. When the girls double-teamed her this afternoon, coming up with every reason imaginable to hit the beach, Jenna hadn't argued. She'd been so busy with her career, then settling in with the girls, she couldn't remember the last time she took time to play. Besides, they all needed to work off their excess energy.

The beach here in Cypress Pointe was beautiful. Puffy clouds, rolling along in the swift air currents, swirled a murky gray in the sky, tossing Jenna's short, pixie-cut hair. Meager bursts of sunlight occasionally brightened up what started as a gloomy day. This morning, the temperature hovered in the mideighties before steadily rising to the sticky ninety-degree dog days of August. Humidity topped the charts. All part of living in Florida, Nealy assured her when Jenna complained. Just another aspect of her new life.

Going from a single, independent career woman to a new mother at twenty-nine had created a huge learning curve. Oh, she loved the girls, no doubt about it. After these months together, she couldn't imagine life without them. Still, she was plagued with doubts. Could she do this, especially while they were still grieving Carrie's sudden death? Could she love the girls as much as their mother had? Fill the void of their mother's absence? Carrie had been awesome with the girls. Could Jenna do the same?

A few other children joined the twins, probably also needing a break after being indoors for days. This would be the first chance for the girls to make friends. Jenna crossed her fingers.

As the two started moving out deeper, Jenna straightened and yelled, "Hey, come closer to the water's edge." Bridget, the more adventurous of the two, jumped about in the choppy surf. She grabbed her sister's hand and shuffled back.

Jenna let out a breath. Would her life always be like this, worrying about every little detail of her charges' lives? She thought she'd left her worries and insecurities behind once she'd aged out of the foster system. Apparently not.

Thankfully, the girls followed Jenna's command. The wave swell was nowhere near as strong as on the California coast where she grew up. For right now, insisting the girls stay in the shallow surf eased her concerns.

Rolling her shoulders, she rested on her elbows again, turning her attention to the panorama. To her left was the marina where boats bobbed in the restless waves. Maybe a nice family outing would take the girls' minds off leaving the only home they'd ever known.

To her right, far off in the distance, she could barely make out the Grand Cypress Hotel. She'd taken the girls there for dinner the first night they'd arrived in town at the urging of Nealy, whose boyfriend owned the hotel and restaurant. Jenna wanted the twins to meet the woman who suggested they move to this coastal Florida town to get away from sad memories and a certain tabloid reporter determined to make her life miserable.

Bridget ran out of the water, a bright smile on her usually serious face. "Jenna, can we build a castle?"

"Of course." She dug into the bag of beach toys she'd stopped to purchase on the way there. "Make it a princess castle," she added, handing Bridget the shovels and sand molds. The girls were in a princess phase, which meant begging for new dolls and sparkly accessories to go with them.

"Okay. Just watch how special it'll be." Bridget ran back to her sister, handing over a shovel to Abby. Soon they were both digging in the soupy sand.

A strong tug of affection squeezed Jenna's heart as she watched them play.

For weeks they'd been despondent, to the point where Jenna decided to get counseling. It had helped, even though the girls still had times when they didn't want to talk or be around other people.

High-pitched shrieks sounded as the two playfully threw sand at each other, abandoning the toys to rush back into the water. So much for the castle.

Encouraged by their carefree play, Jenna watched the girls act like children instead of the mere shadows they'd been for weeks on end. Yes, this move was good. Necessary even.

Back in LA, when she first started appearing on television, a tabloid reporter named Rod Hartley turned his attention to her when he searched for stories about rising celebrities in the entertainment industry. As tenacious as a bulldog when hunting a story, he'd discovered Jenna when the network she worked for dubbed her America's Sweetheart Chef to increase ratings.

New to the world of celebrities, and flabbergasted by the attention since she only had a cable cooking show, Jenna couldn't fathom Rod's interest. At first, she was flattered. Rod could often be charming, flirty even, but as time went by, she got a weird vibe whenever he was around.

Jenna shivered at the memory, reaching into the beach tote for the baggie filled with carrots. Nibbling on good, crunchy food tended to calm her. She dumped a few into her hand

and tossed the baggie on the towel beside her. Munching away, she continued to watch the twins while she thought about LA

For a while, Rod pretended to be a neighbor, although he was vague about where he lived, exactly. He always happened to be in the neighborhood at the same time she was, popping up every place she went. Soon, his excuses of coincidence became thin. Years spent in foster homes had sharpened her senses and her senses screamed something was seriously off with this guy.

When the girls came into her life, he became fixated on them as well. She didn't understand why until her agent uncovered the truth about him. Rod had lost his wife and children to his obsession over his career. Now that obsession included Jenna.

The final straw came when he camped in his SUV outside the office building where Jenna and the girls met a counselor for grief therapy. His exploits were already invasive enough, but this time he chased after them in the SUV as they hurried to their parked car. In their haste to get away, Abby had darted out into the road and was nearly run down by Rod as he tried to snap pictures.

His actions were a clear sign to Jenna. She

couldn't let anything like this happen again so she filed for, and won, a temporary restraining order. The girls were so badly shaken up, it was days before they would venture outside again. If Jenna hadn't needed to get to work, she would have stayed inside with them but instead called a sitter to watch them while she went to the studio.

The situation got worse when Rod drove by her apartment after receiving the legal order. Jenna was getting into her car when she noticed the SUV. She squared her shoulders, not about to let Rod see how much he'd upset her life, and glared at him.

To her dismay, he merely smiled, even as she read the anger in his eyes. "This isn't over," he'd threatened, then peeled out of the complex. Jenna sank against the car, her knees like jelly.

Her mind was so caught up in reliving that terrifying final encounter with Rod that she almost didn't notice two seagulls steadily making their way toward the bag of carrots. "Shoo." She waved her hands at the birds, startling them into flight while she tucked the food away.

After that incident with Rod, Jenna called Nealy to vent. Her friend had moved away from LA, and Jenna missed not being able to drop in on her. At some point in the conversation, Nealy suggested Jenna pack up the girls and come to Florida during the hiatus from filming her cooking show. Nealy had spoken fondly about her hometown, and gone so far as producing a list of pros in favor of moving.

Why not, Jenna thought. A change would benefit the girls greatly, and once away from LA, Jenna could decide where their future lay. If they liked Cypress Pointe enough, maybe they'd stay here for good. Within two weeks, she'd packed up and moved to the other side of the country, hoping she'd made the right choice. Jenna smiled, watching the girls dance carefree in the surf, their dark braids, so like Carrie's long, brunette hair, swinging over their shoulders. Even their smiles reminded Jenna of her best friend, adding a touch of mischief to their play. They were so like their mother when she was having a good time. This was just what they needed, to play like the children they were, not two daughters who grieved their mother who'd been killed in a freeway crash. Yes, there would still be many sorrowful days ahead, but Jenna would gladly do all the worrying and heavy emotional lifting for her best friend's children.

The girls waved at her before continuing to splash each other. Jenna laughed and waved back, getting comfortable again as she watched the girls play.

Out of the corner of her eye, a solitary figure, followed closely by a golden retriever, strolled into view. A man with his hands shoved in his shorts pockets. The breeze blew against his T-shirt, a baseball cap obscured his face. She wondered if he too had grown stir-crazy and longed to be outside. He stopped to pick something up from the sand and tossed it into the churning water. The object, a shell or rock maybe, arced high into the air and splashed with a *plink*. When the dog started into the water to retrieve the item, the man called out a sharp command. The dog barked and ran circles in the surf.

Seeing this man all alone struck a chord in Jenna. Probably because she'd spent most of her childhood by herself. She'd survived the foster system, but memories of missing her mother and wishing for a permanent home had never left her.

She shook off the negative thoughts. Today was all about getting away from sadness and enjoying themselves for a little while. Seeing the girls happy, she shoved her cares aside and gave her imagination free rein to conjure up a life for the man standing in the surf, staring into the horizon. Usually pragmatic and focused, she gave in to her fanciful musings.

Since he came from the direction of the marina, he might be a boat captain, his first day back from a round-the-world cruise. He had no family since he traveled extensively. And he had a thing for petite blonde women.

She shook her head at the flight of fancy. Right. It had been way too long since she'd been on a date. Even before she gained custody of the girls, she'd been too busy with her career for a social life. Made the mistake of falling for a man who claimed he'd loved her, only to dump her as easily as he said those three words. A mystery man held more appeal than men she met in real life.

Taking another cleansing breath, she savored the briny air and the feel of the cool sand between her toes. Calm settled over her and she closed her eyes for a moment.

Until she heard a scream. Eyes wide, she jumped up, spotting Abby at the shoreline, pointing to the water. Bridget was nowhere in sight. Freezing momentarily, Jenna came to her senses when Abby cried out again. She scrambled forward, the sand shooting out from under her feet as she sped toward the area Abby indicated. She'd just reached the little girl when a man streaked past her, running through the surf before diving into deeper water.

Jenna headed toward the waves, ready to wade, or swim, or whatever, to get to Bridget, when the mystery man emerged from the water, a coughing child in his arms. He floated to a shallower area, then stood and trudged toward land. Abby remained rigid by Jenna's side, her small hand gripping Jenna's like a vise.

The dog jumped and barked like crazy, following his master.

"Is she okay?" Jenna croaked through the fear lodged in her throat.

When the man nodded, her limbs went shaky as relief swept over her. He spoke to Bridget in a quiet voice, but Jenna couldn't make out his words. Wrapping an arm around Abby, she hugged her close before following the man to dry sand. Once there, he set Bridget down on Jenna's abandoned blanket in a gentle motion, told the dog to hush, and crouched beside her, his hands resting on small shoulders as he murmured in a low, but firm, voice. The coughing stopped, and within seconds, Bridget's whimpers turned into racking sobs.

Jenna tried to push him aside to get to the little girl, but Bridget wouldn't release her hold of the man's hand. He sent Jenna a sharp warning glance before turning his attention back to Bridget. Infuriated, she moved closer. Who was he, a stranger, to keep her from Bridget?

Only the man who saved her life, an accusing voice taunted. Angry with herself for losing sight of Bridget in the first place, she bent down to pick up the man's ball cap. Shaking off the sand, she took a step closer, intending to return it to him and take over the job of comforting Bridget. But before she could intervene, the little girl rose and launched herself into the stranger's arms.

The man fell backward to the ground, taking the brunt of the fall while he protected Bridget. As the dog began to bark again, he glanced up at her and Jenna's gaze tangled with the bluest pair of eyes she'd ever seen. A slight frown marred his forehead, but it didn't detract from his handsome face.

Abby, in tears, ran over to hug her sister. Bridget let go of the man to return her sister's hug. He rose, swiping sand from the seat of his drenched shorts before reassuring his anxious pet with a vigorous rub.

"I don't know what to say." Unnerved by

the events, Jenna's voice choked with emotion. "Thank you, Mr....?"

"Wyatt Hamilton."

She handed him his cap, which he settled on his head. An accusatory glare hardened his eyes.

Jenna felt an unwelcome flush warm her cheeks. "I would have gotten to her in time, but you moved much faster," she said, pushing past the tightness in her chest.

Wyatt looked down at the girls, then back to Jenna.

"Make sure swimming conditions are safe next time you bring the girls here," he said, his voice husky, as if seldom used. Anger punctuated his tone. "Next time you might not be so lucky." He turned on his heel, whistled for the dog and headed back in the direction of the marina.

Jenna's mouth fell open. Shock, frustration and fear weighed heavily on her shoulders.

LATER THAT NIGHT, Jenna softly closed the door to the girls' bedroom, having checked on them for the fifth time. Running her hands through her mussed hair, she walked back to the living room to rejoin Nealy, who sat on the couch waiting for her.

"Still asleep?"

"Yes." Jenna picked up her cup. Despite her still queasy stomach after the day's events, she took a sip of lukewarm tea and grimaced.

"Problem?"

"Too cool." Jenna nodded toward Nealy's cup. "Want a refill?"

"Sounds good."

They both moved to the kitchen, Jenna's motions brisk as she refilled the kettle before setting it on the burner. She reached into a canister for fresh tea bags to replace the used ones she'd just dumped, then leaned back against the counter, fighting against tears.

"What was I thinking?"

"Jenna, quit beating yourself up. Bridget is fine."

She'd managed to calm both girls down at the beach, then they'd packed up and headed home. After a quick bath and grilled cheese sandwiches, they settled onto the couch with a big bowl of popcorn to watch a favorite Disney movie. The girls stayed glued to Jenna's side until Nealy arrived later on and Jenna tucked them in for the night.

"No thanks to me. It's my job to keep the girls safe. A stranger beat me to it."

"You had no idea what would happen."

"And that's the problem. I should have been sure the girls could swim before they went near the water instead of taking their word for it."

Nealy paused before saying, "You can't second-guess yourself."

"And why not?"

"Because you'll drive yourself crazy."

Jenna's shoulders slumped. "What was Carrie thinking, leaving the girls with me?"

"She knew you would love them."

"I'm finding out that's not enough." She threw up her hands. "The only thing I know how to do is cook. Sure, they get three meals a day, but what about the rest? I've never been responsible for anyone but myself. When Carrie was alive, I visited or took the girls on a special play date every now and then. I never stopped to consider their day-to-day needs."

"I think you're getting a crash course."

She was indeed.

"It's only been six months since Carrie died and my heart still aches. She was more of a sister than a friend." Her voice hitched. "I miss her terribly."

Nealy hugged her. "I can't even imagine," she whispered.

Jenna took comfort in Nealy's presence, drinking in her support.

"Did I ever tell you how we met?" she asked as she drew back, swiping at her moist eyes.

"No." Nealy moved away, giving her some space. "I got the feeling you didn't like talking about your childhood."

"Being in the foster system—it can be tough unless you find a friend."

The kettle whistled. Jenna turned off the burner and poured steaming water in both mugs. A slight smile tugged her lips as she remembered her first meeting with Carrie.

"I'd been at this home for about six weeks when Carrie showed up. Thirteen years old with an attitude." She chuckled. "Heavy black eyeliner, a couple of piercings and a wardrobe you'd cringe at. One look from her and I figured she'd make my life miserable."

"Obviously something changed."

Jenna blew on the steaming liquid before taking a sip of tea. "She'd been there about two weeks when she got caught sneaking back in the house after curfew. We shared a room and I watched her climb out the window almost every night, but didn't say a word. Our foster mother, Mrs. Thomas, wanted an explanation, and much to my surprise, Carrie froze. Couldn't think of a thing to say. What happened to the smart aleck I lived with?

"Feeling bad for her, I told Mrs. Thomas, who really wasn't so bad, just overwhelmed, that I'd forgotten my homework at a friend's house and Carrie offered to get it for me. I'm not sure she believed my story but she let it slide. After she left us alone, Carrie demanded to know why I'd stood up for her. I couldn't tell her that my heart went out to this brash girl who'd finally showed a vulnerable side, so I said I did it so she'd owe me a favor. Surprised, because I usually stayed away from conflict, and impressed that I'd stood up for her, especially for a price, she walked over to me and held her fist in the air. I finally figured out she wanted a fist bump. It was a bonding moment for us."

After that, they'd slowly moved from reluctant allies to true friends. Made wonderful plans for what their lives would become once they aged out of the foster system. For the most part, they'd achieved their dreams, until an accident tore Carrie away from Jenna and the girls.

"Maybe I'm not cut out to be a mom."

She couldn't help but wonder if bad mothering was hereditary. Her own mother had an alcohol problem, which made her less than reliable. It took one visit from a caseworker to find

Jenna in a barely habitable apartment, alone, with very little food, for her to move Jenna to a new home. When her mother didn't argue or try to win her back, Jenna began her journey of moving from home to home.

Nealy snorted. "I disagree. I can't imagine those girls with anyone else."

"Is this what life is going to be like? Me making mistakes and the girls paying for them?"

"Jenna, give yourself a break. You've only lived with them for six months."

She ran a shaky hand over her brow. "Carrie and I talked about me becoming the girls' guardian, but I thought that's all it was. Talk." She shook her head. "I didn't think too much about the conversation, but Carrie took it to the next step to assure her children's future."

"And in the time you've had the girls you expect to be a perfect parent? You think you should know everything there is to know about children and never make a mistake? C'mon, the girls are ten years old. I can guarantee Carrie made mistakes, no matter how much she loved and cared for them."

Jenna straightened her shoulders. She could do this. She had to do this. "Okay, I'll admit I'm walking on shaky ground here, but you're right. It's getting better, but still, I need time to get used to being a parent."

"The first step is admitting you have a problem." Humor sparkled in Nealy's eyes as she attempted to lighten the moment.

Jenna grinned. "Oh, I could come up with quite a list."

"Hey, don't put yourself down. I think you're doing great. For a single woman busy with her career, you accepted responsibility for the girls no questions asked and embraced the idea of being a mom. Take this break you have from filming right now to grieve along with the girls. Once it's time for the television season to start up again, things will get better."

"As long as the tabloid press stays away." She shivered. "If not for the exposure from my job and attracting a crazy person, we wouldn't have left the only place the girls have ever lived."

"No, it was that one idiot reporter. If he hadn't been so intent on documenting your life—"

"Which is incredibly boring, by the way."

"—nothing would have happened. You'd still be in LA, filming your cooking show and making guest appearances on talk shows."

"Honestly, on the juicy gossip chart, I rank about minus eleven."

Nealy laughed. "Now that is totally true."

After years of trying to stay invisible in foster homes, never making waves or causing trouble, Jenna had spent her youth feeling like an outsider. Once she grew up, finished school and embarked on her career, she still found herself on the sidelines of personal relationships, with the exception of a handful of people she trusted. As her career took off, she traded obscurity for the limelight, never imagining that her life might be of interest to anyone but herself.

When Jenna gained custody of the girls, it had been a blip in the media radar since she was hardly in the same league as A-list celebrities. Until Rod. It had gotten to the point she couldn't leave the house without him in her face, asking for an exclusive interview or pictures at home with her and the girls. Only the restraining order could slow him down.

"If he hadn't gotten so obsessed with us, we would have been fine back in LA"

"Look," Nealy said. "You're here. You're safe. We have your back. Get that awful reporter out of your mind. He'll latch on to another story and forget all about you."

He had to. Jenna had based her move to Florida on that hope.

"Just be thankful Wyatt came upon you when he did."

At the mention of his name, Jenna remembered the terse man who'd come to her rescue, his act of bravery at odds with his sharp parting words. Her skin prickled with indignation. "I'm grateful for what he did, but didn't appreciate the mini lecture before he took off."

"That's Wyatt Hamilton. I've known him for a long time, but after the rough few years he's had, he's not the most…easy guy to be around."

"Understatement."

"You only talked to him for a few minutes."

"It was a long few minutes." Jenna recalled the memory. His eyes had been so intense, so judging. "Besides, I wasn't thrilled he was doing the rescuing while I stood on the beach feeling helpless. I should have been the one to save Bridget."

"C'mon, Jenna. It's not like he rushed in the water just to make you look bad."

True, logic reminded her, but his quick actions had made her feel incompetent.

"Listen, he's got a lot of baggage, so we all tend to cut him some slack," Nealy said.

Had her annoyance been so obvious? Jenna sighed. "I guess no one is immune to baggage."

"Yeah, but his is pretty horrible."

The crash of ice cubes falling from the freezer ice maker broke the silence following Nealy's statement.

"Are you going to tell me?" Jenna prodded.

"His son died about two years ago. He was only eight."

Jenna's chest tightened. "How awful." She'd just lost Carrie and the hurt was still so fresh, but to lose a child? She'd only had custody of the girls for less than a year but had known them their entire lives. How would she deal with a loss like his? She couldn't even imagine the pain he must live with every day.

"It was a boating accident," Nealy continued. "About six months later, his wife filed for divorce."

"I've heard that happens sometimes when parents lose a child, but a double whammy? No wonder he has issues."

"He's still so torn up."

"You said you've known him for a long time?"

She nodded. "Yes. Wyatt grew up here, so we were all devastated by his loss. My sister told me he disappeared right after the funeral.

About four months ago, a friend of ours, Max Sanders, met up with Wyatt and talked him into coming back. Now Wyatt captains a fishing charter boat, but I think he's only going through the motions, not really living."

"I don't know what to say. Poor guy." Jenna sipped her tea, her heart breaking for a man she didn't know. "Where does he live? I think the girls and I will bake cookies as a way of saying thank-you."

Nealy's eyes grew troubled. "I'd rethink the idea. He's kind of a loner."

"Even loners who disapprove of my parenting skills need to eat."

"Jenna's answer to all and every problem. Food."

"What can I say? It's who I am."

Jenna had discovered her love for cooking early on when she helped out in each foster home she'd lived in. In high school, she'd worked for a catering company specializing in weddings and loved it. Who knew food would turn into a career?

"Which I, for one, am happy about," Nealy said. "You're still going to make your gourmet mac and cheese for the welcome party, right?"

"Yes. You might be an event planner extraordinaire, but you can't boil water."

"We can't all be gifted in the kitchen."

"True." Jenna smiled. "Thanks for throwing a party to welcome us to Cypress Pointe. It's nice of Dane to hold the shindig at his hotel."

"Anything to show off the Grand Cypress. Of course, it does help that he's wild about me."

Jenna laughed. "I still can't believe he came to LA with you to pack up your belongings. If I hadn't seen it with my own eyes, I'd never believe just how crazy Dane is about you."

She also couldn't imagine a love that strong and found herself a bit envious.

"After being apart for so many years, we have a lot of catching up to do. And besides, he's happy to have the party for you."

"I gotta say, I thought the guest of honor only had to show up and meet her new neighbors, not bring the food."

"True for most mere mortals, but you make a mean mac and cheese. Since I've bragged about your culinary prowess nonstop since you told me you were moving to town, you can't show up empty-handed."

"Fine. Besides, you know I would have brought something even if you didn't ask."

"Yep, so why not put my order in?"

Jenna admitted that spending time with

Nealy went a long way to easing her insecurities.

Nealy glanced at her watch. "I need to get going. Will you be all right?"

"Yes. And, Nealy?"

Her friend raised her eyebrows.

"Thanks. For everything."

"Anytime." Nealy swooped in for another hug. "Actually, *all* the time now that you're here in Cypress Pointe."

Jenna's heart lifted with affection for her friend. "I hope I don't become a nuisance."

"Unlikely. Once you figure this motherhood thing out, you'll feel better."

Jenna crossed her arms over her chest, rubbed her chilly forearms. "We'll see."

"Hey, quit with the gloom and doom. You can do this."

"You're right." Jenna dropped her arms. Tilted her chin. "I can do this."

"That's my friend." Nealy walked to the front door. "Don't forget. Tomorrow night. Six. Grand Cypress Hotel."

"Got it."

Nealy's smile softened. "I promise, once you meet my family and get to know the wonderful people in Cypress Pointe, you'll be glad you came." That said, she swept out the door into the hot, humid August night.

Watching her friend get into her car and drive away, Jenna tried to take Nealy's confidence in her to heart. She could do this, right? Be a single mom? But the doubts and worries continued nagging at her. Take today, for example. As much as Wyatt's response made her angry, he was right. She had to do better.

Still, grief weighed on Jenna. As much as she tried to keep a sunny outlook for the girls, at times, the sorrow took her to her knees. Mostly in the quiet, late at night after the girls went to bed and she only had herself for company. Missing Carrie, asking why she'd been taken from them at such a young age, made it difficult for Jenna to find any kind of normalcy in her life. And it was even worse for the twins. As much as Jenna tried to console them, at times her efforts seemed ineffective. Lacking. And with two strikes against her when it came to the girls' safety, she couldn't afford any more close calls.

More unnerved than she cared to admit, Jenna marched back into the kitchen to rinse out the mugs. Resting her palms on the sink ledge, she leaned forward, staring out the window. The moon emitted a small sliver of light, barely illuminating the backyard.

Lately, the direction of her life seemed just as dark. As it had numerous times tonight, the scene at the beach flashed in her mind.

Next time you might not be so lucky.

At the memory of Wyatt's parting words, she straightened her shoulders. No way would she let his prediction come to pass.

Nealy was right. She had to stop second-guessing herself. Enough worrying over the things she couldn't control. Time to focus on what she could do. With the single-minded-ness that had gotten her through years of foster care and then advanced her career, Jenna vowed to be the best mother possible for Abby and Bridget.

CHAPTER TWO

"GUESS WHAT I have planned for today?" Jenna said at breakfast the next morning,

The girls sent each other a questioning glance. The silent twin communication freaked Jenna out. She'd probably never understand it, but whenever it happened, self-doubt twisted in her. Once again, she found herself on the outside. Unsure. Not very motherly.

"Why don't you just tell us?" Abby asked.

"Because it's a good surprise."

Bridget frowned. "You told us you don't like guessing games."

Holding back a sigh, Jenna said, "You've got me there. But for today, let's play."

"We aren't going to the beach again, are we?" Bridget asked before taking a spoonful of cereal.

"No. I think we had enough fun in the sun yesterday."

"Our new school?" Abby asked.

"No. I already registered you so we're good."

Abby pushed the cornflakes around her bowl. "Shopping. You promised we can get new stuff for school."

"I know I promised, and we will go to the mall, but you're still not close."

"I give up," Bridget informed her with a very mature sniff.

Jenna bit back a grin. Was she ten going on sixty? "So soon? We just started."

The girls stared at her.

Jenna threw up her hands. "Now I give up."

"So you'll tell us?" Abby asked with a giggle.

Despite yesterday's close call, the girls were in a cheery mood today. Most mornings the twins would hide out under the makeshift tent they'd built in the bedroom. Missing their mother, the girls sometimes refused to leave their safe place. Jenna learned from the counselor in LA that this was part of their grieving process. Back home she would have tried to coax them out of the tent with the promise of a special breakfast or plans for the day if she wasn't scheduled to film or meet with her agent. Some days her tactic worked, others not so much. Today, the girls came to the breakfast table the first time she called. A small victory in Jenna's opinion, but a victory indeed.

"You knew I'd give up if you did. No point in teasing when you aren't willing to play the game."

Bridget shrugged.

"Fine. Then here's the answer. Bridget, remember the man who pulled you out of the water yesterday?"

Bridget kept her eyes focused on her cereal bowl. "Yes," she said in a quiet tone. "He was really brave."

"Like the prince in the story you read to us," Abby piped in.

"Yes, I guess he was like a prince. Saving my beautiful princess here."

Abby giggled.

A slight grin tugged Bridget's lips.

"Anyway, I was talking to Nealy about him last night and the idea of making a thank-you gift popped into my mind."

"What are we going to make?" Abby asked.

"Cookies. Then I thought we'd deliver them in person. That will give you a chance to thank him yourself."

Jenna moved to the fridge, taking out the ingredients she needed to make a batch of cookies. "Do you know where he lives?" Abby asked.

Jenna, in mid-reach to retrieve a measuring

cup from the cabinet, glanced over her shoulder. "I'll call Nealy to find out." She brought the cup to the counter then turned to face the girls, who had grown quiet.

"What's wrong?" Jenna asked.

Bridget shot her sister a glance then lowered her eyes. "I'm sorry about what happened yesterday."

Abby, her eyes shimmering, met Jenna's. "We might not have been exactly honest about being able to swim."

Jenna rested her hip against the counter and crossed her arms over her chest. "You told me you had taken lessons."

"Well…we were going to. We never got around to it before mom…you know."

Yes, she did. How could she be angry with the girls when they were still grieving? Every day brought a new tangle of emotions. Yet as hard as it might be, Jenna had to lay down some ground rules. She walked to the table and took a seat.

"Look, girls, I know things have been hard, but you have to tell me the truth. If I had known you couldn't swim, I never would have let you in the water by yourselves. How can I take care of you unless you're completely honest?"

The girls exchanged glances again. What Jenna wouldn't give to know what was going on in their heads.

"How about we make a pact to be honest with each other?" she suggested.

Abby blinked at the tears making her eyes bright. Of the two, she showed her emotions more easily. "We miss Mommy."

"I do too." Jenna swallowed. In her own way, she understood the depth of loss the girls experienced. In her case, her mother had chosen to walk away, leaving Jenna bereft and angry. Abby and Bridget felt the same, but at least they had Jenna to turn to for comfort.

Taking a shaky breath, she said, "It's okay to miss her."

She took one of Abby's hands in hers and squeezed. Then she turned to Bridget, whose lower lip trembled. How like her to be the strong twin when her heart was breaking. Jenna drew them all together. "This is it, kiddos. We've got each other now." Turning her tone from sympathy to firm, she said, "So, the pact?"

After a hesitant moment, Abby said, "From now on we promise to tell you stuff."

Bridget didn't utter a word, the tougher nut

of the two. Not surprised, Jenna knew she'd have to keep an eye on her.

They sat holding hands for a long, drawn-out moment until Bridget shifted in her seat. Jenna released her hold, briskly rubbing her hands together as she rose. "Let's get working on our project, girls."

How many times had they made cookies together? More times than Jenna could remember. When Carrie was alive, they'd had frequent sleepovers with Jenna, which always included some kind of baking session.

The girls joined her and they worked side by side, measuring, stirring, then spooning batter on the baking sheet before sliding it into the oven. A dozen cookies later, with the final sheet in the oven, they'd finished the messy part of their task. Standing on tiptoe, Bridget turned on the faucet to fill the sink before squeezing dish detergent into the rising water. Suds materialized as Abby dropped in the batter-covered utensils.

Proud of the girls for cleaning up without her asking, Jenna said, "Hey, you two, I'll finish up. Go play."

"Are you sure?" Abby asked. "We don't mind helping."

"Yep. You've both been great, but I can take over from here."

The girls scurried from the room. As Jenna removed the last batch of cookies and turned off the oven, her cell phone rang. She glanced at the number and frowned. She didn't want to answer, but knew her agent wouldn't stop calling until she spoke to Jenna.

"Barbara. How are you?"

"Cringing at the number of appearances I have to refuse on your behalf."

Tension tightened Jenna's temples. They'd had this conversation one too many times since Jenna informed her agent she was taking time off. "And you'll have to keep refusing until the hiatus is over."

"Absence from the public eye does not make the viewer grow fonder."

"The girls are my priority. I don't know how much clearer I can make the point."

Barbara Samson had been Jenna's agent for four years. An energetic go-getter, she never heard a "no" she paid attention to. Until Carrie died, Jenna didn't have any reason to turn down work. Now that she did, Barbara was persistent about changing Jenna's mind.

Right out of culinary school, Jenna landed a job at a trendy restaurant that became a popular hangout for celebrities. At first, she was one of the minor chefs in the kitchen. She stuck it out there and eventually, her unique culinary ideas became popular with the in-crowd. When one of the local talk show hosts inquired about her, the restaurant owner quickly encouraged Jenna to be a guest on the show. He couldn't pay for better publicity.

Not exactly thrilled at first, Jenna thought long and hard before agreeing. She didn't like crowds or being the center of attention. But when she arrived on the set, she found the hosts and crew welcoming. Her nerves settled down. Soon, she went from being a guest every couple of weeks to guest shots on other shows, including a popular LA daytime talk show. Not familiar with the world of television, she asked one of the hosts for advice. The person mentioned Barbara's name. Jenna called, set up an appointment. Before she knew it, Barbara had booked her schedule tight and, eventually, landed the cooking show.

As much as Jenna appreciated those opportunities, it didn't mean she'd let the woman railroad her into any future projects until she was ready. She'd made good money and put enough away so she and the girls were financially stable until she decided her next move.

"I totally get your stand on the girls," Barbara said. "Doesn't mean you can't fly to LA or New York periodically. You know, to keep your name in front of the public. The girls don't have to travel with you."

"And I won't be separated from them. It's too soon." Barbara went quiet for a moment. As Jenna removed the cookies from the aluminum sheet to cool, she could only imagine the whirl of her agent's mind as she came up with another way to cajole Jenna.

"How about online? You can work from home."

"Right now I don't want to do anything to alert the tabloid news magazines. I won't risk it." She took a breath. "I understand you don't like it, but I'm asking you to honor my decision."

A long, melodramatic sigh came from the other end of the line. "Fine. But I can't promise I won't call if a worthwhile offer comes in."

Jenna didn't expect differently. "Just don't be upset if I turn you down."

"The one you can't resist will come and when it does, you'll be out here on the next available flight."

While Barbara had other clients, she couldn't

afford to let her main moneymaker go on hiatus, no matter how noble the reason.

"Thanks, Barbara. I do appreciate all you've done for me. Just think of my time away as a small vacation. It's not the end of our relationship."

"So, how are things going? You're settling in?"

"Yes. The girls are happy. So far I like this little town."

"Little, as in, are there any museums? Fine dining? Theaters?"

Jenna chuckled. Barbara could be a fine-arts snob. "We manage."

"I couldn't leave LA, no matter how much anyone tried to convince me otherwise."

Jenna fought the temptation to remind Barbara about the tabloid reporter making her life miserable. Jenna viewed his intrusion as a personal attack on her family. Barbara saw him as a necessity for the expansion of Jenna's career. If he tailed Barbara for any length of time, Jenna was sure the woman would change her tune.

"You're a great agent. Hopefully you'll get some new clients while I'm away."

"I've fielded a few calls."

"See. With me gone, you'll have the chance to develop your next big star."

"Yes, there is a strong possibility I can make that happen."

Which could mean Jenna would lose some interesting job opportunities, she thought with a small pang of loss, but the girls were keeping her too busy to regret her decision.

Abby dashed into the kitchen, her ponytail swinging as she grabbed two warm cookies then hightailed it back to the bedroom.

"Hey, no food in your room," Jenna called to her retreating back. The brief feeling of loss vanished as Abby disappeared. Yeah, she'd much rather be with the girls. "Listen, Barbara, I have to run. Thanks for calling."

She ended the call and then checked on the girls, who were happily playing in their room. Satisfied they were occupied by their dolls, she hurried to her room for a quick shower. Afterward, she stood before her closet wrapped in a towel, trying to decide which outfit to choose. She finally selected a denim sundress for their goodwill mission, and placed a quick call to Nealy.

Her stomach turned, nervous at the prospect of seeing Wyatt again. His parting remarks at the beach, although true, had stung.

She couldn't help but wonder how receptive he'd be when she showed up on his doorstep, cookies or no.

WYATT WALKED INTO his cottage, located within walking distance from the marina, tossing his keys on the coffee table. His golden retriever, Cruiser, followed him into the kitchen, jumping up for attention. "Down, boy."

Absently rubbing the dog's head, he poured some kibble from a twenty-pound bag into Cruiser's bowl, then pulled a glass from the shelf mounted on the wall that served as storage. He opened the fridge and poured a glass of orange juice for himself, draining it as he wandered into the small living room.

He stared out the window, at the view of the Gulf water. Before long, the familiar ache he lived with every day enveloped him.

Two years. Two long years since Jamie had died. Eighteen months since Marcie divorced him.

Since the accident, his family had been after him to talk to a professional. His older brother, Josh, moved back to Cypress Pointe with the purpose of keeping an eye on him. A useless move, but Wyatt appreciated the sentiment.

"You need to let go of the grief," Josh and the family told him. "You need to move on."

They didn't understand. If not for the unrelenting pain, he wouldn't feel anything at all. He was so far beyond numb, grief remained the only emotion alive inside him.

A boat motored by. Wyatt stepped out onto the small screened-in porch to watch its passage, running a hand over his grizzled chin. He should shave. Probably get a haircut. But didn't really give a flip.

Why had he let Max talk him into moving back to Cypress Pointe?

After aimlessly traveling the world, taking one job as yacht captain after another, he'd run into Max four months ago. A mutual Navy buddy had invited both of them to his wedding. Since Wyatt happened to be in the States at the time, he attended, hoping a reunion with old friends would help ease him out of his funk.

"You look terrible," Max greeted him at the reception.

He knew Max spoke the truth. After all, he viewed his face in the mirror every morning. Realized the shadows under his eyes and the blank expression were growing more pronounced daily. "Thanks, buddy."

Max scowled. "You can't go on like this."

"Like what? A guy grieving the loss of his family?"

"You're entitled to your grief, Wyatt, but enough is enough. There comes a point when you have to deal with the loss and try to move on."

It was all Wyatt could do to keep his temper in check. Didn't Max see it wasn't that easy? Every day was a struggle to get out of bed and survive. He knew his buddy meant well, knew Max wanted to help somehow, even if it entailed spewing tough love.

"Do you miss Cypress Pointe?" Max had asked him.

"Not particularly."

"Folks in town miss you. Your parents worry."

Like he needed more guilt. "And bringing this empty shell back to Cypress Pointe is going to make things better?"

"You need to be around people who love you. Running sure hasn't helped you heal."

Max had a point. Running had only made him more lonely. More bitter. Less than the man he wanted to be.

After thinking it over for a few days, Wyatt decided Max was right, so he moved home.

Sure, Cypress Pointe was pretty. For the

most part, people stayed out of his business. He found a job he liked. His family, thrilled to have him home again, tried to cajole him into a normal existence, as if his life hadn't been shattered beyond recognition. Friends welcomed him with open arms, inviting him to get-togethers he had no interest in attending. The thing none of them understood was that he wasn't the man he used to be. Never would be. His life had irrevocably changed the day Jamie died and he was still trying to navigate the waters of what constituted this new existence.

And so his self-imposed isolation continued.

But lately, Max had grown more vigilant in encouraging Wyatt to move out of his comfortable seclusion. Meet me for coffee. Let's go fishing. Wyatt recognized the invitations for what they were, attempts to drag Wyatt back into the land of the living. He doubted that was possible.

Yet some part of him knew he had to get out of this rut. Problem was, he didn't have the energy to pull it off. At that thought, a bitter laugh escaped him. Rut was putting it mildly. No change of location or routine would alter the truth. His son was dead and it was his fault.

So for now, running the charter fishing boat

was all he could handle. He'd go along with Max's little outings, just to keep him from nagging. Let Josh and the family think they were reaching him. Give them something positive to hold on to, even though Wyatt knew better.

Not bothering to stifle a yawn, he dropped into an Adirondack chair, kicking up his feet on an old trunk. Cruiser, who'd finished eating, flopped down beside Wyatt for a nap.

This morning he'd risen early for a scheduled charter. A group of businessmen who didn't know a fishing rod from a BB gun had been a challenge, but the guys knew how to have fun. Long hours in the sun, bright red cheeks and hungry stomachs later, he'd motored back to port. He declined their invitation to join them for lunch. He'd rather sit on the porch by himself, staring out over the calm water, than mingle and make small talk.

For fifteen minutes he savored the relative silence until the sound of chattering voices snagged his attention. A knock rattled the screen door.

Cruiser jumped up, on full alert, barking until Wyatt commanded him to calm down.

"Hello. Anyone home?" a female voice called out.

He glanced through the screen. The woman

from the beach yesterday, flanked by her two little girls, peered inside.

Beautiful green eyes stared at him. He bit back a groan and sank deeper in the chair. Mimicking the computerized tone known to all answering machine owners, he said, "No one is here right now. Just leave a message."

"That doesn't make sense," one of the girls said. "He's sitting right there."

So much for his lame attempt at humor. Man, he was rusty. "Means I'm not up for company."

"Then you should go inside and close the door," the other girl said, matter-of-factly.

How he wished he had.

"We'll only keep you a minute." The woman held up a plastic-wrapped plate. "We brought you a present."

Which meant he had to get up to let them in. Swallowing a sigh, he rose and crossed the porch, holding Cruiser by the collar as he opened the door.

"Thank you," the pretty blonde said, her light and airy tone at odds with her worried expression.

All three entered the porch, hovering near the doorway. Okay, his social skills were pretty awful right now, but the way the girls hugged the woman's side, like they were nervous, surprised him. He ran a hand over his chin, glanced down at his old T-shirt, cargo shorts and scuffed boat shoes, and grimaced.

"Sorry, I just got in from work. Haven't had a chance to clean up."

"It's okay. We won't stay long." She thrust the covered plate in his direction. "We wanted to thank you. For yesterday."

"When you pulled me out of the water," the girl on the left piped up.

As if he could have forgotten.

The woman smiled down at the child, ran her hand over her hair in an affectionate gesture before meeting his eyes again.

"My name is Jenna Monroe. These are my girls." She nodded to the one on the left. "Bridget." Then right to the girl with the ponytail. "Abby."

For the first time his mind registered the children were twins, dressed in matching white tops with a big, bold flower print on front, pink shorts and sneakers. In all the excitement yesterday, he hadn't noticed.

He glanced at their mother, wearing a flattering blue summer dress. Self-conscious, he wished he'd showered as soon as he got home.

Realizing the woman still held out the plate, he took it from her hand.

Smooth, Hamilton.

"We baked you cookies," Bridget announced.

Of course they had.

"Can we play with your dog?" asked Abby.

Cruiser, dancing in place the entire time, strained against Wyatt's hold. He looked at Jenna. "Okay with you?"

"If he's good with kids."

"The best."

"Fine."

He let go of Cruiser, who covered them with doggy kisses. The twins giggled and cooed at their new friend.

"Why don't you girls go in while your mother and I talk. There's a basket of Cruiser's toys beside the couch in the den."

The girls ran ahead, talking to Cruiser as they went.

Suddenly remembering his manners, Wyatt nodded to the porch chair. "Have a seat."

Jenna looked around. "There's only one chair."

Right. Because having only one chair discouraged visitors from staying. "I'll be right back." He hurried inside, placed the plate of cookies on the counter, grabbed a kitchen chair and returned to the porch. Jenna was settled in the Adirondack chair, looking as if she belonged there.

Her genuine smile greeted him, sending a warm rush of expectation through him. Surprised by the intensity of the long-dormant sensation, Wyatt set the chair down with a thud.

"I'm sorry for just barging in. I'd have called first, but…"

He dropped into the chair. "You don't have my number."

"I felt it was important for the girls to thank you."

Giggles and a bark sounded from the other room.

"I appreciate you rescuing Bridget, but your parting words…"

What had he said? To be honest, he was so ticked, he couldn't recall his words. All he knew was, he'd been walking along the beach, thinking about Jamie, when the urgent cries had him in the water before he could stop himself.

"The conditions probably weren't the best. I should have been right there in the water with them, but in my defense, I didn't know they couldn't swim."

He frowned. "You're their mother. Shouldn't you know?"

She waved her hand. "It's a long story. I became their guardian after their mother passed away."

"Sorry." His brow wrinkled. "You were probably upset enough without me piling on, but you should be more careful."

Her spine went stiff. "I'll decide what I should and should not do when it comes to my girls."

He noticed her cheeks had flushed pink. "Sometimes I get a little carried away, especially when it has to do with kids around water."

Her anger faded as something more troublesome crossed her face. "I understand."

He read the pity in her eyes and his stomach tightened. Here came The Conversation. Mostly he stayed away from the topic, but in light of yesterday's events, he couldn't let it go.

"You know?"

"Yes. Nealy told me. I'm so sorry for your loss."

No matter how many times he heard the platitude, it made him angry, even when he knew it came from the heart. He met Jenna's gaze. She didn't know the entire story. If she did, her empathy would most likely change to derision.

Although his social skills were rusty from lack of use, he managed to mutter, "Thanks."

An uncomfortable silence fell between them. She stood, smoothing her dress. "We won't keep you any longer."

Following her lead, he called Cruiser. The dog loped out of the house, the girls not far behind.

"He's super friendly," said the girl with a ponytail. Abby, was it?

"And he likes us," Bridget added. "Can we come back and play with him?"

"Now girls, Mr. Hamilton is busy. We can't just invite ourselves over for a visit."

Wyatt nearly laughed out loud. Busy? Not so much. "Cruiser and I like to walk the beach. If we run into you, you can play with him."

The girls hugged the dog. Cruiser basked in the attention.

"Well, we should be leaving." Jenna turned to the girls. "What did you want to tell Mr. Hamilton?"

In unison they said, "Thank you."

He nodded. "And thanks for the cookies."

She gathered the girls. They stepped through the screen door and down the steps. Before rounding the house, she stopped. "Will you be at the party tonight?"

Max had mentioned something about a party but he hadn't listened. "Party?"

"To welcome the girls and me to town."

"I hadn't planned on it."

She tilted her head, the sunlight catching the highlights in her hair, her skin glowing. An indulgent smile curved her lips, throwing him off balance and making him feel warm. "Do you like to eat?"

His mind suddenly went blank. He blinked. What was the question? Oh, yeah. Eating. "What has that got to do with anything?"

"I'm cooking. You haven't lived until you've tasted my secret mac and cheese recipe."

In the past two years, he hadn't lived much, period. Yet this petite woman showed up on his doorstep with cookies, and for a split second he was considering going to her party.

"See you at six?"

What was wrong with him? She may be pretty, her smile the best thing he'd seen in a long time, but his empty porch beckoned. "I didn't say I was coming."

A sassy grin lit her face. "You won't be able to resist." After her final volley, she disappeared from view.

Wyatt ran his hand over his chin again, shaking his head at the small smile forming on his lips.

In less than thirty minutes, Jenna had made him self-conscious about his appearance, her girls had vied for his dog's affection, and, he had to admit, he'd found her company more entertaining than anything in ages.

She was right. He couldn't resist seeing her at the party. For once, he wouldn't be hiding out at home. Alone.

CHAPTER THREE

"C'MON, GIRLS," JENNA called down the hallway from her bedroom as she fastened an earring in place. "We're running late."

She hadn't gotten used to waiting on two young girls to get ready. Always priding herself on punctuality, she'd yet to master getting the three of them dressed and out the door on time.

"Coming," Abby answered.

At the sound of the oven buzzer, Jenna hurried to the kitchen. The aroma of baking cheese met her before she entered the room. Using three different gourmet cheeses, with a bit of bacon thrown in and a topping of artisan breadcrumbs, she'd made the promised mac and cheese dish for the party. Donning a pair of oven mitts, she pulled the pan out and covered it with aluminum foil. Turning the oven off, she walked back down the hallway, stopping at the door of the girls' room. Abby was on the floor, slipping on the new sparkly sandals Jenna had bought for the occasion. Bridget sat nearby, brushing the hair on her favorite doll.

"Ready?"

"Yes," they answered in unison.

Returning to her bedroom, she picked up her purse before performing a quick scan of the space. She worried about forgetting to unplug her hair straightener or another electrical appliance, especially after a fire destroyed one of the foster homes she'd lived in. Satisfied everything was in order, she left the room.

"Front and center," she sang out.

The girls ran to the living room. Jenna smiled as she viewed their matching sundresses, Abby in pink, Bridget in purple. Jenna had pulled their shoulder-length hair into ponytails with matching bows to finish off the look.

Her heart squeezed tight. "Beautiful," she said, crouching to give them a hug.

"We're late," Bridget reminded her.

"Right." Rising, Jenna smoothed the skirt of her red, sleeveless A-line dress. She'd blown dry her hair in a breezy style, not much else to do with the short length, and added her favorite spiky sandals, which gave her petite frame some height. "Let's—"

Her cell rang again. "One minute." She hurried to the kitchen, glancing at the caller ID. Barbara. The woman's timing was impeccable. It was like she knew exactly when Jenna was in the middle of something with the girls and couldn't answer the phone. Funny how her agent's calls had never bothered her before the girls became a permanent part of her life.

"Jenna!" Bridget called.

"Coming." No time to talk now. She would speak with Barbara later.

Tossing the phone in her purse, she grabbed the handles of the mac and cheese pan and hustled the girls out to the car. Soon, they were on the road. She breathed a sigh of relief. Hopefully Nealy wouldn't be too upset with them for being tardy.

As she pulled into the parking lot of the Grand Cypress Hotel, her cell rang again. Irritated now, she parked the car before digging the phone from her purse. The caller ID showed Barbara's name. Jenna quickly pressed the talk button.

"Good grief," Barbara said by way of a greeting. "I didn't think you'd ever pick up."

"Sorry. I was driving."

"Listen, Jenna, I got a call from Kitchen Care. They want you to sign on for the commercial we discussed."

A major sponsor of Jenna's show, Kitchen Care Cookware, a large commercial-grade cookware company, was ready to release a new line of products, and they wanted Jenna as their spokesperson.

"Barbara, I can't do it right now."

"I know you're on a break, but Jenna, this is Kitchen Care."

"I understand."

A voice sounded from the backseat. "Are we getting out of the car?"

Jenna glanced over her shoulder. "Yes."

"Yes to Kitchen Care?" Barbara asked.

"No, Barbara. I have the girls in the car. Let me call you tomorrow."

"Seriously consider this, Jenna. Your decision will affect the show. And your career."

Barbara wasn't being overly dramatic. In the world of cable television, pleasing sponsors was vital to a show's longevity. "I know."

"Fine. I'll wait for your call."

"Thanks." Jenna almost hung up before a last-minute thought came to her. "Barbara, any photos or stories about me in the tabloids?"

"No. Why?"

"Just making sure." She was glad her plan to escape the annoying reporter was working.

"After the incident with Rod, I'm very careful, just as you requested."

Jenna blew out a breath. "Okay."

"Jenna," Abby called.

"I have to go, Barbara. Talk to you later."

After tapping the off button, she got the girls out of the car, picked up the warm pan and headed inside. The name of the room reserved for the party was posted in the ornate lobby.

Nealy swooped down on her as soon as she set foot in the brightly decorated banquet room. A huge Welcome banner took up one entire wall, surrounded by balloons of every shape and color. Tables were scattered about, topped with bright cloths and flower arrangements. A long table, featuring an assortment of appetizers, lined another wall, along with a station set up for drinks.

"Way to be on time," Nealy mock scolded.

"Sorry. I'm still navigating the ins and outs of getting the three of us dressed and ready to go."

Nealy took the pan from Jenna. "You're here now. I have lots of people for you to meet."

Jenna glanced around the room again. "Wow. You really went all out."

"I wanted this party to be special. To usher you into your new life." Nealy crouched in front of the girls. "And I suppose you'd like something more fun to do than talk to old people."

Both girls nodded their heads.

"My nephew Davey and his girlfriend will take you to the game room." She called to a teenage boy as she rose then turned her attention back to Jenna. "If it's okay with you?"

"Can I go with them?"

"Not a chance. Davey's very reliable and we have work to do." Nealy carried the pan to the food table, moving a few dishes around before placing it in the empty space.

Jenna spoke briefly with Davey before he took the girls to the game room, then joined Nealy.

"I have to say, my mac and cheese smells delicious," Jenna teased her cooking-challenged friend.

"You know I hate it when you brag."

"Hey, I like jealousy on you," Nealy's boyfriend, Dane, said as he joined them. "Gives me hope you'll one day learn to master the kitchen so you can feed me."

The women looked at each other and laughed.

Nealy leaned in to kiss Dane, then grabbed Jenna's arm. "C'mon, let's mingle."

And mingle they did. Before she knew it, Jenna met half the population of Cypress Pointe. Everyone from the mayor and the police chief to shop owners and other town notables. The list went on, leaving Jenna to try to remember the barrage of names.

She smiled until her cheeks ached. Chatted about her job, her family and whatever else the fine folks of Cypress Pointe found interesting. The old urge to melt into the sidelines threatened to overwhelm her, but she pushed away the inclination. Nealy had gone above and beyond to plan this party for Jenna. The least she could do was enjoy it.

Parched from all the talking, Jenna poured herself a glass of lemon-flavored water. In a quiet corner she regrouped, appreciating a moment alone.

She peered over the crowd, surprised to discover that in a short time, she already liked living here. Her busy life in LA left her little opportunity to develop close relationships, but she found she was fond of the friendly residents and peaceful atmosphere of Cypress Pointe. Here, the pace was much slower. More conducive to enjoying life, rather than barreling through every second of the day to attain the next goal, as she'd been doing for years.

But can this place hold your interest, a voice inside her whispered. *Can it keep you and the girls safe?*

Until she was here longer, she couldn't answer that question. Only time would tell.

Nealy weaved through the room toward her, talking to a couple walking with her. Jenna smiled, ready for another round of introductions

"Jenna, meet Max and Lilli, old friends of mine."

They all shook hands and exchanged pleasantries.

"Max is the man responsible for bringing Wyatt to town," Nealy informed her.

The handsome man smiled at Jenna. "Heard you had a little run-in with my old buddy?"

She shrugged. "More like he saved the day."

Lilli touched her arm. "You must have been terrified."

"That's putting it mildly."

"Nealy told us about the girls' mother." Lilli shook her head. "What a terrible loss."

"Yes. Carrie should be the one raising her daughters, not me."

"In a perfect world," Lilli said. "But they have you."

"And she's an awesome mom," Nealy interjected.

"As long as we stay away from the beach," Jenna teased, deflecting the direction of conversation. She didn't want credit for something she hadn't yet earned.

"Well, welcome to town." Lilli smiled. "You're going to love it here."

Nealy hooked her arm through Lilli's. "And we have a new friend to add to our girls' night out."

"Watch out," Max deadpanned.

As the women started discussing the merits of a chic-flick evening at home versus a night on the town, minus their men, Jenna felt Max's gaze focus on her.

"Is there a problem?" she asked, uneasy with his intensity.

"No. Just thinking about you bringing cookies to Wyatt."

"He told you?"

"Yeah. He was surprised at the gesture. People around here tend to give him a wide berth."

"I would imagine it's because he's so prickly."

Max chuckled, then quickly sobered. "That, and he hasn't gotten over the death of his son."

"I understand something of how he feels. I

haven't lost a child, but my best friend's death touched me deeply."

He cocked his head. "Maybe you could talk to him once in a while. No one can convince him to see a counselor, but since you're both dealing with loss, he could use a friend."

Sit down with a man still so deep in grief over the death of his son and talk about…what? Life? Moving on? She barely had a handle on it herself.

"I don't know."

"Look, it's just a thought."

A thought now firmly planted in her mind.

After the brief visit with Wyatt today, she had to admit, she found herself more than a bit curious about him. His dark good looks were made more interesting by the light beard dusting his face. Most guys in LA paid big bucks for the natural look Wyatt achieved without trying. His broad shoulders and muscular arms told her he wasn't afraid of hard work. And his eyes. So blue. So troubled. Not that she'd noticed or anything.

Right. Okay, she'd noticed. She was only human, after all. And it had been a long time since a man drew her interest.

But this man? The guy who accused her of not watching the girls closely enough. Granted, he was right, but did she want him holding that over her head? No. Plus, he carried the same baggage, probably more, that she did. Could she deal with his loss as well as her own?

But he had rescued Bridget. The least she could do was consider Max's suggestion.

Soon, Max and Lilli moved on. Nealy went off to take care of some sort of problem in the kitchen, leaving Jenna alone again. She let out a sigh.

"Overwhelming, huh?"

Jenna smiled at the police chief, Bob Gardener, who everyone simply called the Chief. A tall bear of a man with gray hair and a genuine smile, he inspired confidence and respect in those around him.

"Nealy means well."

"Think you'll remember everyone's name?"

She laughed. "I doubt it, but I'm sure the longer I'm here, the better I'll get."

"Stayin' very long?"

She shot him a sideways glance. "Tryin' to get rid of me already?"

He chuckled. "No, ma'am. Just like to keep a finger on what's goin' on in my town."

"Hopefully the girls and I won't give you any trouble. So far we've been law-abiding citizens. I don't see us changing anytime soon."

"Didn't think you would." He hesitated, as if getting his timing right. "Might be worried about others, though."

Her stomach clenched. "Meaning?"

"Heard you had some trouble with a reporter back in LA."

By the way he looked at her, Jenna knew he'd done more than just hear the news. "Then you know I have a restraining order. We came here to get away from him."

He nodded. "If he does happen to show up in Cypress Pointe, I promise, he won't be hassling you."

Relieved to have someone in law enforcement on her side, she said, "I'm hoping that won't happen, but with him…there's no telling what he'll do."

"I'll be ready." He smiled, reassuring her again.

Before Jenna knew it, another hour flew by. Much as she appreciated the people who had come out to meet her, she wanted a few minutes to catch her breath. Maybe a walk by the outdoor pool would help.

She'd just started to head in that direction when she noticed Wyatt. When had he arrived? So busy chatting up her new neighbors, she'd missed him come in. Clean shaven, with his hair neatly combed, he was more handsome than she remembered. Her pulse leaped, despite her intention to remain unaffected by the man.

Tonight he dressed in a gray button-down shirt and black slacks, a far cry from his work clothes. He stood in a far corner of the room, clearly uncomfortable. She bit her lip. Should she go to him? Attempt small talk again? The decision was taken out of her hands when Max approached Wyatt, handing him a bottle of beer. They spoke briefly before Max rejoined his girlfriend. Curious, she watched as Wyatt looked down at the bottle then set it on a nearby table before walking outside.

Okay, she really should leave the man to his solitude, but when had she ever left a hurting person alone? Never. And she wasn't about to start now. She strode across the room, grabbed the bottle and followed him outside.

WYATT TOOK A deep breath of the humid August air. He hadn't shown up for any public gatherings since arriving in Cypress Pointe, and here he was with real shoes on, even though they pinched. He couldn't remember the last time he'd worn anything but boat shoes.

He'd convinced himself that Jenna's promise

of her secret mac and cheese recipe drew him here, but he knew better. He simply wanted to see her again.

So far he hadn't spoken to her. From the moment he arrived, she'd been monopolized by one person after another. Since he'd already had the pleasure of meeting her, he'd wait his turn.

Pleasure? As much as the word had become foreign to him, it fit meeting Jenna. Like no one had done in a long time, she piqued his interest. Was it because she understood what he was going through, having recently lost her friend? Most people didn't get where he was coming from, couldn't understand why he didn't just buck up and face life without his son. She seemed to have a better insight into his state of mind.

Or was he intrigued by this single woman raising two girls on her own? He understood the sacrifice, worry and all-consuming joy of rearing a child. Knew that being a parent was a tough road. Admired her for attempting it on her own.

After engaging in conversation with people he hadn't seen in a while, his shoulders had started to ache with tension. His chest had grown tighter still when his parents had joined him before he stepped outside.

"Wyatt, I'm so happy to see you," his mother had said, hugging him. When he returned the gesture, she squeezed him again before drawing back, her gaze filled with concern. "You're okay?"

"I'm fine, Mother."

"You're eating? Sleeping?'

His father chuckled. "Liz, the boy looks healthy to me."

"Don't pretend you aren't worried, Bryce. You've spent just as many hours wondering how Wyatt is doing as I have."

"Both of you can stop worrying," Wyatt said, trying to infuse humor into his tone. "I'm eating. Working."

"But not sleeping?" his mother asked.

He sighed. "Mom, let it go."

"I'm your mother. I never let go."

Questioning his welfare was part of the dynamic he'd intentionally walked away from. What was wrong with him? They only wanted to help. Be a part of his life. They missed Jamie too. Still, no matter how hard he tried, he couldn't respond to them. His father laid a hand on his wife's shoulder. "Don't push," he said quietly.

His mother's eyes filled with tears. What a rotten son he'd become. She stepped closer to his father as Wyatt began to withdraw.

"Can we at least meet for dinner sometime? If I promise not to interfere?"

"Sure. I'll call you."

"Promise?"

He forced a grin for his mother's sake. "I promise." Guilt and sorrow tugged at him. He hoped someday he would be capable of spending more than a few minutes with his folks, but right now he needed fresh air.

Leaving behind the party chatter, he strode to the far end of the pool area, opened the gate to step onto the lush expanse of grass spreading from the side of the hotel down to the beach. The sweet scent of blooming honeysuckle filled the air. The soft glow from tiered garden lights bordered the neatly manicured foliage surrounding the building. The dim lighting allowed a better view of the moon shining over the calm waters of the Gulf of Mexico. He hadn't realized how on edge he was until the soothing sound of waves lapping against the sand relaxed him in slow degrees.

Heels tapping against the stone path drew his attention from the water. He turned, surprised and pleased to see Jenna walking his way. Pleased indeed.

She held out a bottle. "You left this behind."

"Thanks, but I don't want it."

She lifted a quizzical brow.

Did he really need to explain himself? Probably. A stubborn part of him wanted to tell her to leave him alone, but the tired part of him wanted to talk to someone. Talk to her. So he started, haltingly at first.

"When my son died, I thought it would be easy to get lost in a bottle. You know, just forget." He shoved his hands in his pants pockets and shrugged in an attempt to make light of the situation. "Funny thing is, I don't really like to drink. So it never helped me not remember Jamie."

"That was your son's name? Jamie?"

"Yes." Emotion clogged his throat. "You'd think after two years I could say my son's name without getting choked up, but apparently not."

"You miss him."

"Every day with every breath."

In the garden's soft light, he saw Jenna's rapid blinking. Was she fighting back tears? See, she got it.

"He was a great kid," Wyatt went on. "Full of life. Loved adventure."

"So Jamie wouldn't want you to drown your sorrows in a bottle."

"Probably not any more than your friend would want you to."

"Carrie," she said just above a whisper. "My friend's name."

As if by silent agreement, they strolled farther away from the building. Away from the music and numerous voices, heading toward a large magnolia tree with a bench positioned beneath. Pink luminous blooms dotted the limbs in the dark night. Wyatt bent over to pick up a fallen flower and handed it to her.

Their fingers brushed in the exchange. He lingered, enjoying the touch of her smooth skin. It had been a long time since he'd touched anyone. At Jenna's shiver, he let his hand drop.

They took a seat on the cool wrought-iron bench, leaving a wide space between them.

"Most people don't want to talk about Jamie," he said. "They find it awkward or think I'm not ready."

Jenna tilted her head and regarded him. "Do you think you're ready?"

"Sometimes it feels good to say his name. But other times…" he took a deep breath.

"I know what you mean. I find I have to walk a fine line with the twins. Sometimes we all have a good laugh over a shared memory, but other times the memories make us cry."

"I guess it's all part of the grieving process."

An uneasy silence lapsed again. Jenna broke it first. "So instead of becoming a drinker, you decided to become a brooding, sullen loner?"

He opened his mouth to argue but Jenna held up her hand. "It's not my opinion. I'm only repeating what I've heard."

Was that what people thought of him? Sullen? Brooding? Okay, the brooding loner part was probably true. "Fair enough."

Was this what he'd let his life become? A ghost walker during the day. Going through the motions of his job without any effort. Cutting ties with family and friends. Shoot, Jenna and the girls were the only people to visit him in weeks.

Not a very flattering picture, if he did say so himself.

He was so mired in his thoughts that Jenna startled him when she spoke again. "I have to say, I'm surprised you showed up tonight."

"So am I. After the promise of food, I had to come." He grinned. "I tasted your masterpiece and I gotta say, you did the mac and cheese crowd proud. And this is coming from a mac and cheese connoisseur."

"I'm glad you liked it." She frowned. "But to be honest, meeting all these people is a bit overwhelming. I'm not usually comfortable in big crowds."

"Something we have in common." He noticed she still held the bottle. "Want me to take that?"

"No. I guess I should head back inside." She stood. "I'll take it with me."

He stood as well, sorry the brief interlude had ended so soon. Who would have thought diving into the waves after a little girl would lead to meeting a woman he actually wanted to talk to?

"Hey, once again, I'm sorry if I came down too hard on you the other day."

"Save the lecture," she warned. "Can't say I've earned the status of mother just yet, but from now on I'll be more vigilant about watching the girls."

"Swimming lessons probably wouldn't hurt," he suggested.

"I was thinking the same thing. Do you know any instructors?"

He searched his memory. "There's a YMCA

nearby. Better yet, a town directory with a list of services."

"It can't be just someone I find on a list. I have to trust whoever works with the girls."

"You'll find the right person."

"I think I have." She stepped toward him. "How about you?"

He froze. Teach her girls how to swim? Did she realize what she was asking? No way. Not after how he failed Jamie.

"I'm not a teacher."

"But you clearly swim."

"Well, yeah, but a teacher? I'm sorry, Jenna. I won't do it."

Despite his refusal, she tried to convince him. "The girls think you're a prince."

He nearly choked. "Prince?" Not if they knew the truth.

"They're in a fairy tale princess phase right now, and after your derring-do at the beach, you fall into the knight in shining armor category."

Please, anything but this.

"Living in this coastal town could be dangerous if they don't know how to swim." She worried her lip. "They tend to be a tad headstrong, but after the grand rescue the other day, I think they'll listen to you."

No. They couldn't be trusted with him. "Jenna, I—"

"Wyatt, I don't let just anyone into the girls' lives. They like you. They'd never learn from anyone they didn't feel safe with. You've proven you can keep them safe."

He closed, then opened his eyes. Forced himself to say the words. "Jenna, you realize Jamie drowned, right?"

"I didn't want to…Nealy said it was a boating accident…" She glanced at him with wide eyes. "I'm sorry. I'm making a mess of this."

"Then you see why I can't do this."

"I disagree." She crossed her arms over her chest.

She disagreed? "Why?"

"From what I understand, your son's death was an accident."

He bit back the bitterness threatening to claim him. Kept his tone even when he said, "You don't know the details." Not an accident. As far as he was concerned, Jamie's death fell squarely on his shoulders.

"Maybe not, but if you were such a bad guy, you never would have dived into the water after Bridget. Maybe you need to help my girls in honor of Jamie."

He ran a hand over his chin. "This is crazy."

She shook her head. "This is healing."

Had this petite woman standing before him just used her kids' need for swimming lessons to help him feel better?

He shook his head, more adamant now. "I can't do it."

A shadow of hurt crossed her face, quickly replaced by a flash of determination. "Okay. I'll take care of the girls' lessons on my own."

"Jenna, I—"

She jerked back, putting distance between them. "No need to explain. You don't want to get involved. I get it."

"I'm not saying…" He took a breath. "Jenna, you can't keep bad things from happening."

"But I can make sure I'm prepared." She turned and strode away, leaving him to wonder if he'd just made another life-changing mistake.

CHAPTER FOUR

WITH A WEEK left before school started, Jenna decided to follow through and sign the girls up for swimming lessons. Wyatt may not want to be involved, but his unwillingness wouldn't stop her. After some research, she discovered the local country club held weekly lessons. She called, set up a time with the instructor and checked one more activity off her growing list.

At first, the girls were excited about the idea, until it came time to put on their swimsuits. Suddenly, Bridget had an upset stomach and Abby couldn't find her suit.

Jenna stood in the doorway to their bedroom, a serious frown focused on the girls, who sat cross-legged on the floor, dolls and accessories scattered around them. "Abby, we unpacked your bathing suit. It's in the bottom drawer of your dresser."

Abby dipped her head and glanced at her sister, as if not sure what to say or do. Bridget, however, kept her eyes leveled on Jenna with a stare she'd come to recognize as a "don't push me" look.

"Bridget, do you want some seltzer water?"

She wrinkled her pert nose. "That won't help."

"Hmm. I seem to remember it helped after too many hot dogs and French fries on Friday night."

Bridget shrugged. "I ate too many eggs this morning."

"Then how about the pink stuff?"

The ten-year-old sent Jenna an, "as if," look.

Yes, Jenna knew Bridget's aversion to seltzer. Or any kind of chalky stomach remedy. The thick concoction made her gag every time she attempted to swallow it. She also knew that Bridget's stomachaches usually stemmed from nerves. If they worked out the problem, Bridget was fine.

Still, she had to get the two moving. *Let the battle begin.*

"I see. If that's the case, you won't make miniature golf tonight with Nealy and Lilli. They'll be disappointed, but will understand you're too sick to join them." She shifted her gaze to Abby. "Guess it'll just be you playing golf later while your sister stays home with the sitter."

A frown furrowed Bridget's brow.

Jenna held back a grin, ready to pour it on. She snapped her fingers. "I nearly forgot. We were also going to the mall later. I wanted to look for new school shoes."

She knew her volley would hit the mark. Only ten and already Bridget loved shoes.

Abby rose and walked to her dresser, opening the drawer to remove her swimsuit.

Jenna pulled a surprised face. "Oh, will you look at that. Right where we put it."

Abby grinned, knowing her little trick hadn't worked. So much for the truth pact. As she began to change, Bridget gathered up her own suit, which was lying on the bed. "I'm not super sick. My stomach will feel better soon."

"That a girl."

"I don't see why Mr. Hamilton can't teach us," Bridget groused. Since the day at the beach, Wyatt had become her hero.

"I told you, he's not up to it right now."

"I wonder if he'd let us play with Cruiser?" Abby asked. "Do you think he'll let us come over again?"

"Mr. Hamilton is a busy man." Or not, but Jenna wasn't about to figure out the man's schedule. Time to change the subject. She glanced at her watch. "Ten minutes and we're out the door."

As the girls got ready, Jenna went to her bedroom, reluctantly thinking about Wyatt. Once Bridget mentioned his name, her mind focused on his anguished expression under the moonlight when he'd refused to give the girls swimming lessons. Sympathy tugged at her. As much as she'd hoped he'd instruct the girls, she had to admit, she understood why he couldn't. Too much too soon after his son's accident.

The counselor she and the girls had been seeing in California urged her not to get stressed over the grieving process, since it varied for every person. There was no time limit, no set-in-stone method to deal with loss. Even the stages of grief were sometimes different for people.

Her mind flashbacked to the beach. Bridget flailing around in the water.

On the other hand, she resented Wyatt's accusation that she was reckless with the girls' safety. Clearly, he had lingering issues after his son's death, and she had her own learning curve to deal with. She'd only recently gone from taking care of herself to being in charge of a family of three. Given her own insecurities as a caregiver, she didn't appreciate his negative outlook.

Shaking off the thought, Jenna retrieved the beach bag from the closet and tossed a tube of sunblock inside.

While Jenna still grieved Carrie, she'd gotten to the point where she had to put the cares and concerns of the twins first and foremost in her life. Yes, she would have liked Wyatt to work with the girls because they'd established a rapport. He could have looked at the lessons as a way to kick-start him into living again, but honestly, she didn't know the man well enough to intrude on his privacy. If he kept those emotional walls intact, she never would.

She should probably keep some distance from Wyatt. By his own admission, he wasn't very social, so that solved the problem of running into him. Yet, he stirred…something…in her. Something she hadn't felt in a long time. Something she'd thought buried after François humiliated her. The world-renowned chef had ended their relationship after her cooking show became successful. She'd foolishly believed he loved her, had thought his group of friends were also her friends. But his large ego and notorious jealousy had them siding with him.

But Wyatt… She couldn't put her finger on

it, but she sensed he was different than most men she knew. You didn't grieve so deeply if you were self-absorbed. He was both hurting and guarded. A dangerous combination for a woman who'd always taken care of the other foster kids she happened to be living with. Yes, she'd grown up and achieved a bit of success, but the need to be a part of something more, of her own family, hadn't dimmed with time.

Besides, this vague emotion for Wyatt was no reason to place herself, or the girls, in the path of a man still mired in grief. Jenna needed to keep them surrounded by joy as they began a new chapter in their lives.

Stop thinking about him. He'd made his intentions clear. And she had to focus on her own job, being a good mother.

As she passed their room, Jenna told the girls, "You'll have a good time with Katie, the swim instructor. She sounds like she's lots of fun. I'll go pack our towels."

"If you say so," Bridget grumbled.

Jenna sighed. No matter what it took, she'd make sure the girls liked the lessons.

Thirty minutes later, they stood poolside, the sharp scent of chlorine muted by the rich, tropical aroma of suntan lotion. Both girls wrapped their arms around Jenna's waist like she was the only thing between them and certain disaster.

"C'mon, you two," she cajoled. "We'll have a blast." Well, they'd have a blast if they actually got into the water. "You told me you wanted lessons. What's wrong?"

Bridget looked up, fear shadowing her big brown eyes. "I'm scared."

Extracting herself from the girl's tenacious hold, Jenna crouched down so they were eye to eye. "I know you are. That's why you need lessons. But you'll soon feel comfortable in the water."

Bridget didn't look convinced. She glanced at the huge in-ground pool. "We'll stay in the shallow end, right?"

"Absolutely. And I'll be there with both of you."

She removed the cover-up over her one-piece bathing suit in case the girls wanted her in the pool. If joining them in the crystal-clear water made them feel safe, she wouldn't hesitate.

Katie appeared, chatting easily with the girls. While Abby seemed to warm up to the teen with a winning smile and long brunette hair, Bridget crossed her arms over her chest and glared.

The sense of missing the mark overwhelmed

Jenna again. How could she make Bridget see the lessons were good for her? She tried to imagine what Carrie would have done in this situation, but came up blank. Every time she thought she was making headway, she found herself back at square one, questioning her place in the girls' lives. Swim lessons were just a small part of what Bridget and Abby would be involved with as they grew up. If she couldn't handle this, what did the future hold for them?

She shook off her dismal thoughts, taking the lead to move down the cement pool steps and stand by the waiting instructor, splashing the warm water around her. "The water's perfect. Let's at least get your feet wet."

Bridget shook her head, turning tail to walk to the chaise where they'd placed their towels.

Jenna held back a sigh. The hot August sun beat down on her back, and she wished she'd kept her sunglasses on. The glare from the pool, along with the girls' attitudes, gave her the beginnings of a headache.

Abby sat on the pool edge and dipped her feet in the water.

"I know the first lesson isn't very fun," Katie said, loud enough for Bridget to hear, "but once you see how simple swimming is, you'll want to paddle down to the other end on your own."

Jenna doubted that, but she silently applauded Katie's enthusiasm.

She and the teenager kept up a running dialogue, hoping at least Abby would give in and lower herself into the water. Between Bridget's mutinous pout and Abby's hesitancy to move beyond the edge of the pool, Jenna was ready to give up for the day. Pasting an encouraging smile on her face, she sluiced through the water toward Abby, stopping short when she caught a glimpse of Wyatt heading toward them.

Dressed in a pair of navy trunks, he strode with confidence, his broad shoulders and lean build tanned from hours in the sun, his dark hair gleaming in the bright daylight. His shuttered gaze met hers just before he slipped sunglasses on.

Jenna swallowed hard, a hundred different thoughts running through her head, the main one being, *he's here.*

WHEN WYATT EXITED the locker room door to the pool area, he took a deep breath. He couldn't remember the last time he'd been to the club. Probably when he'd taken Jamie for a day of swimming. His son had loved the water, most likely a genetic trait since Wyatt and his brother, Josh, had been water rats for as far back as Wyatt could remember.

Since the night of the welcome party for Jenna, Wyatt had woken with nightmares. Not the usual, of Jamie crying because Wyatt couldn't save him. No, these new dreams were different, centered on Bridget flailing in the water and Abby yelling for someone to help her sister. He'd shot straight up in his bed, a sheen of sweat bathing his skin, his breaths short and jerky. He'd run a hand over his chest, Jenna's voice filling his head with accusations of him not wanting to protect the girls.

It wasn't that he'd refused her request just to give Jenna a hard time. He simply didn't think he had it in him to teach the twins the one skill Jamie hadn't quite mastered. The one skill that might have saved his life. Jamie was confident in a pool, but he hadn't spent much time in deep sea water. Unable to stay upright in the strong Gulf current, despite the life vest he wore, he'd gone under before Wyatt could get to him.

Last night, when he heard Jenna's voice in his head, *if you were such a bad guy, you never would have dived into the water after Bridget,* he decided to let go of the fear rendering him useless. He'd called Nealy to find out if Jenna had scheduled lessons, figuring Jenna would flat-out refuse his offer after he pretty much dissed her parenting skills.

He moved through the maze of lounge chairs set up for sunning and tables with umbrellas scattered around the pool deck. He noticed one of the girls sitting on the edge, dipping her feet in the water. The other sat yards away on a chaise, her body stiff with tension. He assumed it was Bridget, figuring she might be afraid of the water after her close call at the beach.

The young instructor coaxed Abby into the pool, rewarded when the girl slipped into the water. While Abby seemed more willing to give swimming a try, Bridget plainly refused. From the defiant look on her face, she wasn't going anywhere.

He bit back a chuckle, more nerves than amusement. Seemed the little one had a will of steel.

His stomach in a knot, Wyatt tossed his towel on an empty chaise and went toward them, almost stopping short at Jenna's surprised expression.

Once her shock dissipated, her brows angled

in suspicion. Yeah, he deserved the look, but he wasn't backing down.

"Hey, Abby," he said in a quiet tone as he approached. "How's the water?"

Abby turned around to look up at him just as Bridget jumped off her perch on the chair, eyes bright as she ran to him.

They both called to him at the same time.

"Mr. Hamilton!"

"Where's Cruiser?"

He smiled down at Bridget. "Cruiser is at home. And if it's okay with Jenna," he turned his attention to her, "you can call me Wyatt."

"I think Mr. Wyatt would be better," Jenna replied in a curt tone. Oh yeah, she was miffed at him.

He nodded then rubbed his hands together. "So, how's the lesson going?"

"Bridget won't come in," Abby informed him.

Understanding her trepidation, he turned to Bridget. "True?"

Her smile slipped a bit. "I'm…um…"

He held out his hand, and after a moment's hesitation, she placed her smaller one in his. Ignoring the rush of emotion at the trusting gesture, he led her to a waist-high wall at the outer edge of the pool area, giving her a boost before joining her to sit on the sun-warmed cement.

"You don't want to go in the water?" he asked.

"I do, but what if I go under again? I couldn't breathe last time that happened."

"That's because you didn't know how to swim. I believe Katie will show you what to do if you get pulled under again. She's also going to show you how to use your arms to stroke through the water and kick your feet."

Bridget frowned. "She's okay, but you really know how to swim."

He chuckled. "So does Katie or she wouldn't have her job."

"Well, this is a pool, not the beach."

"You have to start somewhere. This is a perfect place to practice."

"Did you start in a pool?"

"Yes. In fact, my brother and I learned how to swim right here."

Bridget's eyes went wide. "This exact pool?"

"This exact pool."

"You learned to swim here before you swam at the beach?"

"We had a good instructor, listened to everything he taught us. Before we knew it, we were swimming in the waves by ourselves."

He and Josh had spent hours in the water, horsing around and having a great time. In the summer, they'd gone swimming from sunrise to sunset, their skin turning a mellow brown, the chlorine lightening their dark hair. In the winter, their mother had to threaten them to get out of the pool, their skin all pruney and lips blue from the cold. And when they got older? He and Josh had participated in every form of water sport from competitive swimming to surfing, strapping their boards onto the car roof to drive to Daytona Beach at the mere promise of big waves. Wyatt had always loved anything to do with the water.

With a frown, he realized he couldn't remember when he'd last thought about those good times. All his water-related memories focused on Jamie drowning.

Shaking off the uncomfortable revelation, he said, "My brother and I raced against each other on the swim team in high school."

"You can do that? Race in the water?"

"Sure. But you have to start with the basics."

He and Bridget watched as Abby stood in the water up to her waist, moving her arms back and forth in imitation of the instructor. Jenna's eyes zeroed in on him, as if waiting to see if she needed to come to Bridget's rescue.

He'd never let anything happen to the little girl, but Jenna didn't know that.

"Will you be close by?" Bridget asked. "Just in case?"

"Why do you think I wore my bathing suit?"

"To go swimming, silly."

"Yes, but I hoped to be here for you too."

"Really?"

His voice hitched. "Really."

Quietly, Bridget glanced up at him, her voice small. "Do you think I can be good at swimming?"

"I think you can be good at whatever you put your mind to."

After processing his words, she grabbed hold of his hand and yanked. "Let's go. Abby is already ahead of me."

Wyatt helped her from the wall and followed her to the water. *You can do this*. Despite his mind screaming at him to run, to get away from this emotional land mine, his heart knew he was doing the right thing by being there for Bridget.

Jenna glided to the side in time to help Bridget slip into the water. The youngster hopped a few steps to join her sister as Katie welcomed her. Jenna rested her elbows in the gutter, kicking her feet and refusing to meet his eyes. The drain made a sucking sound as Wyatt lowered himself into the pool beside her. With an inward sigh, he stood watching the twins' progress.

The day had heated to just below scorching. While the air temperature should have bothered him, instead what worried him was the rush of attraction he felt as he stood next to Jenna. He'd only known her for a few short days, yet he couldn't seem to control his reaction to her.

Finally, she spoke, still not facing him. "Why are you here?"

Right to the point. He nearly chuckled at the indignation lacing her voice.

"Would you believe me if I told you I had a change of heart?"

She skimmed her hand over the top of the water in a nonchalant motion. "You mean you're not here to criticize my parenting style?"

"Fine. I deserved that, but c'mon, you can't be mad because I was concerned."

His remark earned him an evil eye.

"Not one word," she warned.

As he moved his own hand through the water, their arms brushed, resulting in a jolt of longing. He tried not to pay attention to her soft skin turning pink under the strong rays of the sun, without much luck. "How about a truce instead?"

"I suppose. After all, you did show up." She looked at him questioningly. "How did you know we'd be here?"

He shrugged. "Small town."

She shook her head and muttered, "Nealy."

"Don't be mad at her. I figured you wouldn't appreciate my interference."

"You're right about the interference. You talked Bridget into the water, so I won't complain this time."

"Good to know."

Her shoulders slackened a bit. As much as he'd tried not to notice how fine she looked in her bathing suit, the movement showed off the graceful sweep of her neck.

"I know this was difficult for you. Thanks for coming anyway."

He nodded and swallowed hard, breathing deep to decrease the strangling pressure in his chest. Then he changed the subject. "The girls are naturals."

Abby went under with her nose plugged. Bridget, not quite ready, edged closer to him.

The little girl turned to him. For his approval? Support? He remembered the same expression on Jamie's face. Removing his sunglasses, he laid them on the cement deck behind him, then plugged his nose before dipping underwater. When he came back up, Bridget followed his lead.

He shook the water from his hair, keeping an attentive eye as Bridget resurfaced, gasping for air, but okay.

"This buddy-buddy thing you have with Bridget is kind of getting to me," Jenna commented in a light tone.

"Jealous?"

When Jenna's entire body grew stiff, he knew he'd scored a direct hit. "Don't take it personally. She's probably a little attached to me for rescuing her at the beach."

Jenna's lips pressed tight.

"Hey," he said softly. "It's not a contest."

"You saved Bridget's life and you've got a dog. How can I compete?"

He thought she was teasing until he glimpsed the dismay in her eyes.

"Hey, I'm not trying to one-up you."

She blinked furiously. "I know."

Did she? He ran a hand through his damp hair. What had he gotten himself into?

Before he had a chance to say anything else, she turned to him. Her blond hair seemed lighter in the bright sunlight, setting off her green eyes. He found himself having difficulty following the thread of their conversation when she looked at him, all serious and cute at the same time.

"I'm sorry. If being around you makes Bridget happy, then I shouldn't complain. Of the two, she's the most quiet. And the most stubborn. Since her mother died, I don't like to push her into talking about her feelings or make her participate in anything she's uncomfortable with. Maybe she'll open up around you."

"I'm not sure I have much to offer."

"Sometimes all you have to do is listen."

"I can listen, but Jenna, that's about all I can do. I have to be honest with you, I don't want to hurt you or the girls." It was important for her to understand this, before they really became friends or expectations weren't met.

Jenna shrugged, keeping her attention solely on the girls. "I think you've made that pretty clear, Wyatt."

The tension in his shoulders eased. Good, she got it.

He squinted against the glare coming from the water. After a few more dunks under the surface, Bridget seemed to get past her fear. He felt a smile tug at his lips as he watched her splash around with her sister and instructor, acting as if she'd been born with fins.

Truth be told, he'd missed being around kids. Shutting himself off had been a necessary coping mechanism after the accident. The subsequent downhill spiral had become his life. He did not intend to be emotionally vulnerable again, but time had proven that staying away from people hadn't sped up the grieving process, either.

Being here today, he sensed that maybe it wouldn't hurt for him to try a new way of coping. Get out a little more, be around people. While the pain had receded a small degree, he knew he still had a long journey to get back to any sense of normalcy. If there even was such a thing.

Before long, the girls got tired of teasing each other and beckoned the adults to join in their game. Jenna swam to them, her lean arms cutting through the water in good form. Wyatt remained where he was, watching them clown around, until Bridget splashed her way over, asking him for pointers. When she tugged at his arm, he finally gave in and took turns showing the girls how to go underwater without holding their noses. Giggling, the girls gave it a try. Abby succeeded. Bridget snorted water and went back to pinching her nose with her fingers. After a few coughing jags, they began to stay underwater longer on each try. Soon the lesson ended with the twins hanging off his arms, laughing as he carefully swung them around.

He and Jamie horsed around in the pool, just like this. Marcie hadn't liked it when the two of them took off for the day, leaving her home, but she didn't like getting wet. Or put in a situation where her hair might get mussed. So unlike Jenna, who joined in the fun.

He shook his head. Wondered for the hundredth time since Marcie left for the glitz and glamour of LA and the movie industry what he'd ever seen in her. Yes, they'd been smitten when they met at the naval base where he was stationed, but he soon found out that falling in love and marrying someone you barely knew could be a disaster waiting to happen. At least it had been for them. And before they could fix their mistake, Marcie had gotten pregnant. They stayed together for the sake of their child, but Marcie had always felt left out, never part of the bond Wyatt immediately established with his son. It explained why it didn't take long for her to leave him after the accident.

He couldn't imagine Jenna taking off when

times got tough. After all, she'd taken in her friend's children to raise as her own. His admiration rose steadily, along with the knowledge that she managed to twist him inside out.

Abby wiggled loose and hopped away, calling for him to catch her if he could. As he turned to go after her, he barreled into Jenna. Their legs tangled and their feet slipped on the pool bottom. Just before they both went under, he saw Jenna's eyes go wide.

Afraid he might have hurt her, Wyatt grabbed her arm and yanked her to the surface.

She came up sputtering. "What on earth…?"

"Sorry." His chest rose and fell rapidly. "The girls and I got a little carried away."

Steady on her feet now, Jenna rubbed the water from her face and ran her hands through her hair to slick it back. His gaze took in her pretty features, the wide green eyes, the sprinkle of freckles over her high cheekbones, the curve of her kissable lips. Kissable? As if singed by the thought, he loosened the fingers still wrapped around her arm. "Sorry."

She laughed. "Remind me to stay out of the way when you three are playing."

The lilting sound washed over him. He yearned to brush his fingers over her satin skin again. Instead he took a step back. "I didn't…"

She glanced up at him. Their eyes met and held for longer than was comfortable. He glimpsed questions there, along with an interest.

He let out a shaky breath. Tried to control his skyrocketing heart rate.

"Are you guys okay?" Abby called from the side of the pool.

The question shattered the intense...whatever...going on here. Jenna shot one last glance at Wyatt and the tension between them was gone. "Yes," she called back. "No thanks to the boat captain over here."

He glimpsed the sparkle in her eye and relaxed. Right. Humor. He'd been out of it far too long if he couldn't pick up on a joke.

"Usually I keep life vests handy, just in case."

"Good to know, but I won't be chartering *your* boat anytime soon."

He chuckled, a rusty sound he almost didn't recognize.

"Maybe Mr. Wyatt should give Jenna lessons." Bridget giggled as she climbed out of the water.

His eyes met Jenna's again, and he caught a flash of surprise before she looked away. No doubt about it, that was indeed interest he glimpsed. Not as the twins' mother. Not as the woman who wanted to engage him in their lives. No, this interest was purely personal. Unexpected.

And, he realized, welcome. To him, at least.

CHAPTER FIVE

"WHAT'S UP WITH YOU?" Nealy asked Jenna as the excited twins dragged a laughing Lilli into the toy store. The girls had regaled the three adult friends with a steady commentary on the upcoming school year, Wyatt's dog and their swimming lesson since arriving at the shopping mall. "You've been quiet since you picked me up."

"Have I?"

Nealy raised an eyebrow. "You can't tell if you're quiet or not?"

"Of course, I just didn't realize it was noticeable."

"Abby asked you about a new outfit three times." Nealy dropped onto a nearby bench, depositing the large bags emblazoned with store logos by her feet. "And every time they mention swimming lessons, you zone out. Too much sun?"

No, more like too much Wyatt.

And there it was, the reason she'd been so

quiet. She couldn't stop thinking about Wyatt showing up earlier for the girls' lesson. Just when she'd decided he wasn't going to pull himself out of the self-imposed solitary life, he did the exact opposite, much to the twins' delight.

"Judging by Bridget's hero worship of Wyatt, I'd say you have a certain man on your mind."

Jenna lowered herself to the bench beside her friend. Loud conversation, shouts of laughter and a crying baby echoed under the high, vaulted ceiling of the shopping center. Teenage girls scoped out the best buys for back-to-school bargains while flirting with the packs of boys roaming the two-story structure. At one end of the mall, the scent of popcorn wafted from the cinema. From the other came delectable scents from the food court.

Once Jenna had gotten the girls home from their swim class, they all took quick showers and dressed in T-shirts and shorts for a few hours of retail therapy. They'd picked up Nealy and her friend Lilli, scouting for last-minute sales before the new school year began. Abby, a natural born bargain hunter, led the way. Bridget bent Nealy's ear about their swimming lessons and how she wasn't nearly as afraid of the water as she originally thought. Jenna had lagged behind, her mind dwelling on the events of the day.

In the short time they'd been in Cypress Pointe, Jenna and the girls had found themselves surrounded by new friends. Though Jenna worked with many people on her television show, she'd never formed any lasting connections. Even before the twins came to live with her, she'd put in long hours and went home to her quiet apartment. Granted, François's shabby treatment of her had made her gun shy when it came to dating again, but to be honest, she hadn't really put herself out there.

Now she had resumed her friendship with Nealy and made friends with Lilli, Max and Dane, feeling comfortable with the circle of people she would allow in the girls' lives. If she had to give this part of her life a name, it would probably be relief. As much as she liked to be independent, at least they weren't alone in this place they called home for now.

"So," Nealy asked. "What's up?"

Of course, having close friends meant she was required to reveal her innermost thoughts. "I just have a lot on my mind. With school starting next week, I have a million things to do."

Nealy leaned back, a grin curving her lips. "Why don't I believe you?"

"Why would I lie?"

"I'm not saying you're keeping something from me, but c'mon, you are distracted."

Jenna blew out a breath. "Promise you won't blow this out of proportion."

Nealy's hand flew to her chest and she decreed in her best Southern drawl, "Little ol' me? Why I don't know what you're referring to."

"How about the fact that since I've been in Cypress Pointe, you've called me every day to check on us."

"After what you went through in LA, do you blame me? You and the girls were so frightened."

"I appreciate your concern, but we're fine."

"Fine, but distracted."

"I'm...it's..." Jenna gave in. "It's about Wyatt."

Nealy pumped her fist in victory. "I knew it."

"When I asked him to give the girls lessons at the party the other night, he turned me down flat."

"Yeah, he still isn't ready to be around people."

"And I get that, I do. I found an instructor and made arrangements. On my own."

"So what's the problem?"

"He surprised me when he showed up. I accepted his refusal, gave him the space he clearly needs, then he showed up anyway. Does he think I can't properly take care of the girls? After Bridget's close call at the beach, he had to oversee me?"

"Wow. You have thought this through." Nealy blinked. "I have no idea about his intentions. All he said when he called was that he changed his mind and wanted to attend the lessons."

"It just seems odd to me."

"So did he help?"

More than he probably knew. After all, he was the one to get Bridget into the water. "He showed the girls how to stay underwater without holding their noses. They goofed around and the girls had a good time."

"How about Wyatt?"

She shrugged. "It seemed like he still held a part of himself back. Like he wasn't sure being there was a smart idea but he came anyway. The girls got him to join in on their games, but I'm not sure he enjoyed it."

"Easing back into life is difficult for him."

"I know because the girls are going through the same thing. Now I wonder if it's a bad idea for the girls, especially Bridget, to get too accustomed to Wyatt's presence. What if he decides it's too much pressure to be around children because of the memories of his son?" She paused. "I don't want the girls hurt any more than they already are."

Not to mention herself. It would be easy to spend time with Wyatt. Despite his reticence around people, once he let a bit of his guard down, he was funny, intense and way too good-looking for Jenna's peace of mind.

When Wyatt had bumped into her in the pool, he'd caught her off guard. Getting tangled up with him had sent chills over her body, which had nothing to do with the temperature of the water and everything to do with an attractive man's touch. She didn't have the time or energy to get all wound up in a guy.

"You've just met Wyatt. You're making this issue bigger than it has to be."

"You sure?"

"Don't overthink things. Be glad you're here, in Cypress Pointe, safe and sound."

If only it were that easy. Growing up in foster care had shown her that you couldn't always depend on other people. Yes, they had just met Wyatt, but she could see Bridget's young heart reaching out to him.

She hadn't expected the immediate bonding. She'd just thought teaching the girls to swim would help Wyatt's reticence around people, and the girls would have a teacher they liked. Win-win for both. In retrospect, she should have given the suggestion more thought from the beginning. Recruiting Wyatt might not have been in any of their best interests.

How many times had she formed a temporary attachment with an adult in her childhood, only to be disappointed when something, or someone, got in the way and her life changed yet again? She didn't want the girls to feel as bereft as she had, especially while they were still dealing with their own loss. It was her job to protect the girls from emotional stress, and that's just what she intended to do.

"Jenna, please don't write Wyatt off," Nealy said. "For the first time since he's been back home, he's trying, he's willing to be around people again. I know I can be pushy, but when he first got here, he refused to go out at all."

"I agree, you can be pushy, and I get what you're saying, but I'm still going to be cautious."

"That's all I can ask for. Wyatt needs people

in his life who care about him. Who knows, maybe time spent with the girls will be good for all of them."

Caring was one thing, this budding attraction another. Okay, so he'd touched her in the pool. Steadied her when her feet slipped out beneath her. No reason to mistake her heated reaction for something it wasn't. He was being polite, making sure she wasn't injured. Any decent guy would have done the same.

So why did he bother her so much?

"Look, Nealy, you know I've always taken care of myself. Now, with the girls, I have to be more vigilant about who I let into their lives."

"Yes, but you don't have to do it all alone."

"Sure, I do."

Jenna knew she sounded stubborn. And she *was* being stubborn. Nealy was only pointing out that she had friends to rely on. Since Nealy came from a close-knit family, she had a built-in support system. She didn't understand how Jenna had been forced to fend for herself, growing up way too early, taking on too much responsibility when she should have been a kid having fun. Her deeply ingrained need to take care of life on her own terms overshadowed every decision she made. Jenna didn't see that changing anytime soon.

"Listen," Nealy said. "Before the girls get back, I have something to discuss with you."

"Sounds serious."

"It is. I've been tossing this idea around for a while, but after folks raved about your macaroni and cheese at the party the other night, I decided to ask you to join me in my event planning business."

"What do you mean?"

"I'd like us to work together. I haven't been able to find a decent caterer since I came back to Cypress Pointe. Every time someone books an event, I worry about the quality of the food. You told me you worked for a caterer once. Think you might want to do it again?"

"Nealy, I have a job."

"A job in California. What are you going to do when the hiatus is over and you have to return to the cooking show? Move back there? Or hire a live-in sitter here so you can fly to the coast when you need to?"

"To be honest, I've been putting off thinking about that."

"Look, with our combined experience, we'd be awesome together. If you decide to cater for me, you'll have flexible hours to be with the girls."

"I like the sound of that."

"You've already gone through huge changes in your life. Why not take it to the next level? Work as well as live here."

Jenna thought about her agent. She'd been delaying any discussion with Barbara about future work. *Intentionally?*

"You have to admit," Nealy nudged her. "This is a fabulous idea."

"According to you, all your ideas are fabulous."

Nealy grinned. "I don't expect an answer right now, but at least think about it. Especially the next time Barbara is nagging you to go back to LA."

To be honest, the idea interested her. If she and Nealy worked together, essentially she could be her own boss. And she liked the idea of being present for the girls.

Before they had a chance to discuss the topic further, Abby came running over, holding up a red bag. "Look what Lilli bought me."

Abby pulled a stuffed unicorn out of the bag.

"How cool," Jenna cooed, repeating the gesture when Bridget showed off her white stuffed kitty. "Did you thank Lilli?"

A chorus of thank-yous filled the air.

Jenna said, "Lilli, you didn't have to."

"Are you kidding? We had a blast." She

opened her own bag and pulled out a green stuffed frog. "The girls insisted. They said if I kiss him, he'll turn into my prince." She held the frog closer. "He does have eyes like Max."

"I can't wait for you to show him your new prince," Nealy teased.

"He loves everything I love," Lilli replied.

Nealy rolled her eyes at Jenna.

"Like you should talk," Jenna countered. "Dane is a pretty good guy."

"He is," Nealy said, a dreamy expression flitting over her face.

A stab of longing pinched Jenna's heart. Happy that her friends were in loving relationships, she couldn't deny the little blip of hope that someday she'd find her own prince and live happily ever after. Until then, she would love Abby and Bridget with every ounce of her being.

"Fall in, troops," Jenna said, rising and collecting her shopping bags. "What do you say to a burger before we hit the miniature golf course?"

WYATT GLANCED AT his watch. "You said seven, right? It's ten minutes after."

Max grinned. "When women are shopping

there is no time limit. They'll get here when they get here."

Okay, it had been a while since he'd had a woman in his life. Even then he'd never grasped the nuances of shopping fever. "There's five of them. How late will they be?"

Dane laughed. "Chill, man. Nealy texted me. They're almost here."

He should have stayed home. Had planned on it until his buddies showed up on his doorstep, tag-teaming him into joining the group for a night out. Suddenly, staying home alone seemed downright depressing and he'd agreed to come along. But as the minutes passed, he grew nervous. After the way he left things with Jenna at the pool earlier, he wasn't sure what to expect.

"In the meantime," Max said, "what do you guys say to a friendly wager on the golf game?"

"Twenty bucks," Dane suggested.

"Per couple."

Wyatt frowned. "I'm not part of a couple."

"Right." Max rubbed his chin. "Then it'll be just us guys."

"Deal," Dane said.

"I'm in," Wyatt replied. "But I gotta say, this

will be a piece of cake for you both. I haven't golfed in years."

"It's mini golf," Dane countered. "How hard can it be?"

How hard indeed? After the swimming lesson today, he hadn't been able to get Jenna off his mind. For years he'd been solo and now? Now he was interested in a woman. Enjoyed the remarkable sound of her laughter. How could he concentrate on miniature golf? Guess he'd find out when Jenna arrived and he had to choose between playing the game or keeping his eyes on her.

A soft breeze rustled the palm fronds lining the sidewalk. It was high summer now, and the sun still shone brightly in the blue sky. The aroma of grilled steak from a nearby restaurant had Wyatt's stomach growling. Dinner had consisted of peanut butter slathered on a slice of bread.

Shouts of laughter from the families already on the course distracted Wyatt. Miniature golf. So normal, yet suddenly so foreign to him. He hated how everything in life had altered since Jamie had died. He couldn't explain the hollowness inside, just knew something was… missing. Memories lurked everywhere, blatant at times, catching him off guard at others.

Wyatt knew one day he'd be able to deal with the pain and disappointment of losing his son, but that day wasn't here yet.

Maybe the few hours spent with Bridget and Abby had caused his current melancholy. He'd enjoyed their company earlier, but standing here in a place filled with happy families made him wonder if he could make it through the evening listening to the twins jabber on about kid stuff. Stuff Jamie should have been enjoying along with them. What had seemed like a good idea thirty minutes ago now had him second-guessing himself.

A white minivan pulled into a parking space a few feet from where the men stood. Doors opened and women of different ages spilled out. His gaze moved to the driver's side and stopped on Jenna. Her smile slowly disappeared when she saw him. She shot Nealy a decidedly annoyed look.

Although not surprised, he didn't deny the letdown at her reaction.

"You didn't tell me Jenna had no idea I was tagging along," he said to the guys.

"That's because we didn't know," Dane said. "I assumed Nealy would tell her."

"Yet you failed to mention this possibility to me?"

"Yeah, there is that."

Wyatt closed his eyes and pinched the bridge of his nose. What had possessed him to come out tonight? This was exactly why he preferred to be by himself. No surprises. No acting all pleasant when the only thing he wanted to do was sit on his porch and brood, watching the boats bob in their slots at the marina. He liked hanging out with his dog. Cruiser's only expectations were food and a walk on the beach.

Simple. Uncomplicated.

He opened his eyes.

Unlike the pack of women headed his way.

"Mr. Wyatt!" Bridget cried out as she ran to him, Abby fast on her trail.

"Hey there."

"Jenna didn't tell us you were coming." Bridget's excited smile lit up her face. She turned to Jenna. "A surprise?"

"Oh, yeah," Jenna muttered. "A surprise."

She didn't have to sound so unhappy about it.

He directed a raised brow at her. She shrugged, her obvious annoyance mixed with resignation. Yet still, beneath her grumbling, he detected the simmering attraction from this afternoon. Was she fighting it? That would explain her mood. When he caught and held her gaze with his, the powerful flash of interest was undeniable. He wanted to punch the air with his fist in victory, but decided he'd already managed to annoy Jenna enough for one day.

Instead, he smiled, sending the message that he'd figured her out.

She blinked. Her cheeks colored, proving him right. In a sudden hurry, she followed the group to the admission window to purchase their game and pick out a colored golf ball and putter.

"I wanted a purple ball," Abby announced.

"No way," Bridget said. "I called it in the car."

"Calling in the car doesn't count. You have to be right in front of the window."

"Says who?"

"Says—"

"Girls," Jenna cut in. "There are no purple golf balls here."

"Why not?" Abby asked.

"I don't know."

"Just get another color," Bridget told her.

"I don't want another color. Jenna, can you find a purple golf ball?"

Wyatt caught the frustration straining Jenna's features.

"Honey, you'll have to pick another color," Jenna reasoned.

Abby stomped her foot. "Purple is my favorite."

"Purple is stupid," Bridget stated.

Before Jenna could intervene, the girls started an all-out argument on the merit of different-colored golf balls. The tension around Jenna's eyes had Wyatt butting in before he realized what he was doing.

"You know why they don't have purple, don't you?"

The girls stopped mid-argument and turned to him.

"Because it's a stupid color?" Bridget repeated.

He chuckled. "Because it's the color of royalty. Only princesses get to use purple."

Abby frowned. "You're making that up."

Wyatt laughed.

"So what if he is?" Bridget smiled up at Wyatt.

"Sorry, girls. They have other colors to choose from."

"How about pink instead?" Abby said.

Max leaned over the counter and held up a fluorescent pink golf ball. "You're in luck, kiddo."

"Yay." Abby marched over to take her prize from Max while Wyatt produced a bright yellow ball for Bridget. She took it without complaining.

Wyatt waited until everyone, except Jenna, was out of earshot.

"You have your hands full."

She sighed. "I think maybe today was too much for them. Swimming, shopping and golf? What was I thinking?"

"You wanted them to have a good time."

"I did." She grinned and his unease lessened.

"Listen, I didn't mean to just show up unannounced," he told her. "The guys failed to mention you had no idea I'd be here."

"I figured that by all the sly looks passing between the adults."

"If you want me to leave…?"

"Only to disappoint Bridget and no doubt start another argument? No way."

Right. No more tension.

She hurried to catch up with the others.

Before long they'd settled into the game. The guys talked trash. The women cheered each other on in their attempt to beat the men. Wyatt watched Jenna's eyes narrow every time one of her twins hung on his words. He figured a smug smile would turn her off, so he listened to the twins and kept his distance from their guardian.

They'd reached the fifth hole, a tricky layout with a sharp right angle and working windmill, when someone's phone blared a symphony of clanging chimes.

Jenna pulled her cell from her pocket and glanced at the screen. "It's my agent. I need to take this."

Wyatt watched her walk a few paces away for a private conversation before turning to the group. "What does she need an agent for?"

Six sets of eyes blinked back at him.

He held his hand out. "What?"

"You do realize she's on television," Max informed him.

"Television? Doing what?"

"She's a chef. Has her own cable show."

"So she's a celebrity?"

Max nodded. "I guess you could call her that."

Great. Just what he didn't want to know.

His ex had talked endlessly about going to LA to make it big in movies. She had tons of magazines on the film industry scattered around their living room. Went on and on about who was in what movie. She'd even taken acting lessons from a local who had once worked on Broadway. Her aspirations had enticed her away from her husband and young son to the point of becoming a tangible third party in their marriage.

Wyatt ran a hand through his hair. Their last big fight had been over her plan to leave, with her male agent no less, right before they'd lost Jamie. Soon after, Marcie left for good too.

Here he'd been thinking Jenna's job solely entailed being the girls' guardian. To be honest, he hadn't even considered she had a career. If he had, it would have been some normal nine-to-five gig allowing her time at night with the girls. And now to find out Jenna's career was in the same world Marcie had left him for? Great. "Buddy, I know you've been incommunicado for a while, but really? You didn't know who Jenna was?"

Wyatt glanced at Max. "Not a clue."

Max chuckled. "Rich."

Jenna returned a few moments later, slipping her cell into her pocket. "Sorry about that."

"Everything okay?" Nealy asked. Wyatt didn't miss the worry in her eyes.

Jenna waved her hand. "Barbara is after me to do a commercial for a sponsor of the show. I'd have to fly to LA and I don't want to leave the girls, especially with school starting next week."

The disappointment swimming in Wyatt's stomach lessened. Okay, Jenna might work in LA, but she had her head on straight when it came to the twins.

"They can always stay with me if you have to go," Nealy volunteered.

"Jenna, can we stay with Nealy?" Abby asked.

"It'll be fun," Bridget squealed.

The girl's rapid-fire requests soon turned into a chant. "Nealy. Nealy. Nealy."

Jenna held up her hand to silence the girls. "Enough. We'll talk about it later."

The two turned away, but not before exchanging a glance of displeasure Jenna couldn't miss.

The girls' slight had to hurt.

"It's your turn," Wyatt reminded her in a quiet tone.

"Thanks." She met his gaze but couldn't quite hide her distress. "I should enjoy this night before duty calls." He let the group move well ahead of them, leaving him alone with Jenna so they could talk.

"Are you talking about duty taking you away from your family?"

"To support them, yes."

"I don't know if I could have traveled and left Jamie for any length of time."

She took a step back as if his words had physically struck her. "If it was for his well-being, I'm sure you would have. Besides, you had your wife to help take care of him."

A bitter smile curved his lips. "You'd think."

Jenna's brows rose. "She didn't help?"

"Let's just say she had stars in her eyes. The Hollywood film industry kind of stars."

"Oh." With a slight frown, she took hold of the putter and stepped up to the tee area to take her swing. Her orange ball rolled down the artificial turf, narrowly missing the moving blade of the windmill and skimming the lip of the cup. Turning to watch, the twins cheered, but Wyatt noticed the tension in her tight shoulders.

When she stepped away, he took his turn. His steady aim sent the putt straight down the green and through the turn, until the golf ball knocked into a moving blade. His shot veered off course, tumbling down the slope at a far distance from the cup. The group milled about at the end of the green as each of them completed the hole.

Jenna lingered behind the others.

"Good shot," he said as he walked beside her, the soft scent of her floral perfume wafting his way. Even though he'd intentionally isolated himself from others, he hadn't forgotten how much he enjoyed the femininity of a woman. Her perfume seemed to wake up a side of him he'd almost forgotten.

"I don't want to brag or anything, but I am good at mini golf," Jenna said.

"Is that so?"

"And I'm good at my job. If I have to travel, I travel."

Wyatt ran his hand through his hair. "I didn't mean to insinuate you don't put the girls first."

Her eyes narrowed. "I think you did since you made it clear you never would have left your son."

"I guess I'm a little touchy on the subject of the welfare of children."

"I'm assuming you worked before the accident?"

Her question surprised him. "Yes. But I made sure I took a job that didn't require traveling."

"Well I don't have that luxury." She pressed her lips together for a moment. "I'm sure if your job did require traveling, you would have gone to benefit your family."

"I'll never know, since I worked here in town."

"Nealy said you ran a fishing charter?"

"Actually, I owned the boat. A number of boats, to be exact. Sold the fleet after Jamie died."

Jenna's shrewd eyes met his. "So you were gone for long hours every day?"

"Yes. But I came home every night."

Jenna's cheeks flamed red.

"I think we've gotten off on a touchy subject here. What do you say we play golf instead of discussing parenting methods?"

"Good idea."

She moved away, taking her last shot before joining the rest of the group. More than a little rattled by Jenna, Wyatt took three tries to sink the ball. Max and Dane had a field day razzing him, but the only thing that bothered him was the hurt mingled with frustration in Jenna's eyes. His social skills were worse than rusty. Where was Mr. Suave when he needed him?

The play went on for a few more holes. By the last one, Dane and Max were a single point apart while Wyatt lagged behind by five. Taking the win seriously, Dane got down on one knee to read the line and take full advantage of his putt.

"You do know you aren't going to make the shot," Max taunted. "The last one is the hardest."

"Keep talking, Sanders. I plan on keeping my twenty."

"Twenty what?" Nealy asked.

"Dollars. We've got a wager going."

"And you neglected to tell me?" She jammed a hand on her hip. "I'm in."

"Me too," Jenna said, high-fiving her friend.

Lilli shook her head. "You all are way too competitive."

"Yeah, yeah," Max grumbled. "You in?"

"And let you guys take all the glory?" Lilli scoffed. "Not a chance. I'm in, too."

All at once, the play turned serious. Even the twins sensed a change in the air and kept their chattering to a minimum. When the final score was tallied, Jenna came up the winner.

"Oh yeah," she said, doing a little celebratory jig. The twins joined her while Max and Dane scowled.

"I'm not surprised she won," Wyatt told his friends as they returned their putters. "I'm finding out she's pretty tenacious when she wants to be."

"I demand a rematch," Max announced.

"Anytime." A big smile graced Jenna's face,

knocking Wyatt even more off balance. "But right now, I'm more than happy to take your money."

Once the guys determined a strategy to win next time, a jovial mood enveloped the group. Jenna pulled her keys from her pocket. "Okay, girls. Time to head home."

She looked around but there was no sign of them. "Abby! Bridget!" she called frantically.

No response. In silent agreement, the two couples took off in different directions to search for the girls.

Jenna stood rooted to the spot, her face pale. "I can't believe this," she whispered.

Wyatt touched her arm. "They're kids. They have a tendency to wander off."

"You don't understand. The last time Abby left my side she was almost hit by a car."

He took her chilly hand. "Let's check the parking lot."

They each took a section of the lot, calling the girls' names with no answer. They met on the path back to the admission booth.

"No luck," Wyatt said, frustration pounding in his heart. He should have kept a better eye on the girls. That parental instinct never went away, did it?

In the dimming light, he noticed Jenna's face had grown even whiter.

"They can't have wandered off too far, could they?"

He put his hand on her shoulder. "Let's see if the others had any success."

They'd taken two steps when the girls rounded the corner of the snack shack, something wiggling in Abby's arms.

Jenna hurried over, crouching down before them. "Where have you been?"

"We heard a baby kitty crying and went to see if it was okay." Abby held up a meowing calico. "I think it's hungry."

Jenna closed her eyes for a half second before focusing on the girls. "Do you realize how worried we were?"

By this time, the other adults had returned and gathered around the twins, who now had deer-in-the-headlights looks.

"Sorry," they said in unison.

"Don't ever do that again," Jenna whispered. "You scared me."

"We said sorry." Abby hugged Jenna.

"We should have told you but, um…" Bridget looked up at the adults. "We were afraid you'd say no."

"Or we might have offered to come with

you." Jenna let out a long breath, followed by a nervous chuckle. "Next time, let me know."

"Okay."

Abby waited a split second. "Can we keep the kitty?"

"No."

"Why not?"

"Because it might belong to someone else. Let's go to the office and find out."

Bridget crossed her arms over her chest.

"You're mean," Abby muttered.

Jenna took the wiggling kitten from Abby's grasp. "Next time maybe you'll think before you act."

Wyatt followed Jenna as she led the way to the ticket window. When the woman inside saw the kitten her eyes went wide. "What are you doing with Smoky?"

"My girls found her out by the fence."

The woman's face turned red. "Oh my goodness, I didn't realize she was gone. Last time I looked she was sleeping."

Jenna handed the kitten to her owner. "She must have escaped."

The woman's smile was rueful. "She is a little escape artist."

"I'm just glad the girls found her."

The woman hugged the kitten to her chest and beamed at the twins. "Thank you, girls."

"You're welcome," Abby whispered, tears glimmering in her eyes. Bridget put her arm around her sister, turning so their backs were to Jenna. Wyatt couldn't miss the despair in Jenna's eyes.

Now that the girls were safe, the group headed to their cars. Wyatt helped Jenna get the girls into the van. As he slid the door shut, she said, "Did I react too strongly with the girls?"

"You were right. You couldn't reward them for running off." He reached out and touched her arm. "Parenting isn't for the faint of heart."

"I'm guessing it doesn't get any easier?"

He stared out over the parking lot, studying the burnt-orange horizon, before turning back to her. He swallowed. "I can't say for sure, but I do know it's the best job you'll ever have."

CHAPTER SIX

THREE DAYS LATER, Jenna found herself back in LA, exhausted after the grueling six-hour commercial shoot her agent had arranged. The sponsors were pleased with the results and Jenna's willingness to fly to the coast on short notice. Unfortunately, it also prompted Barbara to propose additional work. Jenna refused, reminding her agent she had a family waiting at home.

"You're passing up opportunities that might not come our way again," Barbara reminded her, the tone of her voice so strained it sounded more like a dire warning.

Rubbing the tension in her neck, Jenna said, "I realize that, Barbara, but I need to get back. The girls start school on Monday and I want to be there."

"You aren't helping me here."

Jenna tuned out Barbara's arguments, wondering if this was what she had to look forward to in the future. Jetting back and forth across the country for a few hours' work? Worrying about how the girls were doing without her? Nealy's suggestion of working together sounded better as the long day progressed.

Her agent blew out a frustrated breath. "All right. I can see you aren't going to budge. In that case, we'll need to strategize and find ways to work around your new home."

"Thanks. I appreciate your staying with me, even if it is driving you crazy."

Barbara grinned. "Just remember that when I propose my next ideas."

"I will."

When Jenna arranged the move to Florida, her emotions had been at a high point. She really hadn't considered the logistics. Now she understood why Wyatt made a point of not traveling for his job. He wasn't being judgmental, he was being…a parent.

Had she been too hasty in her decision-making? Had she not thoroughly considered all her options?

The grief counselor had warned against making major changes so soon after Carrie's death, but Jenna hadn't listened. So here she was, questioning her current situation and fretting about the future. All because she had no clue how to be a good mother. What she did know was that she desperately loved the twins and would do anything in their best interest.

If they'd stayed in LA, she wouldn't have to travel for her job. Barbara was right about one thing. If she wanted to keep her career relevant, she would have to compromise. Do commercials, maybe some appearances. The idea didn't sit well, especially since she'd been reporter-free since arriving in Florida. From her friends in the business, she'd found out that Rod still had his sights on his latest interest, Pamela somebody.

What a headache. After a two-hour dinner meeting with her agent, Nealy's offer sounded like a dream come true.

She had some serious decisions to make.

Finally, Barbara drove her to the hotel. All Jenna wanted to do was take a shower and fall into bed. She entered the lobby and was digging for her room key in her purse when she heard a familiar voice.

"Well, if it isn't my favorite chef."

Jenna jerked her head up, surprise and revulsion cascading through her as she watched Rod casually get up from an armchair, acting as if they'd just seen each other yesterday.

"Shame on you for leaving town without telling me. Imagine my surprise when a stranger stepped out of your apartment." He made a tsking sound. "I was concerned."

"How did you—"

"Find out you're in town?" He sent her a self-satisfied smile. "I always know what you're up to."

Stunned, she had no idea what to say.

"You know," he continued, unfazed by her evident alarm, "I thought we had a good thing going."

She ran a clammy hand over her skirt. "Rod, we don't have anything going. We never did. This has always been a job for you."

"No, Jenna. You're wrong. We have an unmistakable chemistry. I've been waiting for you to realize the truth."

"The truth? There is no chemistry. There will never be any us." She cleared her dry throat. "If you don't leave right now, I'll call the police. You're violating the restraining order."

A red flush covered his cheeks, but he smiled at her. "I know things got out of control for a while." He shoved his hands in his pockets. "I didn't meant to cause you any harm. You have to believe me."

At this point, she didn't know what to think.

He seemed sincere, yet she couldn't ignore the niggle of disbelief.

"I am sorry. I'll leave you alone now."

She watched him exit the lobby, a small laugh escaping her. He'd gone, just as she asked.

Drama over. Now she could move on to the more important aspects of her life, such as raising the girls in peace.

DEPLANING IN TAMPA after the red-eye from LAX, Jenna dragged herself and her overnight bag through the noisy airport. All she could think about was a good cup of coffee and a hot shower. Still contemplating Rod's change of heart, she decided to take it as a good sign. He'd moved on, and so would she. Glad the nightmare was over, she'd get a hold of the police chief when she got home to inform him of the latest development.

Breathing easy, she spied the girls waving at her, standing alongside Nealy. In that moment, she forgot her fears. What she desperately needed was their little girl hugs.

"I missed you both so much," she said, savoring their tight embraces and sweet scents. Jenna hadn't realized how much she'd missed them all until she saw their smiling faces.

"We missed you too, but we had fun," Abby said between hugs.

"We swam in Dane's pool and ate at the hotel," Bridget informed her. "And Mr. Wyatt showed us how to float in the water."

Jenna raised a brow at Nealy. Her friend shrugged. "We were hanging out and I invited Wyatt to join us. So sue me."

Torn between laughing and reminding her friend that Wyatt wasn't the most social of guys, Jenna decided to let the girls fill her in on their adventures on the drive home. She'd deal with Nealy later.

"I can't wait for dinner tonight. Will you make something special?" Bridget asked once they were settled in the car and Nealy navigated the traffic out of the airport.

"Anything you want," Jenna answered.

The girls giggled. Nealy shot them a stern glance in the rearview mirror. Before Jenna could ask what was up, Abby started to talk about a girl she'd met who was going to be in her class at school. Jenna felt a huge relief. She had always dreaded a new school year in a new school while in the foster system, so her heart soared as she listened to Abby relate exacting details about the meeting.

"Her name is Nikki and I like her already. We're going to try to sit together in class."

"Hey, what about me?" Bridget asked.

"You'll find your special friend," Jenna assured her. "After all, I found your mom."

"And became BFFs."

"Yes, we did."

At the girls' chatter, the stress of business eased from Jenna's shoulders. Once at the house, Bridget and Abby ran around to the backyard, Nealy popped the trunk to retrieve Jenna's suitcase. With little ears out of hearing range, Jenna plopped her hands on her hips.

"Wyatt? Really?"

"You didn't say they couldn't hang out with him."

"Because I didn't expect him to be around."

"The girls wanted to see Cruiser, so I called him. Then we invited him to swim. No big deal."

"I don't want the girls getting attached to him."

Nealy sighed. "This again?"

Jenna took the handle of her suitcase and rolled it up the driveway. "Yes. We've had this discussion once. Let's not go there again."

"Why? Because you're so convinced he'll

purposely do something like…I don't know…
leave you guys?"

"Not purposely, but he made it very clear
he's emotionally unavailable. I'm just looking out for the future." Her brow furrowed as
she tried to explain some of the issues that
had been circling her brain on the flight home.
"Because of the problems in LA, I might have
rushed us here to Florida a little too soon."

"You aren't thinking of leaving, are you?"

"No. I wouldn't do that. One upheaval is
enough for the girls." Rod's appearance yesterday reminded her she wouldn't risk putting
the girls in harm's way.

"Okay. I can understand the second-guessing."

"As soon as we get here, Wyatt literally
dives into our lives. And what do I do, I push
him to give the girls swimming lessons when
it's abundantly clear he's not in a good place."

"But he's getting better. Since you and the
girls moved here, I've seen him out and about
more than months before."

"But he's still grieving. Once he starts to
get his emotions together, I'm afraid he might
not want to spend time with us. I don't think
the girls can stand another loss in their lives."

"Us?" Nealy grinned. "Hmm. Now I think we're getting somewhere."

Jenna stopped in her tracks. "What's that supposed to mean?"

"Are you worried about Wyatt hurting the girls or you?"

All set to argue, Jenna mounted her defense, but just as quickly, lost steam. "Honestly? Both."

"Not everyone leaves, you know."

"In my life they do." First her mother. People in and out of foster care. François. Carrie. Did she have it in her to trust her heart to anyone ever again? Especially Wyatt?

Nealy shook her head. "You're just as bad as Wyatt. Afraid to take a chance."

"You know how my last relationship ended. Not pretty."

"François turned out to be a jerk."

"A jerk who ended up with all of our friends."

Nealy tilted her head. "It seems losing the friends bothered you more than the breakup."

She was probably right.

The early afternoon sun beat down on Jenna's head and a pesky insect buzzed by. Jenna swiped at it, wishing she could rid herself as easily of her doubts as the flying pest.

When Jenna had met Francois, a dashing French chef, in culinary school, she never dreamed he would notice her. But he had, just a few weeks into the semester. At first they'd started out talking shop, which soon led to longer after-school hours together. When he asked her to the local farmer's market, she'd been honored, especially because he introduced her to the secret places he bought his natural ingredients. Then he asked her to dinner under the guise of checking out a new buzz-worthy restaurant.

It wasn't until he kissed her that she realized she'd been on a date. Before she knew it, her heart had stepped over the line into dreams of romance and happily-ever-after, especially when he promised that together, they would take the culinary world by storm. And to add to her joy, François's friends had become hers as well. Good friends had been few and far between in her life and now that she'd become part of a group of people she enjoyed, she didn't think life could get any better.

Over time, she'd noticed François becoming increasingly short with her, first when she breezed through school with the high regard of her instructors, then when she landed a job at a popular restaurant followed by her cooking show. As a result of her success she lost her jealous beau, along with people she'd thought were her true friends.

Two boys on bicycles pedaled by, their loud voices jarring her from her dismal thoughts.

"Losing François was pretty devastating. I trusted him. Believed him when he said he loved me. I don't want to go through that again."

"I get what belonging means to you. And you have to know here in Cypress Pointe, you're a part of us."

Jenna nodded, touched by her friend's real concern. She might hope, might even let herself believe Nealy's heartfelt words, but experience had proven that as much as she wanted to belong, to be a family, life wasn't that easy. And while Nealy had been a true friend, she had a man in her life. She and Dane planned to build a future together. Would Jenna ever get to that place in her own life?

Better to end the conversation now than talk it to death. "You know I love being here. And I appreciate how you've included the girls and me in your life. I'm sorry I'm overly cautious, but old habits die hard." She ran her hand over her churning stomach. "I've had time to finally catch my breath and think. Right now the best thing for us is to put the brakes on spending time with Wyatt."

Nealy ducked her head. "About that…"

Jenna held up her hand in protest. "Conversation is over. Now let's get out of the sun before I fry. This pale skin needs sun block or I'll look like a tomato."

"I should probably take off." Nealy glanced at her watch. "I'm meeting with a prospective client."

"Great. I hope it works out."

"Me too. Starting my own business is rather nerve-racking. But if we work together…"

"I'm still considering all my options," Jenna said. "Besides, I have faith you'll get the client. And thanks for the ride home from the airport."

Before Nealy had a chance to leave, Bridget came around the side of the house. "Did you tell her yet?" she asked Nealy.

"To be honest, I was trying to avoid it."

A sense of foreboding settled over Jenna. "Tell me what?"

Bridget's eyes went wide. She turned and dashed back the way she came.

"Um, about your plans to put the brakes on Wyatt?"

Oh no. By the guilty look on Nealy's face, this could not be good. "What did you do?"

"Not me. Bridget invited Wyatt to dinner tonight."

"Tonight?"

"I'm so sorry."

Jenna narrowed her eyes. "You are so not sorry."

"It's not so much I'm sorry as I knew you wouldn't be thrilled. Bridget invited him before I had a chance to intervene. She caught us both off guard."

"And neither of you told her no?"

Nealy shrugged, an unrepentant smile curving her lips.

"Is that why she was asking about dinner tonight when we were in the car? Why didn't you say anything sooner?"

"I'm telling you now."

In panic mode, Jenna glanced at her watch, realizing she only had a few hours to come up with a menu, shop for the ingredients and cook a meal before Wyatt showed up. Her heart pounded. From the pressure of coming up with a special meal? Or the prospect of seeing Wyatt again? A little of both, maybe? No, definitely more about Wyatt.

So much for her calm, cool, collected plan

to avoid him. Maybe she could call him and postpone the evening, blaming jet lag. But then she'd disappoint Bridget. She didn't want to do that either.

"This is too much," Jenna quipped. "These girls have us wrapped around their little fingers."

Nealy grinned. "And I don't expect that to change anytime soon. Get used to it, Mom."

"Mom. Right." Jenna shook off the trepidation. She could do this for Bridget.

Nealy drove away, leaving Jenna to enter the house, or rather, the home she'd created for Abby and Bridget. She opened the back door and yelled, "Girls! Front and center. We need to talk."

WYATT STOOD ON the doorstep, staring down at a hastily purchased bouquet of daisies, mentally arguing how sensible it was to actually show up tonight. Along with his dog. Not sure what to wear, he'd thrown on a black polo shirt and jeans.

Sure, he suspected Jenna wouldn't be happy about him coming over for dinner, especially since she'd been out of town when Bridget extended the invitation. He should have declined, but he was finding it increasingly harder to refuse the wide, pleading brown eyes of the little girl. What she'd wanted was Wyatt to come by for dinner and bring Cruiser with him.

What Wyatt wanted was to see Jenna again. Despite all his arguments to himself about not getting involved, the bottom line was he needed to be around a woman who brought the sunshine back into his life, despite his insistence he didn't want that.

So here he stood in spite of the fact that he and Jenna continuously rubbed each other the wrong way.

He closed his eyes. Erased the image of Jenna's surprise when they collided in the pool, the feel of her soft skin against his.

Change that to constantly at odds.

Cruiser whined from his position beside his master.

Wyatt opened his eyes. "Give me a minute, buddy. This isn't as easy as it looks."

The dog stared up at him. If Wyatt didn't know better, he'd have sworn the animal shook his head in disgust.

"Easy for you, everybody loves a dog."

To which Cruiser responded by thumping his tail.

Before reason could take over, he rang the

doorbell and braced himself for the night ahead.

The sound of scrambling feet came from inside and the door burst open to reveal two smiling faces.

"Mr. Wyatt!"

"Hi, girls."

Bridget grabbed his hand. "Come in."

He chuckled as the girls dragged him down a tiled hallway to the bright kitchen. Jenna turned around from the stove, the savory aroma of sautéing vegetables spicing the airy space. "You're here."

She smiled, her face rosy and gorgeous, but he didn't miss the hint of wariness. Only a few days apart and he'd missed her sparkling green eyes. She looked great in an aqua tank top and long flowing skirt in shades of yellow, green and blue.

"I am." He held out the flowers.

"Oh, my." She removed the pan from the burner and turned off the stove. Her hand brushed his as she accepted his gift. His gaze shot to her wide eyes. "How nice. Thank you."

He forced himself to keep from staring at her. *Act natural.* "It's the least I can do. It smells good in here."

Jenna shrugged but didn't hide her pleasure. "Let me put these in water."

She reached up to open a cabinet, removing a cut crystal vase. Once she filled it with water from the tap, she cut the stems before arranging the daises. "Lovely."

He continued to stare at her. "Yes."

She cleared her throat. "I didn't have a lot of time to prepare, so I marinated chicken to grill."

"Sounds great." He stuck his hands in his pants pockets. "It was nice of you to plan dinner, since you just got back from your trip. You could have rescheduled."

"And let Bridget down? She's looking forward to tonight."

Fair enough. Jenna didn't want to disappoint the kids. He got that, so was she just putting up with him for Bridget's sake? It was one thing to do something nice for your children, another to have dinner with a man she might be interested in. Since Jenna wouldn't meet his eyes and hurried about the kitchen in a flurry of activity, he wondered which category he fell into.

With a nod, she finished with the flowers, placing the vase at the center of the table. Then she scooped the vegetable mixture into a bowl, covered it and set it aside. "Let's go out back," she said, gesturing him to follow. On the back patio, the lid of the grill was already open.

He gazed around the backyard, his heart suddenly heavy at the homey sight. Picturesque best described the scene. Lush grass, blooming flower beds with insects buzzing from bud to bud, a new privacy fence. The heat still held the day hostage, but also set free the rich scent of the earth. Bridget and Abby giggled as they raced around, Cruiser barking at their heels. He swallowed hard, knowing he'd never share simple family moments like these with his son.

"Oh, please."

He switched his attention back to his hostess. "What's wrong?"

She pressed the ignition button on the grill numerous times. "This grill is finicky. I turned on the gas, but sometimes it won't light."

"Let me give it a try."

Wyatt checked the control panel, twisted the dials to adjust the gas pressure and pressed the ignition button again. With a whoosh, a fire sprang up along the burners.

"Here you go."

Her mouth gaped open. "Unbelievable. The only reason it worked for you is because I primed it."

He grinned. "Right."

"Let me get the chicken."

While Jenna ventured back inside, Wyatt wandered the backyard. The neatly cut grass cushioned his steps. Coral-hued honeysuckle laced the back fence, the nectar emitting a sweet scent from the tube-shaped flowers. A distracted grin curved his lips. The floral scent reminded him of Jenna. Dodging the girls as they ran past, he came across a long, wide box. Under closer inspection, he noticed a picture glued to the top. He crouched down, to find a picture for an elaborate swing set.

"Jenna is gonna build that for us," Bridget informed him as she ran over. "We picked it out."

"It's pretty awesome."

"I know. I like the playhouse. It's going to be our castle."

"Where we wait for our prince," Abby said as she joined them. "Who is probably Cruiser."

Wyatt laughed. "I'm sure he'll be honored."

"But Jenna has to build it first."

He glanced at the picture again. The set included a small off-the-ground playhouse, swings and a slide. Jenna planned to assemble this alone?

"Hey, what are you looking at?" Jenna called from the patio where she held a platter.

Wyatt rose and walked to her. "The girls were showing me the swing set. Pretty ambitious project."

"I can handle it." She shrugged. "Go big or go home, I always say."

"Do you plan on building it yourself?"

"Sure, why not?" Her eyes narrowed. "You don't think I can do it?"

"I'm not saying that. I have no doubt you can do anything you put your mind to."

"But…"

"If you want to get the set built so the girls can use it in this lifetime, you could use some help."

She frowned, her eyes changing to a deep shade of green and flashing with indignation. "Because women can't build things?"

"No, because with all the pieces, it'll take you forever."

"I'm good with tools," she told him, her voice tight. "I'll get it done."

Yeah, he'd stepped right into it, suggesting she couldn't tackle the swing set on her own, but he liked the fiery challenge in her eyes. "I'd love to hear all about this."

"And I'd love to regale you with my talent for tools, but right now I have to get the chicken on."

Platter in hand, she turned back to the grill.

He silently sighed. He'd made her angry, again, without really trying. While he liked the attraction between them, he warned himself to back off. Reminded himself he wasn't looking for anything between them.

He ran a hand through his hair. So much for tonight being stress free.

"Not again," Jenna muttered from her place beside the grill.

He joined her. "Another problem?"

"The fire went out."

She placed the platter on a small table and stepped closer to examine the dial. "This thing came with the rental house but I am so going to buy a better model."

"For right now, let's figure out what's wrong with this one."

Wyatt knelt down to inspect the fuel line, which seemed intact. He stood to fiddle with the dials again. Jenna hovered, her floral perfume drawing his attention from the task. He tried to concentrate, but the warmth of her body had his thoughts going from the grill to the fact that she made his heart race. He turned, a mistake, when he found his face mere inches from hers.

"What do you think?" She bit her lower lip.

That I want to kiss you.

No, no, no. "I'm not sure what the problem is."

They stood staring at each other for a drawn-out moment before Jenna blinked. Wyatt mentally shook off his lapse of sanity and pressed the ignition button again. Nothing.

"This is ridiculous," Jenna muttered.

Before he had a chance to respond, Cruiser started barking. The girls squealed. Wyatt glanced up to see a cat streak across the top of the fence, heading in their direction. Cruiser followed the fleeing cat, running past a surprised Jenna, his tail whopping Wyatt on the leg before rounding the table with the platter. In his haste to catch his prey, the retriever knocked the table over, sending the chicken into the flower garden. Then he proceeded to trample over it. The dog ended his quest with his front paws on the fence. The cat jumped into the neighboring yard.

"Cruiser," Wyatt shouted just as Jenna cried, "our dinner." She hurried over to look at the dirt-covered chicken.

"Eww. We aren't going to eat that," Abby told her as she hovered nearby.

"Just rinse it off," Bridget said.

Jenna frowned at her.

"What?"

"I don't think the five-second rule applies when the food is covered with dirt and dog prints." Jenna picked up the chicken with the tips of her fingers and dropped it onto the platter.

Wyatt pulled Cruiser from the fence and pointed to the far end of the patio. The dog slinked off, tail between his legs, dropping down at the appointed stop. His tongue lolled out of his mouth as he caught his breath after all the excitement.

For a minute, Wyatt watched Cruiser, then turned to meet Jenna's eyes. The grill ignition button suddenly popped and a flame scurried across the burners. Wyatt couldn't help it. A grin formed, spreading to an all-out smile. Before he knew it, they were laughing at the fate of their dinner.

"Definitely getting a new grill," Jenna said drily.

After turning off the phantom grill, he followed Jenna into the kitchen, where she dumped the contents of the platter into a plastic trash bag.

"So much for grilled chicken." She headed to the refrigerator. "I'll find something else to make."

"Let's just get take-out."

She opened the door and studied the choices inside. "No, I'm sure I can find ingredients to whip up something else."

"Look, I appreciate the gesture, but my dog destroyed dinner. Let me order a pizza."

"But, I—"

Wyatt gently took hold of her arm, pulled her from the refrigerator and pushed the door closed. "No arguments. Just give me the number of your favorite place."

She blinked. "I don't have any numbers. We don't get take-out."

"Never?" If he didn't have half a dozen numbers programmed into his phone he'd starve.

"Never. I always cook."

"Wow. Nice." He pulled out his phone. "I'll call a place I like and have them deliver. Sound good?"

"Wyatt, you don't have to."

"I want to. Leave it to me."

She bit her lip, sending his pulse skyrocketing again. "Okay."

He made the call while she put away the vegetables and cleaned up the kitchen. By the time the two pies arrived, she had plates set out on the table, cold tea poured in tall, ice-filled glasses.

Placing the boxes on the counter, he opened one containing plain cheese that he knew the girls would like, the other a specialty Hawaiian pie he'd come to favor.

Jenna considered her options before a smile crossed her face. She opened the fridge door, took out the vegetables she'd cooked earlier, warmed the bowl in the microwave and spread the mixture over her cheese slice. "Not bad," she said after her first bite.

"Must be a chef thing."

She laughed. Had to be the best sound he'd heard in ages.

After they finished eating, Abby looked at Jenna, her little face solemn. "This is really good. Why don't we ever order pizza?"

"You know I like to make my own."

"Yeah but your pizza doesn't taste like this."

"Thanks." Jenna laughed. "I have to say, this has to be the best pizza I've ever eaten. I don't think I could have made my own version as good."

"I doubt that," Wyatt weighed in.

Cruiser rubbed his nose against the glass sliding door, letting loose a whine. The girls went outside to join him.

"Coffee?" Jenna asked him.

"If you're having a cup."

"After the day I've had, all I want to do is sit on the patio and enjoy the evening."

"Sorry for making your day more difficult."

She waved away his worry as she scooped coffee into the paper basket. The rich aroma reached him as she filled the machine with water.

"It's not you. It's a little something called twins. I swear, I never thought my life would be so hectic."

Wyatt gathered up the glasses from the table and carried them to the sink. "Good or bad hectic?"

She glanced out the kitchen window. "Both. They have me stretched in so many different directions."

They worked together to clean up the kitchen. When the coffee had brewed, they each took a mug and moved outside to the patio chairs. Wyatt sat back in one.

"So, to carry on the thread of our conversation, how are you dealing with your life being hectic?"

Jenna cradled the mug with both hands, watching the girls running around with Cruiser.

"I'm not sure what I expected. I mean, I always planned to have a family of my own one day. I'd been so consumed with my show and my busy schedule of endorsements that I only saw Carrie and the girls every so often. Until the girls came to live with me, I never really considered what having them 24/7 would entail."

"Kids change your life."

From the corner of his eye, he saw Jenna take a quick peek in his direction. "I can't even imagine how it must feel to lose a child."

He supposed he should hate that comment, but when Jenna made it, he didn't mind responding. "He may not be here physically, but Jamie definitely lives in my heart."

Jenna shivered despite the warm night air. "I don't know how I'd cope if I lost Abby and Bridget. They've totally changed my life."

"I hope you never have to find out." He stared out to the backyard, his voice tight. "No parent should have to watch their child being taken away from them, knowing they'll never see or touch or comfort that child again."

She seemed to hesitate, then spoke anyway.

"What happened, Wyatt? If you don't mind my asking."

He clenched his teeth. "I don't talk about it."

"Sorry, I didn't mean—"

"But maybe I should." He took a moment to compose himself. "We were out on my speed boat. Marcie and I started arguing—we did that a lot back then. I took my eyes off Jamie for a split second it seemed like. We hit a big swell and the next thing I knew, he tumbled overboard." He swallowed. Pulled it together. "He went under. I dove after him, but the life jacket didn't work properly and…"

He glanced at Jenna, noting her eyes shiny with tears. Instead of pity, like he normally saw, and hated, he glimpsed understanding there. She'd experienced loss in her life. Losing her best friend and taking in her children had changed her forever, just as Jamie's death had forever impacted him.

"Sounds like an accident."

"I should have been more attentive. It's my fault he drowned."

"I can't change how you feel, even though I disagree. But still, cut yourself some slack, Wyatt. Terrible things can happen to our loved ones. We can't control everything, but in time, the pain will get easier to carry."

Jenna did indeed have a clue about the state of his heart and mind. Because of the recent loss of her friend? He didn't have to explain the deep, painful ache that never eased. She got it.

"Thanks." He waited a beat. "For everything."

She swiped her fingers over her eyes then chuckled. "It wasn't my finest cooking hour, but we made due."

"No, I mean, thanks for not being afraid to talk about Jamie. So many people want to shy away from the subject, act like nothing happened. I don't know if they feel awkward or don't want to stir up any sadness by mentioning my son." Maybe that's why he was drawn to Jenna and the girls. Their shared grief. "To be honest, I like talking about Jamie. It brings me comfort."

Jenna turned in the chair, pulling her knees up to tuck them beneath her. "I agree. Those first awkward moments are the worst. I just want to cringe when I have to explain that Abby and Bridget's mother is gone." She glanced over at the girls, sitting under the tree, paying attention to Cruiser lying between them. "It's worse for the girls."

He went quiet for a moment, lost in his

thoughts. "It's weird, how the emotions ebb and flow. Do you notice it with them?"

"Yes. Carrie hasn't been gone as long as your son, so we're still trying to navigate the emotions."

Wyatt sipped his coffee, the rich roast mixed with a bit of cinnamon sweet on his tongue. The shouts from the playing children lifted his heart. A neighbor's sprinkler system kicked on with a whoosh, followed by the *tick-tick-tick* of the sprinkler head. Instead of shutting out the normalcy, he decided to let go and simply enjoy.

"You are doing a good job," he told Jenna.

This time when she looked at him, he saw humor sparkling in her eyes. "Really? You can say that with a straight face after the fiasco tonight?"

"I will admit, I never know what to expect when I spend time you."

"I promise you, we are not usually this accident prone."

A thought flashed through his mind and he laughed.

"What's so funny?"

"We should call you Calamity Jenna."

She tilted her head. "I could see why you'd think that, but honestly, I do have it together."

"And I've seen the good times as well."

As the sun descended, Wyatt noticed Jenna's hair changed color, from the almost white blond to a honey gold. Since she'd been spending time in the sun, her freckles had darkened. She had that girl-next-door attractiveness he'd never sought in a woman before, but as he covertly studied her, he found the look growing on him.

So yeah, he was interested in the total package. Not only the beautiful woman who caught his eye, but the new mother handling a steep learning curve. Every time they were together, he discovered something else that was intriguing about her. He wanted to find out more. Problem was, his interest in her didn't fit the not-wanting-to-get-involved policy he'd instituted since Jamie's death.

At the time, it had been easy to place aspects of his life into nice, neat boxes to help him deal with his emotions. An available excuse to disengage from his life and keep people at arm's length. Until Jenna. Now he found himself rethinking this attitude, deciding how Jenna could be part of his life. Because one thing he knew for sure. He was interested in the woman.

Cruiser barked, drawing his thoughts back

to the present. The dog bounded about the girls, stopping to sniff the box holding the contents of the swing set.

He decided to take a chance and voiced an idea that had crossed his mind. "So I was thinking. What do you say I come by and give you a hand with assembling the swing set?"

When she flashed him an annoyed look, he held up his hand. "I'm not suggesting you can't do it alone. With the two of us working together, the girls might actually get to use it sometime this century."

"Funny."

"I'm serious. I'd like to help you."

Jenna set her mug on the table between the chairs. She hesitated. He found himself holding his breath as he waited for her answer. Maybe she didn't want him around? Maybe he'd overstayed his welcome?

"I suppose I could use some help. You're right, with our hectic schedules, I haven't even opened the box."

He let out a relieved breath. "I'll check my charter schedule and let you know what day we can get started."

She smiled. "Thanks, Wyatt."

"On that note, we should head home." He stood, whistling for Cruiser.

Jenna untangled her legs and rose from the chair. "It's time for the girls to settle down for the night."

Cruiser came to him, his expectant brown eyes waiting for Wyatt's next command. The girls ran over too, flanking the animal.

"Thanks for bringing Cruiser," Bridget said.

"Yeah. He was our first new friend."

"I'm sure that'll change when you start school," Wyatt assured them.

Jenna clapped her hands. "Hey, you two. March inside. I'm going to walk Mr. Wyatt to the door then I'll be back to start your bath."

The girls waved goodbye and hustled inside. Jenna collected the coffee mugs, depositing them on the counter as she led Wyatt to the front door. He stepped onto the porch and turned to face her.

"Thanks again for dinner."

"I really should thank you. You saved the day by ordering pizza."

He shrugged. "I do what I can."

Jenna laughed. "Mr. Helper, I'll see you when we build the swing set."

He winked at her. "It's a date."

Just before he pivoted on his heel to walk away, he caught the surprised look on Jenna's face. Maybe *date* hadn't been the right word choice, but her shocked reaction had him humming all the way to the truck.

CHAPTER SEVEN

TWO WEEKS. THE TWINS had only been in school two weeks and already Jenna was going out of her mind. There was only so much laundry, housecleaning and reading a person could do. On top of that, she kept thinking about her show. Or going into business with Nealy. And in between it all, thoughts of Wyatt kept popping into her mind. What was she going to do with herself?

It's a date.

Right. A date. With Wyatt. In thirty minutes.

So much for keeping her distance.

Actually, she wasn't quite sure they had a date. Did assembling a playground set constitute a date? Really, it was about as far from romantic as she could imagine. Still, when he'd said *date* before leaving the other night, her heart thumped in her chest and her mind went into overdrive.

Did he mean a real date, date? Like one-on-

one romance? Or did he mean it as a figure of speech? The man continually managed to tie her up in knots. Even the girls picked up on her disquiet. For ten-year-olds, they managed to figure out her moods quickly.

"Just chill," she muttered to herself.

After dropping the girls off at school, she headed to the temporary location Nealy had set up for Cuppa Joe, the coffee shop she co-owned with her grandmother, since a fire had damaged the place. Between her event planning business and the shop, Nealy was working overtime to get the space cleaned up, restored and back to normal. The regulars had rallied to the cause, insisting she somehow keep the business going. The landlord of a vacant store on Main had offered to let Nealy run the business from there until Cuppa Joe reopened.

As much as she would have liked to talk to Nealy about her conflicted feelings for Wyatt, her friend was much too busy for a break. As the only event planner in Cypress Pointe, Nealy had multiple appointments scheduled for later that day. She promised Jenna they'd catch up later.

Fighting nervous jitters, Jenna took her coffee to go, not convinced ordering decaf would make a difference, and wandered down Main

Street. Taking advantage of this alone time, she walked at a leisurely pace, passing brightly decorated shop windows inviting shoppers to explore the treasures inside. She stopped more than once, basking in the quiet morning, enjoying the sights around her.

The more time she spent in Cypress Pointe, the more she was beginning to love it here. The easy camaraderie of the town's people and the slower pace of life appealed to her after years spent in the hustle and bustle of LA. Here she breathed more easily, without the constant fear of a reporter popping up out of nowhere, hunting down a story.

While she was glad Rod had decided to leave her alone, doubts still came to mind from time to time. She guessed she'd always be wary of reporters.

Last time she checked with her agent, Rod was busy stirring up stories in LA, latching on to new celebrities. She felt sorry for those people, but was glad she was out of his spotlight.

Now, she and the girls were free to come and go as they pleased. The number one reason for staying here in Cypress Pointe. No reason to worry about Rod any longer or burden her new friends with that problem.

The wonderful people she'd come to know

had busy lives of their own. As long as Rod kept his distance, she and the girls would be okay. Soon, Jenna reached the far end of the main thoroughfare. She paused before a building sporting a For Sale sign. With one hand shading her eyes, she peered through the grimy window of what appeared to be a restaurant.

She'd thought of nothing besides Nealy's offer to work together since her return from LA. She loved her cable show, but there was always someone telling her what to do and when to do it. Although she came up with all original recipes, the producers wanted to tweak her creations to make them more appetizing, in their opinion. The show had been great for exposure. Readers sent her emails and letters raving about how much they liked her style. She loved sharing her cooking ideas with others, but she missed the one-on-one she'd had in culinary school. Maybe at this point in her life Nealy's idea had merit.

In a short span of time, her priorities had changed. If she'd been by herself, the show would probably still satisfy her. Now, however, her decisions affected the girls. Could the next logical step be to start a catering business? Sure, she'd have to begin from scratch, but the challenge stirred the creative side of her.

And the best part? She'd be available for the girls, not traveling and worrying about them. A major plus.

If she did decide to do this, it would mean not renewing her contract with the network. Barbara would definitely have an opinion and be sure to give Jenna an earful about leaving the limelight.

A car door slammed behind her, jerking her from her thoughts. She squinted through the layers of dust to get a read on the inside. Tables were scattered about, chairs stacked in a corner. In her mind, she imagined the existing dining area transformed into an attractive reception space to meet with prospective clients, as well as adding an office. Closer to the kitchen, she could put out a few tables and chairs to accommodate clients sampling items from her menu.

From this vantage point, she couldn't see the kitchen at all. Really, the idea hinged on whether the kitchen was suitable for her plans. To find out she would have to call the Realtor.

A laugh escaped her. Was she serious about this? "Yes," she whispered. She hadn't been this jazzed since the day she'd been offered her own television show.

Glancing at her watch, she realized she had

to get moving or she'd be late meeting Wyatt. She placed her to-go cup on the wide windowsill and searched her purse for a pad and pen. Once she found them, she jotted down the Realtor's number.

Fifteen minutes later she pulled into her driveway, noticing Wyatt had already backed his truck in. She angled the rearview mirror in her direction to fluff her short hair, check her teeth and run bright berry lipstick over her lips. Satisfied she'd passed her own last-minute check, she went around his truck, following the path along the side of the house. The fence gate gapped wide open. One last smoothing of her sleeveless blouse and she entered the backyard to find Wyatt opening the swing set box.

"Hey, what about teamwork?" she called out.

He spun around, smiling when he saw her. "Just getting the preliminaries out of the way."

She shaded her eyes, the midmorning sun exceptionally bright today. The temperature had risen steadily and she knew her blouse and denim capris wouldn't be the best outfit for spending the day working outside, but she had dressed carefully because they had a date.

"I thought if we got started right away, we'd make some serious progress by lunchtime."

And the date? she questioned silently.

Stop it. He might have used the word *date*, but Wyatt had made it more than clear that dating was not going to be a part of this relationship.

He nodded to the pile of supplies. "Ready?"

Right. *Date* in Wyatt language obviously meant an appointment to accomplish an activity. A decidedly unromantic activity.

Silently chiding herself for letting her imagination, and her hopes, go wild, she said, "Let me go in and change. I'll be right back."

He returned to the job at hand while she hurried inside to change into a tank top and shorts. She slathered on SPF 50 and grabbed her small tool chest from the garage, all the time pushing her disappointment down deep. When she joined Wyatt again, with a sunny smile on her face, he had his nose buried in the instruction manual, a frown wrinkling his brow.

"Please tell me you understand the directions."

"I do. I'm going over the list of parts." He glanced up. Went still for a moment when he caught a glimpse of her more work-suitable clothes. She wished he had removed his sunglasses so she could see the expression in his eyes. Even not knowing what he was thinking, she felt her heart trip.

"You sure know how to pick a project," he told her.

"I do." She held up the pink, camouflage-colored tool chest. "And I have my own tools."

He removed his sunglasses. Blinked at the box. "Pink camo?"

"Who says tools have to be blah."

He shook his head and put his glasses back in place. "Okay."

As she moved beside him, she noticed his tangy cologne. It filled her senses, along with the heady mixture of excitement and jitters. And once again, she wondered about the date remark. Yes, he'd made it clear he wasn't available emotionally, but c'mon, she was human. Yes, he interested her. Yes, it was probably a bad idea to hope for more, considering the girls. But she so wanted to ask him what he meant when he uttered those words. Why couldn't she get her mind straight when it came to this man?

Focus on the job at hand. "So, what have we got here?"

"A full day and more of work."

She opened the toolbox and pulled out a hammer. "Lead on."

"First step, let's get all the pieces out and separated in order of use. I brought a couple of containers to store the hardware so we don't misplace anything."

"Good thinking."

"This isn't my first project," he said, grinning at her in a way that made her squirm.

"Don't get all cocky. No plan is foolproof."

"Says the woman who can't start the grill," he said with a straight face.

"Hey, it's defective."

"Right. You keep believing that."

Jenna enjoyed the companionable silence as they pulled the lumber and parts from the box. Once everything was laid out, Wyatt asked her where she wanted the location of the swings.

"A little left of the center of the yard is good. We get shade from the bordering trees in the late afternoon."

Wyatt carried some of the lumber to the spot and they began to work.

"So how did you get so handy with tools?" he asked as he checked the power level on his cordless drill.

"It's one of the things I learned in foster care."

He looked up at her. "Foster care?"

"Yes. Spent most of my life moving from one home to another."

"Must have been tough."

She shrugged. "I missed my mom, but it's where I met Carrie."

"Do you ever see her? Your mother?"

"No. Once we were separated that was it."

"I'm sorry."

"Don't be." She brushed off the underlying hurt of her mother's abandonment. "My life turned out fine."

His voice was gentle when he said, "She's the one who missed out."

Maybe. Jenna didn't usually think of it that way.

Wyatt focused on the drill again. "So, tools?"

The brokenness she usually experienced when she thought about her mom eased. More than anyone she knew, Wyatt understood that certain topics were not pleasant to discuss.

"In so many of the homes, the foster moms didn't have a clue how to fix stuff, so I kinda learned along the way."

"They didn't mind?"

"Nope. In fact the better with tools I became, the more they asked for my help. And the dads were happy because it cut down on their honey-do lists."

"Must have made you very popular."

Jenna moved the lumber closer to where

Wyatt was working. "With the parents, sure. The kids? Not so much."

"They didn't like you helping around the house?"

"No. It made them look bad if they didn't step up ."

"I can see that." He laughed. "My brother, Josh, and I were super competitive, even with our chores. He never did like it when I bested him."

"Take the times your brother was ticked at you and multiply it. My life in foster care."

He looked up from the two pieces of wood he'd fastened together. "So how did you deal with the other kids' attitudes?"

"That's where the cooking came in. I learned early on that a pan of brownies can solve any problem. Short term, anyway."

"Seems like you did a lot of figuring out on your own."

"It wasn't all bad, but yeah, I learned to fend for myself. So now I can fix just about anything with my tools and whip up dinner without breaking a sweat."

"I imagine the foster moms liked your culinary talent, too."

"Yeah, but I really cooked for the kids. With so many coming from difficult backgrounds, I found making them something special counted for a lot toward keeping peace in the house."

Wyatt looked up from a container of bolts, wiping his forehead with his shirtsleeve. "That explains the cookies."

"What do you mean?"

"For you, cooking is a way of giving to others. You wanted to thank me with your cookies, but I have a feeling you also thought the gift might make me feel better."

Was she that obvious? Apparently. "Busted." She snuck a peek at him. "Did it work?"

"Best cookies I ever tasted."

She should really ignore the heart-squeezing, sappy sensation reducing her to a giddy teenager, but she didn't want to. For just a little while, she'd relish the feeling.

But on the heels of the realization came the reality that with Wyatt's loss, he didn't expect anything more between them than friendship. Unfortunately, she'd let herself read more into his offer to help. Sure, she had his male attention. He couldn't completely hide his interest—after all, he was a guy. But long term? That was a whole different discussion. One they might never get to. So right now, if enjoying the sunny day with a handsome man scored an eight on the happiness scale, she'd take it.

Before long, they'd constructed the frame. Admiring their progress, Jenna finished off the last swig of water in her bottle. "How about a break?"

"Sounds good."

They moved to the shade of the patio. Jenna retrieved fresh water from the kitchen. She'd just handed Wyatt a bottle when her cell phone rang. Barbara's name showed up on the caller ID.

"I should answer this."

Wyatt nodded as he sauntered back to the swing set, giving Jenna some privacy.

"Hello, Barbara."

"I know you asked me to give you a break when you left LA, but I have some news."

Jenna held back a sigh. "Okay."

Barbara paused, uncharacteristic for her frenetic agent. A tingle of unease formed in Jenna's belly.

"It's about the show."

"Do they want me back earlier than we talked about? I appreciate the extended hiatus, but I'm not ready—"

"No, in fact they're giving you more time."

Wait. More time? "That's good, right?"

"Only if we're not worried about the new

show they're going to preview in the open time slot."

"New show?"

"Apparently they found another interesting chef who not only cooks but gives fitness advice as well."

"Fitness?"

"Silly, I know. Who wants to think about exercise when they're cooking? Anyway, I reminded them we have a contract and while they are aware of the terms, they're using the clause stating they can push back your show's timetable if there are scheduling differences. Your move to Florida constitutes scheduling differences."

"I don't know what to say."

"Say you'll move back to LA."

As much as she wanted to respond with a resounding no, she had to be wise. Think through her options and determine how best to proceed. Until she decided whether or not to partner with Nealy, she couldn't shut every door. "Do we have to give a response to the network or are they going ahead with their plans?"

"It was up in the air. I'm thinking they wanted to scare you into returning earlier, but

I can't deny the excitement in the executive's voice about this new premise."

Jenna fought the butterflies in her stomach as she gazed over the backyard. She loved the peace and quiet here, loved that the girls had settled in without too much of a fuss. Yes, they'd only been in school two weeks, but, so far so good. Wyatt had pulled out his cell to make a call and she watched him pace, urgently trying to ignore the jolt of pleasure his presence managed to ignite in her. They'd worked well together, even had a bit of fun, but she knew better than to get ahead of herself. Right now, his scowl as he spoke didn't bode well for the remainder of their time together. Still, there was something about the man...

"Jenna? Are you still there?"

"Can you give me some time? I need to check into some things here."

"What kinds of things?" Worry laced Barbara's voice.

"Just an idea my friend mentioned. In light of what's going on with the network, I need to be prepared for the worst."

"I warned you this might happen, Jenna. In this business, it's all about opportunity and timing. I'm not sure about the timing of your move."

"C'mon, Barbara. You know why I left."

"Yes. Rod tailing you was problematic. But he's found other stories to focus on."

"Do we really know that for sure?"

"I've been keeping tabs on him in hopes that once he lost interest in you, you'd come back."

"And you know for sure he's moved on."

"It appears so. There is a new girl making news in town. She's signed on to one of the celebrity dance shows and he's been following her rise in popularity. Actually, she's given him access to her life, so she's making his job easier."

"Why on earth would she do that? Why would anyone want him interfering in their life?"

"Because she's thinking long-term, my dear. Rod is part of her strategy to make it big."

Jenna shivered. "Well, more power to her. I just hope she knows what she's doing."

"Not your problem. You have your own career to worry about."

Jenna knew Barbara was concerned about her biggest client moving far away from the limelight. And while Jenna loved her work, she didn't see it meshing with her family life.

"I'll get back to you soon, Barbara."

"Before you make any decisions, talk to me," she said before signing off.

Jenna set her phone on the patio table. Grabbing her water bottle, she made her way back to Wyatt. As much as she wanted to keep working on the playground set, this newest development took the wind out of her sails.

"Problem?" Wyatt asked, removing his sunglasses when she joined him. She glimpsed the concern in his eyes.

She rubbed her temples and grimaced.

"Sorry. None of my business."

"No. It's fine." Right now she didn't want to dwell on her problems. She'd do plenty of thinking later, most likely much later while she tossed and turned in bed. "I could ask you the same. I saw you talking on your phone. Looked pretty intense."

His eyes grew shadowed, his answer terse. "Family."

Okay, she didn't get all the dynamics with Wyatt, but she was learning. One-word answers meant change the subject.

"Gotcha."

When he raised a brow, she said, "Work issues."

"Ah. Does that mean you're moving back to LA?"

"Why would you automatically assume that?"

"The troubled expression on your face. You've got a weight-of-the-world vibe going on."

She almost laughed, except he'd hit too close to home.

"Nothing I won't survive."

He picked up his drill. "If you ever need someone to talk to…"

"Thanks." She grabbed her hammer and paused. "Actually, I would like to ask you something."

"Shoot."

"You've lived in Cypress Pointe a long time. Do you know anything about the restaurant for sale on South Main?"

"Duke's Grill?"

"I'm not sure. I didn't notice a sign on the building."

"It's got to be the same place. Guy named Duke Skinner used to own it. Before Cypress Pointe became a tourist destination, it was the favorite restaurant in town. I worked for him one summer when I was a teenager."

"Why did he close down?"

"Not sure." He looked at her curiously. "Why do you ask?"

Should she tell him? All morning thoughts of the restaurant space had been hovering on the fringes of her mind. After Barbara's call, she realized she had to check it out in order to consider all her options before dealing with the television executives about her cooking show.

"A long time ago I used to work for a caterer. Nealy knows this, so she suggested we work together. She'll plan events, I'll cater."

"Sounds interesting."

"I haven't quite figured out how that would impact my current career, but if I decide to join Nealy, I'd stay put in Cypress Pointe and have time for the girls."

"Is your own business something you want?"

"Yes." Even as she said the word out loud, she acknowledged the truth behind it. "This morning when I walked by the restaurant, it hit me. We could do this. The location is great. I could transform the dining room to make it inviting for clients. Of course, I'd have to check into the kitchen first, so I jotted down the Realtor's number."

When he didn't say anything she went on. "I want a stable home life for the girls. Traveling back and forth to LA isn't going to cut it and honestly, I'm not sure I want to go back." She bit her lower lip. Wow. She'd said that out loud too. "Having my own place here in Cypress Pointe might be good for us."

"Do you know anything about running a business?"

"Before I got involved with the cooking show, I played around with the idea of opening a restaurant one day. I took business classes, just in case."

"So your answer is…?"

She laughed. "I know how to run a business in theory."

"Theory and real life don't always go hand in hand."

"I know. That's why I'm torn about checking out the place."

"On the other hand, you'll never know what you could have if you don't try."

"You're a philosopher now?"

He grinned. "More like meddler. You don't have to listen to my advice."

"There was advice in there somewhere?"

"Convoluted, but yeah."

"So what I'm hearing is that I should go for it?"

"Check out the space. See if it's something that appeals to you, something you can work with. Then decide."

"Solid advice. I guess I'll give the Realtor a call."

He glanced over her shoulder then met her eyes again. "I could come with you if you want. A second pair of eyes might help."

Her heart fluttered at his offer. "I'd appreciate it. I have to admit, I'm kind of nervous at the prospect of trying something new when I have a pretty sure thing in LA"

"But if you don't look into it, you'll always wonder, what if."

She had to admit, he was right. Saying all the right things.

"Agreed. I'll call and set up an appointment. How about later this afternoon?"

"Impatient?"

"No. I have decisions to make, so the sooner the better. Besides, I figure the Realtor will jump on it and you're off today, so it works."

"I can make it later this afternoon."

"Great. It's a big step. You might ask questions I wouldn't think of."

"Glad to help. It's good to have dreams and ambitions."

She raised an eyebrow. "Dreams and ambitions are good for you, too, you know."

"My life changed after Jamie died." He

picked up the drill to check the bit. "But not only because of my son."

Jenna ducked under the beam they'd assembled for the side A-frame. She got his grief for Jamie, she just wished he could move forward with his life.

"It didn't help when my wife left me for the fame and fortune of Hollywood." He paused a beat. "And for her agent."

Surprised that Wyatt was laying it all on the line, Jenna forgot to lower her head as she backed out and hit the beam with a thud. "Ow!"

"Hey, are you okay?"

She rubbed the back of her head. "I'm not gonna fib. That hurt."

"Let me see."

"I'm fine. Don't worry about me."

"Humor me." Wyatt came up behind her, gently brushing her hair away from her scalp, lightly touching the area. "Just because you like being independent doesn't mean you shouldn't ask for help now and then."

"It's less about independence and more about embarrassment. I'm always so clumsy around you."

"It's endearing."

"Embarrassing."

He chuckled, moving closer. She could feel his body heat along her back as he checked out her head. "I can feel a bump starting."

She swallowed. "Any blood?"

"No."

She turned to tell him she was grateful for looking, but he stood so close, the words died on her tongue as she felt his breath on her cheek. His gaze met hers before moving to her lips. She inhaled, waiting for his next move. She really wanted him to kiss her. But if he did? So many conflicting thoughts ran through her mind, all overpowered by her wanting this man to kiss her.

"You're thinking too hard."

"Sorry. I can't help it."

"Sure you can."

In slow motion, he leaned down to capture her lips. She froze, until he stepped even closer, his hands moving from her head, down her neck to her shoulders. She returned the kiss, resting her hands on his hips.

They stood under the hot Florida sun, sharing what Jenna knew was the most important kiss of her life. Birds sang nearby. A lawnmower droned in the distance, but all she could focus on was the warmth and mastery of Wyatt's lips. No other man had ever come close to stirring her the way he did.

But Wyatt doesn't do permanent, a pesky voice reminded her.

She broke the kiss, staring up at him, thinking it was the best kiss ever and that Wyatt wouldn't let this turn into a relationship. The doubt in his eyes spoke of his reticence.

He dropped his arms to his sides. "I couldn't resist."

She backed up, not sure what to do next. She'd wanted him to kiss her, and he sure did. But to what end? He'd made it clear he didn't want an emotional entanglement. After everything she'd been through lately, she wasn't sure her heart could take being broken. Because Wyatt definitely had the power to bring her to her knees.

"Um…" Jenna glanced at her watch, searching for any excuse to cut the awkward tension between them. "It's almost noon. Want me to throw something together for lunch?"

"Is that professional jargon?"

"Hardly, but you know what I mean."

"I do, but I'll have to pass." He gathered up his tools. "I need to be somewhere, but thanks for the offer."

She tamped down the disappointment of his

refusal as her curiosity rose. Where could the man who barely left his cottage need to go? And when did it become her business?

Switch gears already. "It's the least I can do after you helped get this playground set started."

"It's for a good cause. The girls will love it." They walked to the patio. "Let me have your phone."

She tilted her head in question.

He held his hand out.

She handed him her cell. He punched in a series of numbers. "Text me when you set a time to view the restaurant and I'll meet you."

She stared at his number, sensing that giving a little of himself away, even just a phone number, was a big deal for him. Her pulse leaped. Silly, but there it was. "Thanks. I will."

"It's a *date.*"

She rolled her eyes.

"What?"

She waved her hand. "It's nothing."

He crossed his arms over his chest, waiting.

"Okay." She laughed. "I finally get your meaning of the word date."

He frowned for a second before enlightenment dawned. "Oh, when I said date you thought…"

Her cheeks burned. "Sorry."

"No, don't be sorry. I guess I should have been clearer."

Yeah. The whole not getting emotionally involved thing. Even though he'd kissed her. Why did he kiss her, exactly? She wanted to ask, but was afraid of his answer. "I shouldn't have jumped to that conclusion."

He paused, his body language screaming discomfort. "I'll be more careful next time."

If there was a next time. Argh. She sounded like a love-starved twit. Now would be a good time for the ground to open up and swallow her whole.

"So, ah, text me."

"I will." She graced him with a wide, unconcerned smile to cover her embarrassment.

He replaced his sunglasses as he disappeared around the corner of the house. In the silence she cringed, the voice inside her head reminding her Wyatt didn't do forever.

AFTER A QUICK SHOWER, Wyatt dressed in a pair of dark jeans and button-down shirt. He rolled up the sleeves before heading back out into the heat and the confrontation he was dreading.

Josh had insisted they needed to clear the air. Wyatt didn't know why. He'd been up front and honest ever since Josh moved to town. He didn't need his brother's help. Sure, he appreciated the gesture, but he wasn't a kid. But Josh had been adamant, threatening to come by Wyatt's place unless he agreed to meet. At least in a public place Wyatt could get up and leave anytime he wanted rather than being cornered in his own home.

He hadn't seen his family since the welcome party Nealy had thrown for Jenna at the Grand Cypress. He knew they worried about him. Understood their helplessness. He hated that his grieving burdened them. But he wasn't ready to talk. Or plan a future without his son.

He drove to the Grand Cypress, the designated meeting place, dreading every minute of the conversation to come. He parked, stretched out the tense muscles in his neck before heading to the outdoor restaurant by the pool. His brother, already at a table, stood and waved him over. As he approached, he saw his parents were there as well.

"Son," his father said in greeting.

Wyatt glared at Josh then turned to his parents. "Mom. Dad. What a surprise."

"It's about the only way we get to see you these days."

"I've been busy."

"That excuse is getting old, son."

He hated hearing the hurt in his father's voice. Growing up, they'd been a close-knit family. Even after he'd married Marcie and they'd had Jamie, the family stayed in regular contact. His parents and brother had adored Jamie. They were also hurt by the loss of their grandson and nephew. Maybe that's why Wyatt dreaded being around them. Not just because of the memories, but the fact that he couldn't do a thing to ease their pain. He loved his family, but their hurt tore at his already shredded heart. He couldn't help them until he helped himself.

Wyatt took a reluctant seat at the table.

His mother laid her soft hand over his. "You know we love you."

"I've never doubted that."

"But we worry."

He felt like he was being dragged under a rogue wave, losing his breath under the water without any hope of rescue. He knew his family cared and felt like a jerk for his reaction to their concern.

"I've told you I'm okay," he said with a bite in his tone.

Josh snorted. "And you expect us to believe you? We have eyes."

Wyatt scowled at his older brother. "I didn't ask you to leave your big, fancy computer company to come home and baby me."

"Even though you haven't asked, truth is, I sold it for other reasons. And I wanted to come home."

"Boys," his father interjected. "You're getting off track here."

"What is the track?" Wyatt said in a tight voice. "If you don't mind my asking?"

"Making sure you're okay," his mother answered. "I know you're still grieving, honey, but we want to help."

"Helping me would be leaving me alone. I need to sort this out myself."

"By cutting us out of your life?"

He glanced at his mother's soft, blue eyes. Saw the tangled emotions reflected there. "Is that how you see it?"

"How could we not? You've shut us out, Wyatt."

Yes, he had, because he couldn't carry the pain for everyone and not buckle under the weight.

Josh held up a hand before Wyatt could respond. "We get that it's not about us, but that doesn't stop us from missing you."

Shame slammed into his solar plexus.

For the first time in over two years, he looked, really looked, at the faces of his family. Josh still held on to anger. His parents' concern ranged from worry to frustration. He'd unwittingly placed those burdens on his family. He'd been so mired in his own grief he hadn't considered their point of view.

"I'm sorry. I didn't realize how much my actions have affected you all."

His mother squeezed his hand. "We don't want to rush you, but we want the old Wyatt back, don't we, Bryce?"

"Liz…" his father warned.

Never going to happen, but Wyatt kept the truth to himself. "I'll admit I've closed myself off."

"Become a hermit is more like it," his father said.

"I can't be around people, dealing with the awkwardness and pity. And with you guys fussing all the time, it's tough."

His father cleared his throat. "I'll admit, we might have gone overboard, but we were trying to protect you."

"From what? Jamie's gone. His death was my fault. You can't change the facts or protect me from the guilt."

Tears glittered in his mother's eyes. "It was an accident," she whispered.

"Which never would have happened if I hadn't been distracted."

Silence settled around the table. No one could deny his heart-wrenching words.

His father spoke first. "Son, you have to forgive yourself."

Yeah. He knew that. Easier said than done.

"Remember," his mother added. "Jamie loved you."

Which only made the guilt burrow deeper into his gut. He couldn't speak, couldn't move. His heart hardened like a lump of stone.

"Maybe we could start spending some time together," Josh suggested. "Slowly, at first. Work up to the grudge matches we were notorious for."

His mother glanced at Josh. "As if you have the time."

Glad for a diversion, Wyatt pounced on his mother's comment. "What's up with you, Josh?"

Josh took a sip of water, an obvious delaying tactic.

"Your brother has been keeping himself busy, as well," his mother replied with a frown. "Seems he had a little out-of-town adventure."

No wonder Wyatt had had a reprieve from his brother's meddling. "What kind of adventure?"

His father's brow wrinkled. "An adventure involving a woman."

Wyatt forced a grin. "If I remember right, those are the best kind."

"We aren't here to talk about me," Josh countered.

Just then Wyatt's cell phone pinged. He pulled it from his shirt pocket and read the text.

4 PM. WORK FOR U?

He grinned. Jenna's timing was perfect. How like her to relieve the tension. He had to admit, it had felt good working with her this morning, focusing on something positive rather than brooding on his porch.

His thumbs moved over the screen. SEE U THEN.

"Have you got something more important going on than lunch with your family?" his father asked.

"Sorry. Just confirming an appointment for later."

His mother smiled. "With a therapist?"

Wyatt ground his back teeth. Would they ever quit?

At least when he was with Jenna she didn't pry or push him to make strides he wasn't ready for.

"No. I'm meeting a friend."

"Friend." His dad's expression lightened. "A female friend?"

"Yes. She's considering purchasing some property and wants my advice."

"Because you're such a real estate mogul?" his brother teased.

Wyatt grinned back. "Right."

"Would this be Jenna by any chance?" Josh fished. "Heard you've been hanging around with her."

"Oh my," his mother cut in. "The lovely television chef we met at the party?"

"The one and only."

Josh crossed his arms over his chest. "Now this is interesting."

Wyatt shook his head. He had to admit, since Jenna's text the tension had decreased not only around the table but in his chest as well.

A genuine smile touched his mother's eyes. "It's a start."

"Jenna's a friend, so don't get any ideas."

"We only—"

"No ideas. When I'm ready, you'll know."

He had to cut off their wishful thinking, because no matter how much better he was doing, he still had setbacks. And setbacks meant uncertainty. He wouldn't give them, or Jenna, false hope.

CHAPTER EIGHT

"So what do you think?"

Madeline Haynes, a stylish woman in her midfifties, dressed in a very expensive tailored suit and matching pumps, held her leather organizer to her chest and focused on Jenna.

She'd led Jenna and Wyatt on a grand tour of the building, which included the main seating area, kitchen, restrooms and storage areas. Jenna took notes as she asked the Realtor questions about the property. The musty smell of disuse had bothered her at first, but as fresh air breezed in through the open door, she realized she'd replace the stale odors with the magic of her cooking.

"This is a prime location," Madeline went on to say. "Easily accessible. Plenty of foot traffic whether you open a restaurant or catering business. Granted, there are some internal issues we need to address, but I'm sure we can negotiate an amicable resolution and get you in this place quickly."

Jenna recognized a practiced sales pitch when she heard one, but she had to admit, the space was what she'd expected. The location was great, but she'd pay for the exposure. The kitchen needed minor upgrades, and she'd have to turn the current dining room into an office/showroom for the catering business.

"I like what I see. Can you give me a few minutes to talk to my friend?"

"Certainly." Madeline shot Wyatt a curious look. "If you don't mind, I'm going to step out to the sidewalk while you look around. Call me when you're ready to leave."

"So," Jenna said, turning to Wyatt. "I guess this place isn't quite the same as when you worked here?"

"I don't remember there being any cobwebs or all this dust."

"The place does need some work, but I'm hoping it's mostly cosmetic."

"I'm not a food prep expert, but this place has potential." He stopped in the middle of the room, peering at the ceiling. "Of course, you'll need an inspection, but the bones of the building look pretty solid."

"Already have it down as number one on my list."

Wyatt had joined her as the Realtor unlocked

the door. She hadn't realized just how nervous she was until he strode down the sidewalk in her direction, dressed in a casual button-down shirt and jeans. Her heart had gone haywire at the sight, but she'd also felt her anxiety lessen.

Stop it, she'd admonished herself. This attraction to Wyatt was getting out of hand. He'd made it clear he didn't want a relationship, so why did her heart do somersaults when she knew better?

She'd dressed in a lavender sundress and spent extra time on her makeup for the appointment. In fact, she'd taken the time to look her best for Wyatt. A girl had that prerogative.

"Did Madeline give you the name of an inspector?" Wyatt lowered his arms after knocking on the wood surrounding the door frame, just in time to catch her in the act of checking out how nicely his shirt stretched over his broad shoulders.

Her cheeks grew warm. For a moment, they stared at each other, the only sound a car horn on the street. She looked away, focusing instead on the dust floating in the stream of sunshine coming through the window.

Jenna cleared her throat. "Yes, but I'm assuming the guy works for her."

"I can get the name of a reputable inspector from my dad."

"Thanks."

Wyatt walked to the window. "This is a big undertaking."

She joined him, shrugging. "I'm not afraid of hard work."

A slight smile flitted over his lips, generating a rise in her body temperature. "As you've proven."

"I sense a 'but' coming."

He shoved his hands in his pockets as he turned to her. "Look, I'll be the first to admit I don't have a clue about the food industry, but I did own a fleet of charter boats. The responsibility of owning your own business is a 24/7 job. A lot of work, with a lot of rewards, but time-consuming. Have you thought about how that will affect Abby and Bridget?"

"Yes." She blew out a breath. "I spent too many hours at the studio filming, and the girls weren't usually welcome there. The producers didn't want them underfoot, so I had to find someone to watch them after school. I didn't like that arrangement." Her gaze swept over the interior of the building. "If I decide to start a catering business, I can make my own hours. At least I have the say about whether the girls can be here after school, which of course is yes."

He nodded. "A check in the pro column. Others?"

"I can take my vision and execute it my way. Come up with my own menu. Hire my own staff. Create an environment to my liking as well as our lifestyle as a family."

"Any cons?"

"Long hours, at least at first, until I figure out how to run the business. I take on the financial risk, which means I can be successful or lose everything."

"Trust me, it's a big risk."

"Yet you sound like you enjoyed owning your business."

"I did. If it hadn't been for losing Jamie, I wouldn't have sold it."

Silence settled between them. Jenna tried to read Wyatt's mood, but he'd been quiet since he arrived and she couldn't get a handle on him. Had his previous appointment made him contemplative? Or was it her awkward admission earlier about them having a date?

"It's not a decision to make lightly," he said. "You have to consider a great many things."

She looked down at her notes. "And by that you mean, am I up to this? Taking on a business while juggling everything else going on in my life?"

"No matter what you do, you'll figure out your priorities. It comes with the territory."

She glanced over the empty space again. "I have to say, I'm intrigued by the idea of having my own business."

"It's perfect. This is what you do, cook for people. Now you can do it on a much more personal level."

She hadn't looked at things that way. "I still have commitments back in LA"

"Get your agent to help you."

"Trust me, she is not going to be on board with this."

And then there was keeping out of the public eye so the media wouldn't visit Cypress Pointe and focus on her once again.

"Go for your dream," Wyatt told her.

She glanced around the open space. "It sounds easy, but whatever I decide changes our lives. Again."

"Then I guess your next step is bringing the girls in on the decision."

Her stomach tightened. They'd been through so much. Would the girls be on board for a new adventure? "That will be a conversation for tonight."

"I'd like to be a fly on the wall."

She hesitated. "You could come by."

Wyatt shook his head. "Thanks, but I just came from seeing my family and I've had enough conversation for today."

"I'm guessing it didn't go as you expected?"

His shoulders went straight and stiff. "Yeah."

Judging from his one-word answer, she didn't think he'd offer any details and she wasn't about to prod.

"Besides, you should talk to the girls alone."

Alone. Lately, she hated the word. While she'd been on her own for most of her life, now with the girls, she didn't relish figuring out major life decisions single-handedly. So far Wyatt was the only one she'd brain stormed with, but at the end of the day, she'd still go home and figure things out on her own. Even before she talked to Nealy. No point getting her friend's hopes up if the girls weren't on board. "I'll fill you in on the outcome of our family meeting later."

He glanced at his watch. "Listen, I should go."

"Oh, yeah, please don't hang around if you have plans. I'm going to walk though one more time."

"You're sure?"

"Positive. Thanks for stopping by. It was good to have someone to talk to."

"Anytime. I'll get back to you about finishing the swing set."

"Great." She couldn't resist adding, "It's a date."

He chuckled and walked out the door.

Sighing, Jenna shook off the loneliness shrouding her. *Enough.* She didn't need a man to make her life complete. While nice, it wasn't imperative. At least Wyatt now had a friend who didn't remind him of the past. If that was her role in the relationship, she'd live with it.

Hiking her chin, she took a final pass through the kitchen, jotted down a few more notes about the building as well as additional questions for Nealy. Once she'd finished, she headed toward the door, stopping short when she glimpsed a woman standing there.

"Can I help you?"

"You're Jenna Monroe, right? I recognized you from your television show."

Jenna smiled. "Yes. How can I help you?"

The woman, probably close to forty, smiled tentatively. Her dark hair showed a hint of gray, and, her slender build bordered on skinny. She wore a white blouse, black pants and black shoes. In her hand she clutched what looked like an apron. A waitress?

"My name is Michelle Lewis. I used to work here when Duke owned the place." She stepped inside, a wistful expression on her face as if she hadn't traveled these floors in a long time. "I watch your cooking show."

"Thank you. Always good to meet a fan."

Curiosity burned in Michelle's eyes. "Are you thinking of buying the restaurant?"

"Thinking about it. I still have some decisions to make."

Michelle's expression betrayed a combination of hope and wariness. "Look, I know you don't know me, but if you do decide to reopen the restaurant, I'd appreciate hearing about it."

The woman gazed around the open space. "I have so many memories tied up in this place. Duke had plans, and well, he never followed through on them." She held up the apron. "I've been working down the street, but to be honest, my heart is here."

"Do you mind my asking why?"

"I suppose that's fair since I'm kind of presumptuous showing up here." She grinned. "Duke and I were together for a long time. He'd already opened the restaurant by the time we met."

"When you worked for him?"

"Exactly. I never meant to fall for him." She chuckled. "If you ever meet him, you'll understand why. He's not comfortable around people."

Gee, Jenna knew another guy with the same problem.

"But he loved to cook. I like people, so we fell into an easy working arrangement. Over time, we took to each other as well."

"Romantically, you mean?"

Michelle nodded.

"So what happened?" Jenna tilted her head. "Obviously he closed the restaurant."

"One day he didn't show up to open. Usually he was here at sunrise, prepping for the day. One day turned into two and soon he was gone a week. I panicked. No word. Nothing. I closed the doors, but then he showed up. Acted as if nothing had happened. But he was never the same.

"Soon, he began taking days off on a regular basis. The restaurant lost its popularity and before long, he closed for good. I tried to persuade him to keep going, but whatever caused the change in him was too much."

"You never found out why he acted so strangely?"

"No. Eventually we broke up. He left town." She reached out to run a finger around the edge of one of the tables. "But this place is still special to me. If you decide to reopen, will you let me know?" She pulled a pen and paper from her purse, scribbling on it before handing it to Jenna. "I'd like to work here again, help you, no matter what you decide to do with the place. I'm a hard worker and I won't let you down."

"I'm sure, but—"

"Was that Wyatt Hamilton leaving a little while ago?"

"Yes."

"He can give me a reference. I'm friends with his mom."

"I think we're getting ahead of ourselves." Jenna looked at the paper, then back at Michelle, whose eyes were wide with expectation. "But I will let you know either way."

"Thanks." Michelle took one last, long look around the room. "Thanks."

Jenna saw the woman out before Madeline reentered the building. "So, have you come to a decision?"

"I need more time."

"I understand."

"I'll call you," Jenna said. The girls would

be home from school soon. She'd give them a snack and have them tackle their homework before discussing the future. If all went well, she'd talk to Nealy. Then Wyatt, to get his take on Michelle.

As much as the idea of talking to Wyatt appealed to her, she remembered his mood when he left. Lately, any excuse to speak to the man had her blood racing, despite his warning about personal involvement. But if she called him to ask about Michelle, it was business, not personal. Yeah, he had her tied up in knots. Not good. Not good at all.

"So if you open a catering place," Abby asked Jenna later that evening as she helped clean up after dinner. "Does that mean when we go there with you it's like eating out?"

She and Bridget still sat at the kitchen table while Abby flitted about. "Absolutely."

She'd laid out her ideas, Nealy's offer and her chance to start something brand new. So far, the girls were on board.

"So you wouldn't have to go back to California?" Bridget asked.

"I would until I fulfill the contract for the cooking show." Her gaze went back and forth between the girls. "Do you want to move back to LA?"

"No," Abby answered first. "I like it here. School is fun and I'm making friends."

"Bridget?"

"I like it here too. It's far away from...you know, where we lived with Mom."

Even though the girls had been doing much better lately, Jenna didn't miss the shadows in their eyes from time to time. To be expected, she supposed, but she didn't want to add any more pressure to their young lives.

"You both know that I'd take you back if it's really what you wanted."

The girls exchanged a glance. "We didn't like the people following us, you know, with the cameras," Bridget offered. "It was weird."

"And scary," Abby added.

Jenna leaned her elbows on the table and clasped her hands, silently agreeing with the girls' assessment of life in LA. "So, what do you say, then? Do we go for it?"

The girls shot each other another glance. Jenna, not normally a nail biter, squeezed her folded hands hard just in case.

They both nodded.

"We think it's a good idea," Abby said.

Jenna blew out a sigh of relief. Excitement

swirled in her belly. She'd make this work. For all of them.

"We could work for you," Bridget volunteered.

"When you get older. Right now you have homework and school to keep you busy."

"No fun," the youngster groused.

"True, but if you want to have your own business one day, you have to do well in school. It's not easy. You have to know things, like math and English. Things you can only learn in school."

Bridget shot her sister an uneasy glance. "About that."

Jenna tensed. "Is there a problem?"

Abby closed the dishwasher door with a bang. "I'm going to my room." She hustled out of the kitchen before Jenna could lecture about the rough handling of the appliance. She turned her attention on Bridget.

"What's going on?"

Bridget shuffled to her backpack, dug inside to pull out a wrinkled paper. "I didn't do good on my math test this week."

Jenna glanced at the grade. Sixty-five marked in red ink. "I thought you were comfortable with the material when we reviewed the other night?"

"I was." Bridget took a seat at the table, frowning. "I thought I was."

"So what happened?"

"I don't know. I started answering the questions and then they got harder and I got scared and wrote down the first thing I thought of."

"You don't normally get scared by tests."

Bridget stared at the tabletop.

Studying the paper, Jenna searched for the problems Bridget got wrong. She soon realized Bridget had answered these same questions correctly when they prepped for the test.

"Do you want me to talk to your teacher?"

"No," Bridget responded, her answer quick and adamant.

"Is something wrong at school?"

"No," she said, just as quickly. "I'll do better next time."

Jenna didn't like the distress in Bridget's voice, or the shiver of unease she felt. "If you keep having problems, we'll talk to Mrs. Roseman about getting extra help."

Bridget merely nodded.

"Don't get discouraged. It's the beginning of the school year. We just moved here. You've had to get used to a lot of changes." She leaned over to hug her young charge. "Things will get better."

Stiff in Jenna's arms, Bridget didn't move. Troubled, Jenna pulled back, her hands on Bridget's shoulders. "You're sure everything is okay?"

"I have to do my homework now."

Jenna kissed the top of Bridget's head. "Call me if you don't understand something."

The little girl slid from her chair, scooped up her backpack and hurried down the hallway to her room. Jenna sat at the table, knowing deep inside something beyond math was going on with Bridget. What, exactly, was the problem? Her dilemma boiled down to this—did she push Bridget for answers or let her work on whatever was going on by herself? But what if she left Bridget alone and the situation got worse? Dropping her head in her hands, she closed her eyes, silently asking Carrie for advice. Knowing an answer from her friend wasn't possible, she shook off her little pity-party and called Nealy with the news that she'd decided to start a catering business.

Nealy shrieked, "I'll be right over," and immediately hung up.

"Okay," Jenna said to thin air. She glanced at the stove clock. Just after seven. Knowing her friend, Nealy would be brimming with ideas, ready to discuss them regardless of the time or the fact that it was a school night. In anticipation, Jenna gathered her notes and financial papers, just in case.

Sure enough, the doorbell rang fifteen minutes later. Jenna hurried to the door, surprised to find not only Nealy, but Dane standing on her front step. Nealy held up a hand and launched right into her speech. "I know I didn't warn you, but after we hung up, I realized we could use Dane's help."

Jenna stepped aside to let them in. "And just what kind of help do I need?"

"Financial advice. He's the best."

Jenna led her friends into the living room, motioning for them to take a seat. "I'm sure he is, but I thought we might have other topics to discuss first."

"You're right. I got ahead of myself." Nealy plopped onto the couch. "So you're okay with the idea of us working together?"

"I am, but we have things to iron out first. I still need to finish my obligations in LA before I can concentrate fully on catering. I'll have to start slow."

"Nealy doesn't go slow," Dane said with a grin.

"I know, that's why I want to be clear up front. If we do this, we each run our own businesses separately. You call me for events, or vice versa, and we decide which ones to book. That way we don't clash about business decisions and end up ruining our friendship."

Dane nodded. "Smart."

"I can see the wisdom in that," Nealy said. "Even though I toyed with the idea of us being partners."

"It's not that I don't think we can work together, it's just that with both of us owning our own businesses, we have more leeway accepting projects we're interested in."

"And you get to keep your coveted independence."

"That too."

"So you're in?"

Jenna took a deep breath. "I'm in."

Nealy whooped, jumped up and pulled Jenna from the armchair to give her a big hug. Laughing, Jenna returned the gesture. Nealy stood back and announced, "We are going to rock Cypress Pointe! Once you move into Duke's Place, we can get started. I already have a few events lined up. You can look over the list, see which ones appeal to you."

"Listen, Nealy, I can't help worrying that I'm aiming too high."

Nealy shot her a glance that said Jenna was

clearly dense. "You're thinking about buying Duke's Place. It's perfect."

"*Thinking*, being the operative word."

"You know Dane buys properties and fixes them up. He'll look at the specs, see if it's a good investment."

Jenna knew all about Dane's hotel construction business. The man was very successful at what he did. What could it hurt to have someone else take a look at the details? She'd never done anything like this before, never had anyone interested in helping her wade through the waters of a major life decision.

But jumping into a business without any experience? She didn't want to be so independently minded that she messed things up because she refused good advice.

"Let me get you the information I have," Jenna said, collecting the papers from the Realtor to hand over to Dane. He sat back, concentrating on the documents while Jenna perched on the edge of the armchair, biting her thumbnail.

"You look like you're waiting for bad news," Nealy teased.

"It could be bad news," Jenna retorted.

"You told me you did your research."

"I did. But only as far as the properties on

Main Street. I mean, I don't necessarily have to be right on Main. I could find another location." She started on her nail again and forced her hand down. "I was also going to look into what goes into starting a business, then draw up a plan."

Dane looked up. "I can help you there. It'll make it easier to figure out the financing."

Nealy grinned. "He helped me prepare a business plan when I decided to focus on my own event planning company."

Jenna admired how devoted her friend was and smiled. "Yes. You told me." Grabbing Jenna's arm, her friend pulled her into the kitchen. "Better we talk in here while he's concentrating."

"Want something to drink?" Jenna offered.

"No," she said in a hushed voice. "I want the skinny on your day with Wyatt."

"We just decided I'd start a catering business so we can work events together and you want to talk about Wyatt?"

Nealy shrugged. "I'm a multitasker. I can be excited about business and still meddle in your personal life."

Jenna laughed, not at all upset about her friend delving into her personal life. She pointed out the window over the sink. "We started assembling the swing set."

"So was he chatty while you worked? Did you have a good time?"

"Surprisingly, yes. We had a good time for a non-date." Jenna hadn't yet confided her little misunderstanding to Nealy.

"I told you he's a good guy."

"He is. But he's not ready to date for real."

"And you know this how?" Nealy's tone took on an inquisitive edge.

"He told me."

Nealy looked confused.

"We had a laugh over my misconception of his meaning of the word *date*." She glanced at her friend. "He may be getting out more lately, but deep inside, he has reservations about starting new relationships."

Nealy's smile faltered. "Darn. I was hoping you might kick-start some fun back into Wyatt's life."

"I don't think he's opposed to fun, in general. He just hasn't found how to have fun and not feel guilty over it." She leaned back against the counter. "He has to come to terms with that by himself."

"Hmm. No prodding him along?"

"No. Grief is different for everyone. And in

Wyatt's case, I'm pretty sure the added guilt is making the whole process more difficult for him."

Nealy crossed her arms over her chest. "Hey. I'm sorry if it seems like I'm pushing you two together."

"You are." Jenna laughed. "Look, he's made it clear he's not emotionally available. As much as he interests me, I respect his wishes."

Her friend nodded. "I understand. I just want everyone to be as happy as I am."

"I am happy. The girls keep me busy. I may have a new business venture. What more do I need out of life?"

Someone to share it with would be nice, an evil inner voice taunted. Yeah, well, she'd tried and clearly romance was not in the cards for her and Wyatt. As much as she liked him, enjoyed his company and the shiver of anticipation whenever she spent time with him, she wasn't about to court trouble. That led to heartache and she'd been there, done that. She didn't need another T-shirt proclaiming her mistake.

Dane walked into the kitchen, the folder of information in his hands.

Jenna's stomach dipped. "Well?"

He placed the file on the table. "The asking price is fair, considering the market. I'd like to take a look at the property. There are always upgrades needed in older buildings, especially one that's been empty for a while, but I don't see that as a reason to back away from the deal.

"And I'd stay on Main Street if I were you," Dane continued. "You'd have a few things going for you. First of all, you have a name. Folks will be drawn to your business because they've seen you on television. That gives you an upper hand right there. Two, you can cook. I know that myself, so you'll have a product the public will want."

"The downside?" Jenna asked.

"You've never run a business before."

"I can learn."

"Oh, if you do this, you'll learn fast," Dane warned. "The good thing is, you've got us to help you."

"I still have a contract with the network for my cooking show. Other commitments." Jenna ran a hand through her short hair. "My agent's going to go crazy when she finds out I'm even considering this."

"If you want this bad enough, I'm sure you can manage to do it all."

"I'm glad you're so convinced."

Dane put a friendly arm around her shoulder. "I've juggled a lot in the past. It can be done."

"You have us now," Nealy said. "We're family and family works together."

Jenna pinned Dane with her gaze. "Anything else I should know?"

"Based on your personal assets and public persona, I can't imagine you'll have much trouble getting financial assistance. In fact, once you come up with a business plan, I'd like to run it by my uncle. We might be interested in investing."

A weight lifted from Jenna's shoulders. "Really? You'd consider that?"

"Why not? You have the talent and determination. Stop by the hotel and we'll get started."

Jenna shook her head. "I have to say, this whole thing is a little unsettling. I never imagined when we moved here that I'd start my own business."

"Then there's only one last thing to do," Dane told her.

"Which is?"

"Ask yourself just how serious you are about your future. If you want to move ahead, don't let anything stop you."

She wouldn't. As of right now, the catering business was a go.

If only her relationship with Wyatt was as easy.

CHAPTER NINE

BACK IN LA THE FOLLOWING WEEK, Jenna was booked with back-to-back meetings. And Barbara and the producers had several discussions about how the cooking show would work despite Jenna's cross-country move. The producers were less than eager to hear she would continue to live in Florida. Thankfully they didn't fire her. Instead, they suggested an intense shooting schedule to film as many episodes as possible, allowing Jenna to reduce the number of trips she'd have to make to LA. She didn't complain, relieved they were willing to work with her. She still had this job. For now.

She hadn't been back for more than a day when Rod tracked her down despite the fact she'd checked into a different hotel than last time. He wasn't very subtle as he trailed her to the meeting with the network executives, then dinner with Barbara.

Her agent noticed her pushing at the food on her plate.

"You're quiet. What's up?"

Jenna placed her fork on the table. "It's Rod. I'm pretty sure he's been following us all day."

"Really? I haven't seen him. I thought the last time you were in town he assured you he'd leave you alone?"

"He did. Apparently he's changed his mind, which worries me."

"What are you going to do?"

"If you don't mind, head back to the hotel."

And wait.

SHE WASN'T SURPRISED when, true to form, Rod sauntered into the lobby a few minutes after her. She'd thought ahead, calling the police in advance of his arrival.

"Expecting me?" A wide smile crossed his face as he came up to her.

How could he behave so casually, as if everything was okay? "Rod, you told me you'd stop following me."

He blinked. "Why would I do that? Jenna, we have a connection. That will never change."

Alarmed, she scanned the lobby for security. "I'm warning you, Rod. Stop following me."

"Hey, as long as I'm not close, I can take pictures. Just like today." He winked. "I'd forgotten how uptight you are."

She lifted her chin. "Look, I've had enough. Back off."

He seemed truly surprised by her vehemence. "You're kidding, right?"

"What part of leave me alone don't you understand?"

"You don't mean it."

"I'm serious, Rod. So serious, in fact, that I called the police."

He quickly glanced around the lobby, but then relaxed. "Nice try."

"They're coming."

As if on cue, the outside doors slid open and two uniformed officers walked into the hotel. One nodded at Jenna when he spied her.

Rod whirled on her. "Are you crazy? Why would you call them?"

"I don't know how clearer I can be. I never want to see you again."

As the officers approached Rod, his face flamed red and his eyes turned stormy. He held up his hands in surrender. "Look, guys. No need to get carried away here."

"If you'll come with us, Mr. Hartley."

In a split second, a calm mask fell over Rod's features, much more scary than when he was angry. "Wrong move, Jenna. We could have worked this out."

"Again, there's nothing to work out."

"Are you okay, Ms. Monroe?" the officer asked.

Despite her shaky legs, she nodded. "I'll be fine."

"You messed up," Rod called over his shoulder as the officer led him away.

Jenna's shoulders slumped as she expelled a breath. She'd done the right thing. Made a statement. Once she returned to Florida, she wouldn't have to look over her shoulder or wonder what Rod was up to. She'd proven she wasn't afraid to use the restraining order. And with Rod spending some time in jail, he'd know she meant business.

AFTER A MONTH of sleepless nights, endless negotiations, pacifying her agent and making trips back to LA, Jenna held the keys to her new business.

"Everyone, welcome to Jenna's Place."

The group of friends consisted of Nealy and Dane, Lilli and Max, the twins and, surprisingly, Michelle. The waitress still wanted to help Jenna with her catering business, even if the position was only part-time to start with. They all clapped and wished Jenna well as she ushered them inside.

"Really?" Nealy said. "Jenna's Place? You couldn't come up with anything more original?"

"It's just for now. I have a bunch of ideas."

"Like?" Nealy prodded as they moved inside the building.

"Jenna's Comfy Kitchen. Southern Charm Catering. The Comfy Gourmet. Comfort Food Catering."

"Yikes. You need help."

"Is that so? Who made you the catering name police?"

"If I don't step in, you'll be arrested for lack of creativity."

"Ouch," Dane said as he walked by.

Jenna laughed. "Yeah. They are pretty lame."

Nealy patted her shoulder. "We'll come up with something snappy, don't worry."

Easier said than done. The girls were excited about the new venture, but Jenna still had her concerns. Next came the ever-growing list of permits, licenses and inspections. What had she gotten herself into?

"Thanks for giving up your Saturday to help me out. I appreciate it, everyone."

Michelle rubbed her hands. "I can't wait to dig in."

Only one person was glaringly missing. Wyatt. She'd called to tell him about the closing and to invite him to the cleaning party, secretly hoping he'd want to join the group. But he'd been distracted when they spoke and rather vague about his intentions. She'd tried not to take it personally, but had anyway. Later, when Bridget asked if he was coming, Jenna could tell the little girl was disappointed too.

"You won't be so enthusiastic after I give you your tasks," she told everyone.

"I want to mop," Abby announced, and everyone laughed.

Jenna jogged to the far corner to grab the mop leaning against the wall. She brought it back to Abby. "Have at it."

"Where are the rest of the supplies?" Nealy asked.

"In my car trunk. I'll be right back."

Jenna walked to the back door, propping it open with a two-by-four. The men helped her carry the supplies inside. Once the items were unpacked, she consulted her list and assigned tasks. That done, she went to the kitchen, wanting to tackle it first.

She loved the large commercial kitchen. The previous owner, Duke, had planned the layout for maximum results. After the inspection, she was relieved to learn the industrial-grade stove and refrigerator worked. Electrical and plumbing were up to code. The walk-in freezer was a bit on the small side, but she'd already bought shelving to make the space work for now.

She ran her hand over the food-prep area, coming away with fingertips covered with dust. The greasy buildup would be the biggest job to tackle today.

"Can you believe you're a business owner?" Michelle asked as she filled a bucket with water and soapsuds.

"It hasn't sunk in yet."

"You'll love it. Duke and I did."

Jenna had hoped to meet the elusive Duke at the signing, but he'd taken care of his end of the deal without making an appearance.

"I'm sure I'll be asking you lots of questions as we get started."

"Does that mean you're going to hire me?"

Jenna beamed. "As if you didn't know."

Michelle's laughter rang out in the room. "I knew it."

"Don't make me regret it."

"Who, me? I'm going to be the best employee you've ever hired."

"So far you're the only employee I've ever

hired, but I'm going to hold you to that promise."

Wyatt's reference for Michelle, along with those from other restaurant owners, was solid and her enthusiasm was infectious. There was one small issue, however.

"Michelle, you do understand that this isn't going to be anything like Duke's Place. It will only be a catering business." Jenna knew the woman had an attachment to the past, but she had to move her new employee into the future.

"I'm sorry. I know you're making changes. I…" Michelle blinked rapidly. "This is a little hard to take in."

"I can't imagine." She crossed the room to give Michelle a quick hug. "Look, we might be catering, but we'll do Duke proud."

Moisture glistened in Michelle's eyes. "Yes. We will." She took the bucket and exited the kitchen.

Jenna leaned her hip against the counter. Michelle had already proved valuable as a sounding board during the past few weeks. While Jenna had been waiting for the deal to go through, she'd spent her time planning different types of menus down to the smallest detail, making lists of supplies, and setting up appointments for inspections. Even though it had been years since she'd worked for a catering company and cooked for large crowds, she hadn't been this enthusiastic about a project in ages.

"Hey, just because you're the owner doesn't mean you get to slack off."

Jenna smiled as Nealy joined her. "You're awfully bossy."

A twinkle lit Nealy's eyes. "Guilty."

"But I appreciate everything you've done."

"It wasn't much."

"Um, yeah it was. You got Dane involved, which was major. You've scheduled some easier events to get me started and most of all, you've given me support. What more could I ask for?"

"Wyatt to be here?"

Jenna frowned. "You had to ruin my good mood by bringing him up?"

"Even though you didn't say it, I know you were disappointed that he didn't join us today."

"I'm not disappointed." She held up a hand to fend off Nealy's argument. "I don't need his help. I have all of you guys here."

"Sure. Keep telling yourself that."

She had and she would. Getting any closer to Wyatt was too risky. He'd made his intentions clear. Friendship only. Besides, she wouldn't want him, or anyone else for that matter, to be a part of her life if they didn't want to.

"Change of subject." Taking hold of Jenna's arm, Nealy dragged her out back.

"Is there a problem?"

"No. I don't want anyone to overhear this conversation and if I don't tell someone soon, I'm going to burst."

Jenna's eyes narrowed. "Am I going to like this?"

"You're going to love this." Nealy shot a look over her shoulder. "Do you remember I told you about how Max and Lilli worked together on a wedding-themed fashion show and ended up falling in love?"

"Yes. A very romantic story."

"Well," she blurted, "Max is going to ask Lilli to marry him and he wants us to throw a surprise engagement party."

Jenna's hand flew to her mouth. "Oh my gosh. This is awesome."

"I know."

"Lilli has no clue?"

"Nope."

"Even better." She grinned. "Our first job together."

"I already have a ton of ideas."

"Great. Think they'll want you to plan their wedding too?"

"Maybe. If Lilli's mother has any say in it, though, they'll probably want to elope. But I refuse to let that happen."

"Either way, I'm excited for them."

Dane popped his head out the back door, his brows angling as he glimpsed the two women together.

"You two better have a good reason for hiding out back here."

Nealy blew him a kiss. "We'll be right in."

"I'm surprised you haven't told him yet," Jenna commented as they headed inside.

"Later."

"In the meantime, I thought I asked you to clean the restrooms?"

Nealy shuddered. "I love you like a sister, but no way. You get that pleasure."

"Back to work then." Rolling her shoulders, Jenna marched inside to grab a plastic bag and a large pair of rubber gloves. "Out of my way. I have a job to do," she said as she passed Nealy.

"That's the spirit. And quit thinking about Wyatt," she added in a whisper.

Jenna filled a bucket of soap and water to carry from the kitchen to the restrooms. Cleaning therapy. Definitely the best method to get a certain male off her mind.

Which worked for about an hour. Then she found herself wondering where Wyatt was and what he was doing. She stood before the now squeaky-clean sink, staring at her reflection, and rolled her eyes.

"Stop. It. Now," she muttered, knowing all along she probably wouldn't listen to her inner self when it came to Wyatt, but deciding she had to give it a serious try.

CROUCHED NEXT TO THE charter boat docked beside the pier, Wyatt wiped the engine grease from his hands. Another hot, humid Saturday. Instead of lending Jenna a helping hand, he'd chosen to be out in the summer heat, doing boat maintenance. Why did he think this was a good idea?

"Because you're an idiot," he told himself.

"No one's going to argue with you." At his brother's voice, he twisted around.

"Sneaking up on me?"

Josh grinned as he looked down. "I wasn't intentionally trying to be quiet. So caught up in your thoughts you didn't hear me?"

Wyatt stood and tossed the greasy towel at Josh. "What do you want?"

"Just wondering why the gang is at Jenna's place and you're not?"

"What do you know about her place?"

"Thanks to the local rumor mill, I know she's going to open a catering business and her friends are helping her clean the old restaurant. It's been empty for a while now." Josh arched his brow. "What's your excuse?"

"I have my own work to do."

"Work you couldn't do on any other day?"

"Why are you bugging me about this?"

Josh grinned.

"What?"

"You haven't gotten worked up about anything in a while. Good to see you can still generate some sparks."

Wyatt scowled. His brother always knew how to push his buttons. "I'm not worked up. I'm busy."

"Sorry. Have to disagree, bro. Anytime Jenna's name comes up you get, what's a good word? Antsy?"

"I only talked with you about her one time."

"Yes, you did. And it made you come alive."

"You need glasses."

"You need a reality check," Josh fired back. "Do you really want to do this?"

"I'm free all afternoon."

Wyatt shook his head then finally laughed. "You always were relentless."

"Why do you think I used to beat you at our swim meets?"

"I think you're mistaken."

"I think you've forgotten." Josh took a seat on a nearby piling. "About a lot of things."

Terrific. Another intervention. "So you're here to straighten me out?"

"Nah. There's no point. You won't listen. I just like giving you a hard time so you'll smile again."

Wyatt glanced at his brother, judging the weight of the other man's words. Okay, Josh meant what he said. Wyatt's shoulders relaxed. "You know I love our family, right?"

"We never doubted it."

"Good." He nodded his head. "Good."

"We get that you're still having trouble. Just know that Mom and Dad are concerned."

"I do know."

"Then you'll come to their anniversary dinner next Saturday."

"Anniversary?" Wyatt had forgotten. "I'm not sure—"

"It'll make them happy."

He hesitated before answering. "Yeah. I'll be there." He crouched down again.

Josh jumped off his perch. "Excellent. And bring a date."

Wyatt's head shot up. "What?"

Josh shrugged, clearly unconcerned about Wyatt's reaction. "Merely delivering the message."

Wyatt glared at his brother.

"What could it hurt?" Josh said quietly.

"You have to ask?"

"Not every woman is like Marcie."

"I know."

"Do you?"

Wyatt stared out over the water. The heavy scent of diesel mingled with saltwater. A gull swooped into the water after food, leaving a ring of waves in its wake.

"In my head, yeah. Not so much in my gut." Just like he knew Jamie would want him to be happy.

"You guys were on the outs even before she left."

"Proof positive that I'm not good at relationships."

"Wrong. You and Jamie were great together."

"He was my son." Wyatt swallowed. "I loved hanging out with him."

"Maybe you just need to find the right woman."

"And take the chance of screwing up again?" He shook his head. "I don't think so."

"We all screw up, bro. It's what you learn along the way that matters. Look, I don't know Jenna, but obviously something about her has gotten your attention. So go out a few times. Test the waters. You don't have to marry her."

Wyatt cringed. "I don't want to marry anyone, but with Jenna, well it's complicated. She's got kids."

"So? You love kids."

"These girls are special. They lost their mother and are still grieving."

"You're stubborn, so I know you're going to argue this point to the grave, but Wyatt, you weren't responsible for Jamie's death. It was an accident."

"It doesn't feel like that to me. What if I'm with those girls and something bad happens to them?"

"Wyatt, *anything* can happen in this life. You can't look for danger behind every door."

"Maybe if I had, Jamie would still be alive." His jagged voice was the only clue to the storm waging inside him.

Josh stepped back and long seconds passed.

At last he said in a calm tone, "And maybe the accident was out of your hands. Are you going to turn away from every relationship, women or kids, because you can't protect them every second of every day? Unrealistic, bro."

"Maybe, but that's how I feel."

"Then you have a choice. Close yourself off to all relationships and have no life or just stay friends with Jenna and her kids, but please, do something."

Just friends. Why didn't the thought appeal to him? Because he wanted a deeper kind of relationship but wouldn't put his heart on the line. Something about Jenna drew him, no denying it. Question was, could he be with her and not get emotionally involved? He'd already warned her he didn't want to go there, but what if he took a chance? There was only one way to find out, and it was something he hadn't been willing to do since Jamie died and Marcie left him.

"Are you bringing a date?"

Josh frowned.

"Cuz at lunch the other day Mom mentioned something about you and a woman."

"It's complicated."

Wyatt chuckled. "Isn't it always?"

Josh slapped him on the back. "Yeah. Which means I will be bringing a date."

Wyatt smiled as he watched his brother walk away. It felt weird, like his facial muscles hadn't been used for a long time and were only now coming to life. Truthfully, he found himself smiling more and more lately, without the usual accompanying guilt. Jenna's influence? The twins? He'd give credit where credit was due, because he did like being in their company. Maybe more than was wise under the circumstances.

But Josh's words still rang in his ears. *Please do something.*

His brother might have a good point.

CHAPTER TEN

TUCKERED OUT AFTER a long day of cleaning, Jenna and the girls showered and enjoyed a light meal at home. Jenna's lower back ached, but in a good way because of all she'd accomplished today.

With everyone's help, the catering kitchen and dining room were spotless. The used restaurant tables and chairs were gone thanks to her ad online. With the dining space now empty, Dane would send his construction team to build walls separating the office and meeting room for clients as well as the food tasting area. The painters Jenna had hired to give the place a fresh coat of paint would come in and finish the job. She'd chosen a shade of sunny yellow for the walls to complement the new, dark wood furniture she'd ordered.

The girls had gone to their room to play with their princess dolls, leaving Jenna to tidy up the kitchen. On the hutch in the corner, the twins had piled their schoolbooks and homework. As she walked by, her hip bumped the corner of a book. Before she could stop it, the entire pile tumbled to the floor. She crouched down to gather up the mess, and an envelope, with her name on it, fluttered from the pile.

Curious, Jenna replaced the books on the hutch then slid her fingernail under the flap to open the envelope. She removed a letter from Bridget's teacher, informing Jenna that Bridget's test scores were low, her attention in class was spotty and she'd been disrespectful to school authorities.

Shocked, Jenna dropped into a seat at the table to reread the letter. That's when she noted the date. One week ago. The teacher had listed her concerns before finally asking for a meeting. At the bottom of the letter was an area for Jenna to sign and send back her response.

Bridget had kept the letter from her for a week. What was going on? And why hadn't she noticed that Bridget was really struggling?

Because you've been too caught up in your new business venture.

Her cheeks burned with shame. Here she'd told anyone who would listen that she wanted to be a good mom but she was shirking her duties. The butterflies that had been at bay lately started flapping with a vengeance.

Letter in hand, she walked down the hallway, intending to have a little sit-down with
Bridget. Jenna found her under the blanket fort
in the corner. Her heart squeezed, but she kept
her voice firm when she said, "Abby, would
you please take your dolls to my bedroom. You
can turn on the TV if you want."

Abby glanced at Jenna, then Bridget.
"Why?"

"I need to talk to your sister."

"I don't mind staying."

"Please. For a few minutes."

Abby's face went pale, but she gathered her
toys and shuffled from the room.

Jenna took a seat on Bridget's bed, patting
the empty space beside her. "Come join me."

Bridget gently laid her princess doll on the
floor and joined Jenna. She averted her eyes,
as if she knew what was coming.

Jenna held out the letter. "Care to explain
why you didn't deliver this to me?"

"How did you find it?"

"It fell from your schoolbook."

"You shouldn't be in my stuff."

"You shouldn't have kept this letter from
me."

Bridget's lips went taut.

"Your teacher says you're having problems

in school. I remember you didn't do well on that test, but I thought you had promised to do better?"

Bridget crossed her arms over her chest.

"If you were still having difficulty, Bridget, you could have come to me and we'd get you extra help."

"I don't need help."

"She thinks otherwise." Jenna read from the paper in her hand. "She says you're failing math."

"Math is stupid."

"Math is necessary, as are good grades. Why didn't you tell me?"

"Like you'd care."

"What? Of course I care, Bridget."

"You said when we moved here things would be different. You weren't going to work so much, but you've already been away on business trips and now you're at the building all the time."

"I did say that and I meant it, but honey, I still have to work. To provide for us."

"Mom didn't work all the time."

Jenna tried not to let Bridget's reminder tug at her guilt. Carrie had been an assistant manager in a bookstore the hours the girls were in school, making sure she had plenty of time to spend with them when they were home. They didn't have much, but had been happy.

"You know I want to provide for you the very best I can."

"Then work but leave me alone."

"You can drop the tone." Jenna straightened her shoulders. "I won't leave you alone. We need to deal with this problem."

"I don't want to go to school."

"Not an option."

Bridget grabbed the letter from Jenna's hand, crumpled it up and threw it on the floor. "Problem solved."

This was not going well. If Jenna didn't know better, she'd think Bridget was failing on purpose, just to get attention. "I'll call your teacher on Monday and set up an appointment for the three of us to sit down and talk."

Bridget stayed silent.

"I don't know what's gotten into you, but it's going to stop."

"You can't tell me what to do. You're not my mother."

Ever since she got custody of the girls she was afraid one of them might throw those words at her someday. And as much as she thought she'd be prepared, the reality was nothing like she'd imagined. And she'd imagined the worst.

She stood. "No TV until we talk to your teacher."

Bridget jumped off the bed and disappeared under the blanket tent, closing the flap. Leaving Jenna on the outside.

Blinking back hot tears, Jenna went to her bedroom to find Abby seated on the center of her bed.

"Have you been keeping your sister's secret from me? We're a family, Abby. We've got to figure this out."

Abby crawled across the bed, tears running down her face. "I'm sorry," she murmured.

Jenna pulled her into her embrace, kissing the top of Abby's head. "I know."

They sat together for a long while before Jenna let go. She gathered up Abby's toys, placing them in the girl's outstretched arms.

"Go get ready for bed. I'll be in shortly to check on you guys."

Abby nodded.

Jenna went to her bathroom, closed the door, turned on the tap and sat on the lid of the toilet. Tears ran unchecked down her cheeks. She buried her face in her hands, releasing the jag-

ged sobs. Her worst nightmare was her reality.
What did she do now?

She cried until she ran out of energy, then
got up to wash her face. Looking in the mirror,
she cringed. Pale skin, covered with blotches.
Mascara clumped around her eyes, her hair a
tangled mess.

"Pull it together. You're the adult here."

Five minutes later she exited the bathroom,
unsteady and unsure, but more in love with
the girls than ever. Tough love wasn't as easy
as it sounded. She had to hold her ground, no
matter the emotional cost.

She'd just rounded the bed when Abby came
rushing into the room, eyes wide, hysterical.
"I went to the bathroom to brush my teeth and
when I came back, I couldn't find Bridget."

"What do you mean you couldn't find her?"

"I checked everywhere. Bridget is gone."

WYATT HAD JUST dried the last dinner dish and
placed it on the shelf when he heard a soft rap-
ping on the porch screen door. Surprise jolted
him when he saw the small figure standing
outside.

"Bridget?" He looked over her shoulder ,
expecting Jenna to appear. "Are you alone?"

"Yes," she sniffled. "I hate Jenna."

Wyatt opened the door and motioned her inside. "Pretty strong words there, kiddo."

"It's true."

The screen slammed behind them.

He led her into the living room and she took a seat on the couch, an adoring Cruiser sniffing his guest. Wyatt stood in the doorway, waiting for her to meet his gaze. "You can tell me what the problem is, but first I have to call Jenna. Let her know you're here."

Bridget's shoulders slumped. "Okay," she said, barely above a whisper.

Wyatt strode to the coffee table and picked up his cell phone. Jenna answered on the second ring, her tone breathless.

"It's Wyatt. Bridget is here with me."

"Is she okay?" Jenna said, her voice catching.

"She's fine."

"I'll be right over to pick her up."

"Why don't you let me bring her home? A little space might not be too bad right now."

"But I—"

"Trust me."

He could well imagine her indecision. Understand her worry.

"You really think it's best?"

"I do."

He heard Abby in the background before Jenna answered.

"Yes, all right. We'll be waiting."

He hit the end button and faced Bridget. "Want to share some Oreos with me?"

Her head popped up. "With milk?"

"Of course with milk. Is there any other way to eat them?" He went into the kitchen to fetch the cookies from the cabinet. He tucked the package under his arm as he removed the milk carton from the refrigerator, grabbed two glasses and carried his stash back to the living room. After placing everything on the table, he poured the milk.

"You know, I don't share my Oreos with just anyone. You gotta be very special for me to part with my favorite treat."

"Thanks, but I'm not sure I deserve a treat."

Wyatt drew out the silence before saying, "So you must have a good reason for scaring Jenna so badly."

Bridget looked shocked. "I didn't mean to scare her."

"How else did you think she'd react?"

"I didn't think about her." She clasped her small hands in her lap. "I was upset and left."

"And of all places you decided to come here?"

"You listen to me."

He picked up a cookie and nodded. "Yeah, I am good at listening." He took a bite, giving her a moment to start talking.

Bridget reached for her own cookie, but held it between her fingers. She glanced around the room, then at him. "Did anyone ever lie to you?"

"Sure, at some point in my life."

"Did you get mad?"

"Probably."

"Did you tell them off?"

He tried to think of a situation to use as an object lesson before answering. "When we were kids, Josh and I built a tree fort in the backyard. We would have our friends over all the time and sleep out. We were supposed to have a bunch of kids over this one night, but Josh didn't do his chores and lied about it. My dad knew he was lying, so he canceled the get-together. I was mad at my father. I didn't lie, so why couldn't I have the kids over? I didn't talk to Josh or my dad for a few days afterward."

"So Josh got caught."

"Yep. Lied right to my parents, even though they knew the truth."

Bridget turned the cookie over in her hand. "Jenna lied to me."

"How so?"

"She promised that when we moved to Florida we'd have this great new life and things would be better."

"They aren't?"

"Well, our house is pretty cool. Everyone here is nice."

"So what's the problem?"

"Jenna promised she'd always be there for us, but she's been on trips without us and now she's going to start catering. When will she have time for us?"

"Is that what you're worried about, that she won't make time for you?"

"Kinda. I mean, my mom is already gone." Bridget sniffled and swiped her eyes, her voice barely audible. "I don't want to lose Jenna too."

"I can honestly tell you that Jenna's not going anywhere. She loves you and your sister."

"But she's busy."

"She has to work. Look, if she has to go to California, it's because she made promises to the people who hired her. If she didn't show up, she'd be in trouble and her bosses wouldn't trust her word. Keeping your word is important."

Bridget nodded.

"But by working here in town, she'll be able to plan her schedule around you and Abby. Be home every night. I bet she wants you to help her with the business too."

"Yeah. We were there today."

"See, she's including you. She wants you to be a part of her plans."

"I guess."

"I'm pretty positive she'd do anything for you."

"How can you be so sure?"

"Because I'd feel the same way if you were my daughter."

Bridget gripped her cookie so hard, Wyatt waited for it to crumble in her hands.

"I haven't been completely honest," she said.

He hid a smile. "There's more?"

"My teacher gave me a note to give to Jenna. Abby knew, but I made her swear she wouldn't tell on me. Then I hid the note because I didn't want Jenna to know about my bad grades. She found it anyway and wasn't too happy."

"That's serious, Bridget."

She nodded again. "I thought Jenna would get mad at me if she found out."

"Mad because you kept the note from her or mad because of what the teacher wrote?"

"Both." Bridget swiped at her eyes. "I

haven't been doing good in school. Math is the worst."

"Does Jenna know you're having problems?"

"She knows I'm having trouble in math, but not the other stuff."

"What other stuff?"

"Abby has some friends, but I don't."

"Can't Abby include you?"

"I guess, but I didn't tell her what's going on. I don't want to make problems for her." She ran her hand over Cruiser's fur. "Some of the kids are mean to me."

Ah, now they were getting to the root of the problem. "How so?"

"They pick on me. Someone found out that Jenna's not my real mom and made jokes about Abby and me being orphans."

Wow. Pretty heavy stuff for a kid to deal with. "But you're not orphans. Jenna is your family."

"I know, but I said some stuff back at them, so now I don't have any friends."

"I know kids can be mean, but there must be one or two you can apologize to. Once they forgive you, realize that your feelings were hurt, they can convince the others to forgive you too."

"You think so?"

"Sure, but you have to start by telling Jenna everything. She won't be mad. If anything, she'll want to help you."

"Things were easier when my mommy was here."

"I felt the same way about my son."

"I heard Jenna talking about him." She paused a moment then looked at him with big, brown eyes. "Think he's in heaven with my mommy?"

Wyatt's throat grew thick. "I think so."

Bridget reached over and covered his hand with hers. "Bet your son doesn't have to worry about making friends there. I think everyone in heaven has friends."

The knot in Wyatt's chest eased.

"I should get you back to Jenna. She's probably wondering why you aren't home yet."

He started to rise but Bridget's voice stopped him.

"Mr. Wyatt?"

"Yes?"

"Thanks."

"Anytime, kiddo."

Wyatt grabbed his wallet and keys then locked up the cottage. They walked to his truck in silence, Cruiser bounding beside them. Once they'd gotten settled inside, Bridget said, "I'm gonna be in trouble when Jenna is finished being worried about me, aren't I?"

"Pretty much."

"That's gonna stink." She sighed. "What I did is kind of like what your brother did. I probably got Abby in trouble for asking her to keep a secret."

"Maybe next time you'll talk to Jenna instead of running off."

"I guess."

"Don't make your sister promise anything she'll get in trouble for."

"Okay," came the small voice in reply.

Wyatt smiled. Jenna was bound to have plenty of worry time in the future.

JENNA GLANCED AT the clock for the fiftieth time in the past half hour. Where were they? By the time she'd paced the living room floor yet again, the doorbell rang. Heart pounding, she ran into the foyer, swinging the door wide open.

Wyatt stood under the porch light, Bridget at his side. Both faces held solemn expressions.

Cruiser barked from the truck bed.

"Thank goodness." Jenna pulled Bridget into a tight embrace. After a few seconds, the youngster's tense body relaxed and her thin arms circled Jenna. Abby ran down the hallway, joining in the hug. Before long, the girls were hugging and whispering to each other.

Bridget looked at Jenna. "I'm sorry."

Jenna ran a hand over the girl's soft hair. "I know, sweetie." She swallowed hard. "Why don't you and your sister go to your room? I'll be there soon."

Hands clasped, the twins scurried off.

Wiping her moist eyes, Jenna met Wyatt's gaze. "Come in."

He took a step inside. Once Jenna closed the door behind him, she found herself in Wyatt's arms. Unable to speak, she relaxed to the rhythmic motion of his hand stroking her back. She held on tight, drawing in his strength and warmth.

"Thank you," she whispered, taking a step back.

He shrugged.

"I can't believe she ran away, but I'm glad she went to you."

"I think she was working off a little bit of frustration."

"C'mon." Jenna led him to the living room and they both took a seat on the couch. "She is so much like her mother. Headstrong and fearless."

The corners of Wyatt's lips tipped up. "Headstrong for sure."

Jenna sank back into the cushions. "She's only ten. I don't even want to think about what she'll be like in her teens."

"She's still trying to juggle her emotions. It's tough to do in the real world when school and friends interfere."

"I thought she was hiding something from me." Jenna glanced at him, searching his face. "Did she…confide in you?"

"Yes. She's having trouble adjusting. Not only in her classes, but with the other kids too."

"Maybe I should have talked to her before laying down the law. It's hard being a disciplinarian."

"Even if you'd tried to get the truth out of her, I think she needed a third party to talk to. Sometimes kids don't want to confide in their parents."

"I so wanted to make things different for the girls." She ran a shaky hand through her hair. "When I was growing up, I didn't have a parent to confide in. The foster parents weren't bad, for the most part, but I held a lot inside."

She stopped herself from revealing more. He

didn't need to hear about her troubles, didn't need him to think of her as needy.

"Jenna, you aren't going through anything other parents haven't been through. You'll survive this rough patch. Bridget's a good kid."

"I know." She took a deep breath. "I just don't want her to hate me."

He took her hand in his. "She doesn't. She was lashing out. You were the closest target."

She looked down at his tanned, capable hand. She couldn't deny the relief she felt, sharing this situation with Wyatt. His calm, steady demeanor went a long way in soothing her doubts and worries about parenting. For once, she was glad to have a sounding board. Raising the girls solo was the toughest job she'd ever had.

"So I haven't scarred Bridget for life?"

His soft chuckle made her heart shift. "I think you'd have to do a lot worse."

"Trust me, I feel bad, but I understand what you're saying."

"Good."

Silence fell between them. Jenna suddenly went tongue-tied, unable to think of a thing to say until Wyatt broke the tension.

"This is off topic, but can I ask you a favor?"

"After what you did tonight, I'd be unable to say no."

"You might after I ask."

"Ask away."

"My folks invited me over for dinner next Saturday. It's their anniversary. Anyway, my brother said I should bring a date and I was wondering…are you free?"

Jenna was so shocked that he would ask her, so pleased she wanted to squeal with delight. With effort she managed to answer calmly, "I don't have any plans."

"Great. Good." He gave her a warm smile. "They've been bugging me to get a life. I know it's last minute, but I could use a little moral support."

"Moral support? You mean this isn't a date," she teased.

"Sure, I mean, it'll be good to go with someone who isn't after me to change my life."

Meaning no romance.

"And you can bring the girls. My folks will love them."

Definitely no romance.

"I'm sure they'll be excited."

Wyatt ran his palms up and down his denim-clad thighs. "Okay then." He stood. "I should get going."

Jenna rose and walked to the foyer. As she reached for the doorknob, Wyatt said, "Jenna, some advice?"

She faced him. "Please."

"Keep loving them, just the way you are. They'll always remember your love."

Her throat went dry as tears misted in her eyes. "I can do that."

He reached out to run a finger over her cheek, catching a single teardrop as it escaped. His gaze held hers, dark and mysterious in the dim light.

"Then you're miles ahead."

Jenna stared into Wyatt's eyes, splayed her hand over his steady heartbeat. The foyer suddenly seemed cramped. The air heated. They stood toe to toe, so close she could feel his soft breath on her skin. His firm fingers circled her arms, drew her closer. He lowered his head, but neither of them made the next move. Unable to stand the suspense any longer, she stood on tiptoes to brush her lips over his.

It didn't take long for him to return her kiss with enthusiasm. His hands moved into her hair, drawing her closer. She circled her arms around his neck, lost in the sensation of Wyatt kissing her senseless. How right this felt. A deep part of her connected with him on a level she'd never experienced with any other man. Her heart expanded. For a guy who claimed he didn't get emotionally involved, his kisses said otherwise. There wasn't anything more involved than sharing a toe-curling kiss.

Gently breaking the connection, Jenna took a step back, her skin cooling at the loss of Wyatt's warmth.

Jenna crossed her arms, hugging herself. "I need to check on the girls."

Wyatt nodded, his dark eyes burning with an emotion she didn't dare decipher. "I understand," he finally said.

She held back a shuddering sigh. "Thanks again."

"Hopefully Bridget won't make a habit of running off."

Wyatt opened the door, took a step and stopped. Jenna held her breath when he turned back to her. "You're a good mother, Jenna. Don't ever think otherwise."

She watched as he went to his truck and Cruiser jumped into the cab. She waited until he'd pulled out of the driveway and driven down the street before locking the door. She squared her shoulders, pushing down the unexpected feelings Wyatt brought out in her. Now for a nice long chat with Bridget.

To her surprise, Bridget, already in her pajamas, came toward her. Silently, she took Jenna's hand and led her into the living room.

"I'm sorry," Bridget said.

"Me, too."

Surprise registered on Bridget's face. "Why are you sorry?"

"I should have talked to you before coming down so hard."

"I don't think moms work that way."

Jenna's eyes welled up again.

"You're supposed to make sure I'm doing good in school. And I shouldn't be mad that you have to work."

"Is that what's bothering you?"

"Well, some of the kids have been kinda mean. About you not being my real mom."

Jenna tamped down her anger. She'd forgotten how tough it was to be motherless. Forgotten how cruel children could be about the most heart-wrenching problems in life. "I'm sorry you're going through this, Bridget. I wish you'd told me." Jenna took a seat on the couch, pulling Bridget onto her lap. "It's never easy being the new girl in school. Whenever I moved to a new foster home and had to switch schools, I was always the odd person out."

"Does it get better?"

Jenna ran a hand over Bridget's soft hair. "In time. You'll find your special friend, just like I found your mother. And about those mean kids? Just walk away from them. Drives them crazy if they think you aren't upset."

Bridget looked down.

"Anything else?"

Picking at her PJ bottoms, Bridget said softly, "I'm afraid you'll get busy with your catering or go back to your cooking show and leave us behind."

Jenna circled her arms around Bridget's slender shoulders and hugged her close. "Never."

"Promise?"

"Promise."

They sat in silence for a long while, Jenna drinking in the little girl smell of soap and crayons. She may not have a chance for anything romantic with Wyatt, but she vowed to protect her relationship with the twins.

"What do you say I tuck you into bed now?"

"You aren't going to yell at me?"

"Sure I am. But not until tomorrow."

Bridget grinned. "Meet you in the kitchen for cereal and a scolding."

CHAPTER ELEVEN

THE NEXT WEEK flew by. Caught up in a flurry of activity, Jenna managed to keep an eye on the girls while getting the business up and running. Nealy helped her with behind-the-scenes projects, like setting a date for the soft opening and inviting local businesses, store owners, associations, churches, anyone who would benefit from Jenna's catering skills.

They'd also gotten details from Max about the engagement party, which he'd scheduled the night after the opening. His plan entailed taking Lilli for a romantic walk on the beach to pop the question as the sun set. After she said yes—he had no doubt he'd get an affirmative answer—they'd make their way to the public beach pavilion close to downtown.

In the meantime, Jenna and Nealy would work their magic to stage the surprise party. Jenna's head swam as she tried to come up with innovative recipes as well as old favorites to wow the guests at both the opening and her friends' engagement party, but she was excited and happy.

About Wyatt's invitation, however, she was a wreck.

She'd never been invited to meet the family of any man she'd dated. True, Wyatt made it clear he only wanted her there for support, but still, the idea of being introduced to his parents made her tense. Unlike Jenna, Wyatt had grown up in a loving, intact home. The closest she'd come to a real home with her mother was just before the social worker took her from their dingy apartment. Although she'd risen above her past, the old insecurities never failed to get to her when she walked into the home of a happy family.

She placed a hand over her stomach to calm the butterflies. "You can do this," she whispered. If anything, she'd rally for the girls. She wanted to be a good example, wanted the girls to know that no matter what kind of home life you came from, you counted. Letting them see her own uncertainty wasn't an option.

Since inviting her to his parents' anniversary dinner, she'd heard from Wyatt once, when he called to tell her what time he'd pick them up. She knew he'd been around, though. At some point during the week, he'd stopped by to finish the girls' play set. She'd called to thank him, but got his voice mail. Rubbing her head, she stared at her closet and forced her brain to focus on one question. What to wear to the party?

She perused her wardrobe, unable to settle on an outfit. Since this wasn't really a date, she didn't want to come off too fancy. Yet it was dinner, a special occasion, so she needed to wear something accordingly. After going back and forth between three different dresses, she finally settled on a flowered print dress, which was fitted to the waist then flared out around her legs. Once she added a strappy pair of sandals, she loved the fun, flirty look. She took extra time on her makeup and hair, hoping Wyatt would like the finished product.

The girls were excited too. Bridget insisted they make a fancy dessert for the occasion. How could Jenna say no? Her relationship with the girls had moved into a new, tentative phase. They were all striving to make the family dynamics better. Bridget promised to let Jenna know if the bullying at school continued. Abby, having been brought into the loop, promised to keep an eye on Bridget. If they needed help, the twins would confide in Jenna and let her, the adult, handle it.

When the doorbell rang, Jenna took one last check in the hall mirror before rushing to answer it. Her breath hitched at the sight of Wyatt, dressed in a dark blue shirt, which brought out the color of his eyes, and black slacks. The sun shone on his dark hair. A welcoming smile curved his lips. Before she had a chance to speak, the girls ran up behind her to greet him.

"Mr. Wyatt. We made dessert."

A rare twinkle lit his eyes. "You do know my parents are providing the food," he said, over their heads, to Jenna.

"Have you known me to show up at a party without food?"

"Not yet."

"It's chocolate cake," Abby went on to say. "With whipped cream and chocolate chips inside."

Bridget tugged at Jenna's arm. "We have to hurry before the topping melts."

"Okay, okay."

She glanced at Wyatt. He smiled. "You look beautiful."

Pleased by the admiration in his eyes, she said, "Give me a sec and we'll be ready to leave."

He nodded. Jenna tried to ignore the shiver

teasing her skin as he talked to Abby in a low voice.

With the girls chattering up a storm, Wyatt took the cake holder while Jenna locked up. Better safe than sorry.

Before long they'd reached his parents' home in a neighborhood of one-story ranch-style houses. The landscaped lawn was immaculate, with bright pink and white impatiens lining the front porch in full bloom. The driveway was filled with cars.

"Really?" Wyatt muttered.

Jenna glanced at him.

"There are more cars here than just my brothers. My mother probably decided to ask other family members to stop by."

"And that bothers you?"

"No, I mean, it's my folks' party. They deserve lots of company to celebrate. I just haven't been to a family gathering in a long time."

He parked by the curb and killed the engine.

"We're here?" Bridget asked, bouncing about in the backseat.

"Yep." Wyatt climbed out and opened the back door for the girls. "My parents' house."

The girls waited in the driveway while Wyatt helped Jenna from the car. "Thanks."

She looked at him curiously. "For what?"

"The moral support."

"I told you we're happy to be here." Jenna bit back her disappointment. Still, what had she really expected him to say when he'd made it clear his emotions were off-limits?

"I know I've shut a lot of friends out of my life. Even my family. It means the world to my mother that I agreed to come today."

Jenna picked up the cake holder from the car seat and stepped to the sidewalk. "I promise, the girls and I will do our part."

Closing the door, Wyatt fell into step beside her. Before they reached the porch, the front door flew open and an attractive woman, who Jenna remembered as Wyatt's mother, greeted them with a big smile.

"Welcome, welcome."

Wyatt introduced Jenna and the girls and soon they were swept into the house, surrounded by extended family members. Someone took the cake from Jenna's hands, replacing it with a glass of iced tea.

Wyatt's father threw an arm around his wife's shoulders. "Liz is so happy you could make it. She's a fan of your show."

"Bryce." Liz batted at her husband's chest.

"She's even whipped up a few of your recipes."

Liz's face colored. "I'm nowhere near your talent, but I try."

"Please, Mom," a tall, handsome man said as he joined them. "You're one of the best cooks I know." He winked at Jenna. "No offense."

"None taken. It's good to know people actually use my recipes."

"I'm Wyatt's brother, Josh."

"Good to meet you."

"And where is your date, son?" Liz asked, looking around the living room.

"She couldn't make it."

"Did you even invite her?"

"Didn't you ask me to?"

Bryce held up a hand. "We have company, remember?"

"Of course." Liz smiled apologetically. "Now that you're all here, we can eat." She hurried off in the direction of what Jenna assumed was the kitchen.

"Nothing too fancy," Bryce told her. "Pot luck. Once we found out Wyatt was coming, Liz got on the phone and asked everyone to bring family favorites. Reminds me of when the boys were younger and we had lots of family gatherings. You'll enjoy it."

"I'm sure I will."

Bryce took off, leaving her with Josh. "Thanks for hanging out with my brother."

She grinned. "It's not a hardship. He's a good guy."

Josh sobered. "Yeah, he is. Wish he'd remember that."

Jenna bit her lip at Josh's concerned expression. Should she interfere or not? "Can I make a suggestion?"

Josh glanced at her. "Go ahead."

"Have patience. Wyatt is never going to be the same man he once was. He's still figuring out life after Jamie. At some point he'll feel more comfortable around your family. Give it time."

"It's been two years."

"And it could take another two years. There's no time limit on grief."

"I've been afraid he'd lose himself in the grief and we'd never see him again."

"He's here today."

"Thanks to you."

She held up a hand. "He probably would have come anyway."

"I'm not so sure."

"Look, it's easy for him to be around me.

I have no history with him. I didn't know his son. He can be open with me."

"Makes sense."

"So, lighten up." She smiled to take the sting out of her words. "Give him space or you will lose him."

"Advice taken." He looked across the room. "Hungry?"

"Starved."

"Let's eat."

Wyatt joined her as she stood in the food line.

"Where have you been?" she asked as he brushed her shoulder.

"Worried?"

"You left me alone with a room full of *your* relatives. The least you could do is stick by me."

"You're great with people."

"Maybe." She tilted her head. "Where were you?"

"Out back. I was showing the girls where Josh and I built our tree fort."

"Sounds interesting."

"Long story."

"Wyatt," she teased, "are you keeping secrets from me?"

"Nothing earth-shattering."

"But the girls are okay?"

"Fine. My cousin has two kids their age. They're having fun."

Just as Bryce said, all the food on the table looked delicious. Jenna tried a little bit of most dishes, but her appetite disappeared when Wyatt took a seat on the couch next to her. When his arm brushed hers, she struggled to suppress her usual telltale reaction to his nearness. But he seemed to relax when he was beside her, even as his family asked how he was, what he'd been up to. Jenna sensed when he'd had enough and she intervened in the conversation, sharing anecdotes about her cooking show and life in LA

Once her plate was empty, she wandered into the kitchen to find Liz bagging up leftover rolls.

"Can I do anything?"

Liz glanced over her shoulder. "No, you're company. Just relax."

Jenna glanced around, looking for a task to keep her busy. "I'm not used to sitting so much."

"I have everything under control."

"If you're sure…"

Liz turned, wiping her hands on a dishtowel.

"If you must, why not get that decadent dessert of yours ready to serve."

"That I can do."

As Jenna attended to the cake, the sound of children's laughter wafted through the open window from the screened porch. Liz craned her neck to look outside, her lips curved in a smile.

"It's so nice to hear the sound of children's voices. I do miss it so much."

Jenna kept busy, saying nothing.

"It was a horrible time when we lost Jamie. Then Marcie left." Liz cleared her voice which had turned raspy. "But to have Wyatt withdraw and then leave…"

Jenna laid down the knife she'd been using to cut slices of cake and moved next to Liz. Silence settled between them as they watched Bryce and the twins engaged in conversation.

Liz wiped her eyes. "I'm sorry for getting weepy. Seeing the girls…having Wyatt home. I guess it's more than I expected."

"I understand," Jenna said. "I'm thrilled when I see the girls happy, but I can't help but miss their mother."

"Wyatt told me about your loss. I'm so sorry."

Surprised by Liz's revelation, she took a moment to reply. "Thank you."

"I see why Wyatt is drawn to you."

Jenna laughed. "Mostly it's because he's helped me out of one scrape or another."

Liz leaned against the counter. Shook her head. "No, it's more than that. You have a very gentle way about you. My son responds to you."

"I don't know. He has seen me at my worst."

"And I imagine you've seen him at his worst." Liz's eyes grew misty again. "I'm glad he has a friend like you in his life.

"I'm not sure if my son is ready to become involved in a relationship again, but if he were, I'd wager you're the woman for him."

"Wyatt isn't there yet. Besides, I have a family to take care of. My plate is full."

Liz placed the towel on the counter. "If you say so."

"I do," Jenna said with enough fervor to make it clear, subject closed.

"Then let me help you with dessert."

Liz announced the cake was being served. The gang descended on the buffet table to get a piece. Jenna searched the room for Wyatt, who was suspiciously missing. She went to the living room, but he wasn't there. She checked the back porch, starting to get worried when she couldn't locate him. A few minutes later, she found him in the guest bedroom, sitting on a full-sized bed covered with a bright yellow duvet, opening a cardboard box.

His hands stilled on the flaps. He pushed them down. A moment passed before he flipped them up to look inside, stopping when he noticed her in the doorway. Judging by the sorrow in his eyes, Jenna didn't have to be told that the contents of the box belonged to Jamie.

WYATT'S BREATHING EVENED out when Jenna came into the room.

"After Jamie died it was too much to keep his things around. I boxed up some of his toys, special clothes, stuff like that. Asked Mom to store them for me."

"Those are special mementos. You should keep them."

"Honestly, I'd forgotten, or willingly put them out of my mind, until Mom reminded me."

Jenna leaned against him to look into the box. The sweet shampoo scent filled his nostrils. He inhaled deeply. Since meeting Jenna, he couldn't get her scent out of his mind.

"May I?" she asked, her bright gaze meeting his. "I'd love to see what you kept."

With the small encouragement, Wyatt pulled out a plastic airplane. A smile touched the corners of his lips. "Jamie was fascinated with planes. I promised him we'd go for a ride one day."

"Did you get a chance to?"

His smile faded. "No."

He removed a few T-shirts with slogans Jamie liked. A baseball cap and jersey. "Although he was only eight, he loved to go watch the Rays play. He'd dress up in his gear, even if we were watching the game on TV."

He pulled out a worn, green blanket printed with frogs. Rubbed his thumb against the soft material. "We got this as a baby shower present. There wasn't a night Jamie didn't sleep with it tucked under his chin." He brought the blanket to his nose and inhaled deeply. Sure enough, he could just make out the little boy scent.

"I've always thought the sense of smell is the strongest when it comes to memories," Jenna said. "There's something powerful about a familiar scent that takes you back to a specific time or place."

Wyatt lowered the blanket.

Jenna reached across, running her fingers over the fabric. "I had a blanket once."

"Just once?" he teased.

"Yep. I don't remember how I got it. I think a friend of my mom's gave it to me." Her gaze grew a little distant as she lost herself in the memory. "Anyway, it was the only thing I had when social services took me from my mother. I hung on to that thing like it was a lifeline. One of my foster mothers had to wrestle it away from me so she could wash it."

"It was a tangible connection to your mother."

She nodded. "That thing got ratty, but I couldn't part with it."

"Do you still have it?"

"No. There was a fire in one of the homes I lived in. We lost most of our belongings, the blanket included."

"I'm sorry, Jenna."

She shrugged, but judging by the tightness of her shoulders, she was still affected by the past. "By that time the emotional link was broken. It was pretty clear my mother wasn't coming for me. I didn't need the constant reminder."

He didn't know what to say. His parents had always been there for him, giving him a safe, stable home. He'd never wanted for anything, until Jamie died. Now, no matter what his parents did, he was never getting his son back.

"Maybe looking through the box was a bad idea."

"Or maybe it's time," Jenna countered.

"I don't know. Some days I think I'm getting better at handling stuff like this. Other moments I can't deal."

"I guess that explains the quiet, broody mood of late."

"Broody?"

"If the word fits…"

He laughed. "Okay. I guess I deserved that."

"But I understand since I know how tough this is. Look, Wyatt, you'll always love Jamie. Nothing will change that, but you didn't stop living when he died. Do you know why?"

He couldn't speak around the lump in his throat.

"Because a lot of people love you. Your folks. Your brother. That's what keeps you alive."

"I don't deserve it."

"Everyone deserves love."

"But it's my fault Jamie's gone." He clenched his fists together. "If I'd been watching him better, I could have kept him from going over-board."

"Wyatt, it was an accident."

"Maybe to everyone else, but deep inside, I know it's all on me."

Jenna went quiet for a second. "Do you blame your ex-wife as well?"

Startled, he replied, "No. Why would I?"

"But don't you see? The same logic applied to you. Neither of you planned for anything to happen. It was a tragic accident."

Wyatt shook his head.

"The guilt will eat away at you if you let it. Do you remember what you said to me the first time we met? When you saved Bridget from drowning?"

"No."

"You told me to make sure swimming con-ditions were better when I brought the girls back to the beach. You said next time, I might not be so lucky."

"Your point?"

"Things happen in life that we have no con-trol over. We learn to live with the bad situa-tions. You losing Jamie. The girls and I losing Carrie. You can't control every single moment in every single day, Wyatt. It's impossible."

He closed his eyes, picturing Jamie disappear over the edge of the boat, the image as clear as day. Maybe Jenna was right. He couldn't control every aspect of life. Bad stuff happened and as a result, Jamie was gone.

"You aren't the first person to say I should accept that it was a terrible accident. My family…friends." He ran a hand over his chin. "Maybe it's time to listen."

"Not only should you listen, you should also forgive yourself."

Wyatt knew that would take more strength than he had in him. But if he listened to Jenna's advice, maybe, in time, the guilt would fade.

He shot her a wry glance. "After how I've acted, I don't know why anyone bothers with me."

"You can't fight love, Wyatt. It's too strong."

She was right. He'd always love Jamie. Nothing, neither time nor grief, would change the deep love he still held for his son. Time wouldn't make things better, but it would help him accept the unacceptable. Maybe one day the never-ending hurt of missing his son would soften into comforting memories of the short time he'd been fortunate enough to have Jamie. For now, he needed the love of his family.

And Jenna, who had more inner strength than any person he'd ever met. He hadn't realized just how much he valued her opinion, how much he looked forward to hearing her wisdom when he wanted to hide from the world. She faced life head-on, punches and all, and still kept a smile on her face. Without her support, he'd have never reached the place where he could consider moving on without Jamie. Suddenly, he wanted to see what the future had in store for him.

Not ready to confide his revelation to Jenna yet, he said, "I'll make sure I let my mom know I appreciate her hanging on to the box."

"It's what moms do," she replied in a cheeky voice.

"So you're an expert now?" he asked, his voice light.

"No, but I'm getting a better idea of what being a mom means every day."

Together, they began to replace Jamie's belongings. Wyatt realized this was a milestone of sorts. "You know, I was dreading being around my family today."

"Really?" A hint of a grin flirted with the corners of her mouth. "I would never have guessed."

He appreciated her humor. It went a long way in keeping his mood from deteriorating any further than it had since he started looking through the box. Yet there was one piece of the grief puzzle still niggling him. Since he'd already confided so much to Jenna, he decided to get it out of his system. "When I see Jamie's things, it reminds me of his laughter. I'm so afraid I'm going to forget what he sounds like."

Jenna placed her hand over her heart.

"Everyone keeps telling me to get on with living my life, and while in my mind I understand that, in my heart I feel like letting go is being dishonest to Jamie's memory. Like the act of letting go means another part of my connection to Jamie will be stolen away. I've already lost so much, how can I let go of the only thing I have left?"

"There's nothing wrong with needing a connection to Jamie. Letting go doesn't mean the memories are lost forever. I've learned that while mourning Carrie. I think you've finally moved to a place where you want the connection to be positive, even though it's tough to let go of your grief."

"Touching Jamie's things just now and not losing it? A huge hurdle for me. It's like I'm finally at a better place for the first time since Jamie died."

Jenna's smile touched his heart. "Go with

your instincts, Wyatt. Only you know what's best for you."

His chest grew tight. She was right. His instincts were telling him to ease off the grief. Enjoy life more. "You know, I always thought saying things like, 'Jamie wouldn't want you to keep grieving' or 'time heals all wounds' were cruel. I mean, how could anyone know how I was feeling? Time hasn't healed, but it does soften the blow. I realize that grief is no place to live permanently. Even at his young age, Jamie wouldn't have wanted me to die with him. I guess living my life will bring him honor."

Jenna squeezed his hand. A tear slipped from her eye and trailed down her cheek. With his free hand he thumbed it away, grateful to have her here with him.

His momentous decision to get plugged back into everyday life might prove tough, but he shook off that fear and said, "So, should we go rescue the girls from my parents?"

Jenna brushed her damp cheek, closing the box as she stood. "Do they need rescuing?"

"Only if you don't want them smothered with affection."

"Right, because no one wants that."

He picked up the box and set it on the

dresser. "It's been a while since my mother's been able to spoil any kids."

"Since it's your parents' anniversary, shouldn't we be spoiling them?"

"Trust me, they're having fun."

"In that case, I want to hear about this fort connection you and the girls have kept from me."

"You mean I can't have any secrets?"

Her expression became serious for a split second then was gone, but he didn't miss it.

"You're a man of mystery now?"

"No, but I like sharing a secret with the girls to make you crazy." He grinned. "A man of mystery is pretty cool, though."

Jenna rolled her eyes. "Fine. Have your little secret. Just know that once I get the girls home, all I have to do is ask the right questions and they'll gladly tell all."

"Then I'll have to bribe them."

"This is a new side to you." Her brows rose. "Should I be concerned?"

He simply smiled.

CHAPTER TWELVE

THE FURNITURE FOR the office and the client meeting area arrived on Monday. Jenna used every free minute to set things up. In the office, she positioned the desk, chairs, computer and printer to her liking before arranging the paper products she'd picked up from the local office supply store. Hands on hips, she surveyed her domain.

"Not too shabby."

She turned to face the client meeting area. "Now this will take a little more finessing."

She shoved the bulky furniture around, finally centering the love seat and two armchairs, along with a large coffee table between them. Below was a colorful area rug. Humming, she brightened the space further by placing a floral arrangement on the table. Pleased with her work so far, she brought the ladder into the client area and hung sheer curtains over the wide windows, creating a homey, comfortable space to meet with prospective customers.

"Now we're cooking." She giggled at her pun.

Late in the afternoon, Nealy stopped by, juggling boxes of colorful brochures and business cards for the newly named Charming Delights Catering. A large bag hung from her arm.

Nealy nodded to the top box. "Take a look. Tell me what you think."

Jenna grabbed it and examined the sample card taped to the box. Her eyes watered.

"What's wrong? You look like you just cut up an onion."

"Nothing. You know I'm wavering between terrified and excited." She released a nervous laugh. "The cards are proof I've actually taken the first step."

Nealy deposited the boxes on the desk, and returned with a handful of brochures. Carefully placing them on the coffee table, she stepped back to observe her handiwork. "I bought a brochure stand and card holders, so when a customer comes in, you're official."

Jenna exhaled. "Official. I like the sound."

"Wait." Nealy hurried to pull something out of the big bag. She shook out a magenta-colored vest with *Charming Delights Catering* stitched in black on the front left side and held it out for Jenna to see. "*Now* you're official."

Jenna placed a hand over her gaping mouth. She and Michelle had scoured every restaurant uniform catalog online until they found the perfect outfit to represent the business. When in the kitchen or meeting customers, Jenna would wear a double-breasted bistro blouse with a mandarin collar. After much debate, they decided on black pants, a long-sleeved white tuxedo shirt beneath the brightly colored vest and a matching bow tie to wear to events.

Jenna's voice finally showed up as she took the vest from Nealy. "Wow. The color is even better than in the picture."

"You'll look both professional and fun. I love it."

"This day just gets better and better."

"So, how are the menus coming?"

"After you gave me the list of upcoming events, I made up different menus based on the type of party." She jogged to the kitchen to retrieve a large notebook. Under the clear plastic cover, she'd placed a beautiful picture of a divinely set dining table she'd cut from a magazine. Inside, she had slipped each menu page into plastic sleeves, making it easy to flip through.

Nealy thumbed through the book. "Impressive."

"Yeah, well, that comes from too many nights not sleeping. Once I got into the spirit, ideas kept bombarding me. I had to write them down. The other day I met with Bridget's teacher and I had to ask for a piece of paper to jot down a dessert idea." She grinned. "But I got us a client. Mrs. Roseman's husband is retiring. She wants to throw him a big party. She'll be calling you." She paused. "Us."

Nealy held up her hand to high-five. "We have it going on, sister."

"We do." Jenna took back the book and placed it on the table. "How are the RSVPs for the opening?"

"Every single business I invited is attending. Doesn't mean a ton of bookings, since most folks in Cypress Pointe will just want to check out what we're doing, but I'm optimistic. Plus, your celebrity status goes a long way."

"I'm not sure how long the status will last. Barbara has been uncharacteristically quiet. It's kind of freaking me out."

"So I guess that means no news from the network?"

"None. And with Barbara's silence, I can't imagine that's good news."

"She has your best interests at heart."

"She does. I invited her to the opening, but she hasn't responded." Jenna frowned. "Do you think she's mad at me?"

"Even if she is, you're doing what you have to for your family. Don't forget that."

"I don't. I feel guilty, though. Barbara really got my career going."

"And she'll still find a way to benefit from it."

"Maybe."

"What's wrong?"

Jenna filled Nealy in on her last run-in with Rod.

"So the cops had him in custody. You brought charges. He's got to see how foolish it is to come near you. That's good news.

He doesn't know about the catering business, does he?"

"I asked Barbara to keep it a secret. Although once I officially open, all bets are off. Between the internet and the other avenues he has to get information, he'll know where I am once he's out."

"He won't bother you."

"How can you be so sure?"

"You're too far away from his sources. His

network of celebrities. He won't come here and miss out on other lucrative stories."

"I hope you're right."

"Why didn't you tell me before today?"

"I kept hoping if I didn't talk about it, it wouldn't be real."

Nealy frowned. "You can't bury your head in the sand."

"I know. That's why I got the police involved. At least there's a record of what he's been doing and some jail time should discourage him from violating the restraining order again."

"For now, focus on what you can control, like getting this place ready and cooking for the guests. The rest will fall into place."

Jenna agreed. Right now she would focus on the girls and her business. Anything more would have to wait.

"Please, don't keep secrets like that again. We're friends, Jenna. That means we have each other's back. Always."

Unable to voice her gratitude, Jenna hugged Nealy especially tight.

JUST AS HE PROMISED, Wyatt showed a new side to himself. As the night of the soft opening for the catering business approached, he made himself available to Jenna. If she needed errands run, he ran them for her. If she stayed late at the office, he stopped by with dinner or took the girls down the street to one of the town's restaurants or to his cottage to do homework. Between ordering supplies and setting up the kitchen to her specifications, Jenna alternated between staying busy and falling into bed at night exhausted.

Setting up the kitchen just the way she wanted had taken hours, but she was pleased with the result. All of the stainless-steel appliances gleamed after multiple scrubbings, from the commercial-grade refrigerator, double sink, range with cast-iron grates and two full ovens and the walk-in freezer to the large prep table. Everything was up to code and ready to use. Although the freezer was the oldest piece of equipment, it worked well, minus the sticking latch.

She'd got a good deal on her cooking utensils and pots and pans through Kitchen Care, her show sponsor. Everything had arrived recently and Jenna had placed each piece in a strategic position. All of the catering supplies, from serving pans and trays to food warmers, china, beverage ware, flatware and linens were neatly stored in a closed storage unit. The purchases had made a huge dent in her finances, but Jenna was pleased with every one. Thank goodness she already had a minivan, otherwise she'd have to look into new transportation.

On Wednesday afternoon before the soft opening, Jenna stood in the kitchen in a short-sleeved T-shirt, shorts and sneakers, reviewing a food order invoice. Slowly, over the last few hours, the sky had grown dark with thick black clouds threatening to dump rain on them. Sure enough, the first roll of thunder sounded, followed by a deluge. Wyatt stomped through the back door after shaking off his drenched slicker, only his boots and the bottom of his jeans wet.

"Hey, you're getting water all over my clean floor."

"I'll mop it up."

"You better. I don't need an increase in my insurance premium if someone falls and gets hurt."

Wyatt hooked his slicker on a peg near the door. "What happened to the happy-go-lucky TV chef? Seems she's been replaced by bossy catering chef."

His words blew the steam out of her. "Am I really that bad?"

"I'm attributing your mood to nerves."

"So I am bad."

"I've worked with worse."

"Lucky you don't work for me."

"No, but as the odd-job guy around here, I have endured greatly," he quipped.

"Wyatt, I'm sorry."

"Don't be. You're a professional. You have high standards. Nothing wrong with that."

"Except when people don't want to be around me. Is that why the girls keep asking you to take them out to dinner?'

"That and the fact they've hardly eaten out since you got custody."

"I may be a teensy bit particular about the food they eat."

"Stop worrying. They're fine."

She glanced at her watch. "Well, tonight they're getting a home-cooked meal."

"Whether they want it or not?"

"Exactly." She smiled at the thought. "There's a parent/teacher open house tonight. We can spend time together before heading back to the school."

Wyatt chuckled. "So why'd you call me?"

"It's the freezer door latch. The sticking is getting worse. Once the food order arrives, I can't be worried about getting in and out of there. And with the girls around, I don't want them getting stuck inside."

"I'll get on it." As Wyatt attended to the task, he asked, "Ready for Friday night?"

"As ready as I'll ever be." She held up the invoice. "I'm going to hit the farmers' market at dawn tomorrow, then be back for the rest of the food delivery. I'll be up to my elbows cooking for the opening."

He moved the latch back and forth a few times and then opened the freezer door. As he did, a puff of cold air escaped, pushing against the vinyl strips acting as a curtain. The condenser kicked on with a loud rattling sound from the top of the unit.

"How is Michelle working out?"

"Great. She's knowledgeable about food service and has cooking experience." She leaned against the prep table. "I feel bad, though. She's always looking at the back door, like she's waiting for Duke to walk in."

It broke Jenna's heart to see the yearning in Michelle's eyes. Was she just as bad? Crazy to have feelings for Wyatt, a man who still didn't want to get emotionally involved? Always looking over her shoulder, hoping he'd changed his mind?

"There was a lot of secrecy on Duke's part,"

Wyatt said. "Makes you wonder what happened."

"Unless the man himself comes around and tells us, we'll never know. But as for Michelle, she'll be here soon to double-check the inventory for Friday night."

Wyatt pushed the plastic dome knob on the inside of the door before closing it. "The door seems to be working fine. Come over here so I can show you how to lock it from the outside."

Jenna placed the invoice on the table and crossed the kitchen, enjoying the cold air lingering around the door of the freezer, along with a whiff of Wyatt's cologne.

"See this hole in the latch?"

She nodded.

"That's the lock. The piece that slides into it seems to be missing." He looked around, reaching toward a small box containing tools on a nearby shelf. He grabbed a screwdriver and held it up. "This will have to do." He pushed it through the hole. "Once this is in place, the door is locked and the girls can't get inside. When they aren't here, just leave it on the shelf."

"That was easy."

"The latch needs a little oil. I'll bring some by next time."

"In the meantime, can you help me drag these shelving units inside the freezer?"

"I live to do your bidding."

"Says the man who keeps to himself."

"Hey, we all have our own idiosyncrasies."

"Just move the shelves."

Minutes later, they'd dragged the last piece inside and stationed it against the wall. Jenna placed her hands on her hips. "That was the final thing on my list. I'm ready for anything now." She headed for the door, pushing the round handle as she went. The door remained closed and Jenna crashed into it. "What the heck?" She whirled around. "I thought you said there was no problem."

He shot her a sheepish look. "There wasn't."

Jenna threw her hands up. "How are we supposed to get out of here?"

Wyatt came up beside her and pressed the handle. The door didn't budge.

"This can't be good."

Jenna shivered, more from Wyatt's close proximity than the temperature. After his emotional breakthrough the day of his parents' party, he'd become more open, more relaxed. She still noticed shadows in his eyes from time to time, but for the most part he was taking his new resolution to move ahead with his life in stride. There had been no more kisses, no more unintentional touches, so she assumed the emotional involvement ban was still in place. She'd kept her distance, afraid to make the first move romantically. Now they were thrown together, stuck in an awful mess. Talk about rotten luck.

"Give me a minute," he groused as he wrestled with the door.

"Wyatt, the longer we stay in here the colder it's going to get."

"Chill, Jenna."

"Funny."

His eyes lit up. "Yeah, it was funny. Just like this situation."

Jenna pounded on the door.

"What are you doing?"

"Michelle will be here soon. If she hears us, she'll let us out."

"As long as the outside latch works."

"Wyatt!"

He chuckled and pounded along with her. After five minutes, they stopped. Jenna rubbed her sore hand. "This is crazy."

"Let's take a short break from making a racket no one's there to hear."

Not wanting to be locked up alone with

Wyatt any longer than necessary, she began pounding again. "I'm good."

He sent her a knowing grin and her stomach dipped. Was she that easy to read?

He followed her lead, despite the fact that no one answered. When their breath vaporized, he stopped. "Tired yet?"

She wasn't, but stopped her pounding and paced the small confines of the freezer, mostly to stay warm, but also to keep distance from Wyatt. After a few minutes, her teeth began to chatter.

"Come here."

Wyatt held his arms open. While she longed to snuggle in his warmth, she hesitated.

"I won't bite."

Maybe not, but the man knew how to kiss. Finally, the chilly temperature triumphed over her common sense and she walked into his arms. She folded her arms so they were between her chest and his and nestled against the soft fabric of his T-shirt. When he closed his arms around her, she sighed.

"Better?"

"Much."

They stood this way for a long, drawn-out moment. Jenna closed her eyes and drank in Wyatt's familiar scent. If they weren't in danger of freezing to death, she could stay this way forever.

"So," Wyatt said, his breath warm against her ear. "The other day. At my folks? I wanted to properly thank you for listening to me."

The air grew heavy and charged and she dropped her head back a fraction to meet his gaze. "Properly?"

"Like this."

His lips brushed hers. Unhurried, he teased her, tenderly at first, until Jenna circled his waist with her arms. Before long the kiss heated her skin, despite the cold air. He ran his warm fingers up and down her arms and she shivered in response, thrilled and wary at the same time.

Soon she took a shaky step away, gulping in much-needed air. She said the first thing that came to mind. "I thought you didn't want to get emotionally involved."

He looked as shaken by the kiss as she was. "Yes, I said that."

"Have you changed your mind?"

"I…" He paused. Stared at the ceiling. "When I told you I wanted to properly thank you, I didn't mean to kiss you. Again. Not that I don't like kissing you," he rushed on. "I do know that I want to be with you. All the time."

He moved closer. "But I can't make promises. Not yet."

She nodded. His admission, at least a step closer to the romantic relationship she craved, would do. "I can wait." She took his face in her hands and they locked gazes. Unable to deny his tempting kisses, she stood on her toes. Pressed her lips to his.

This time Wyatt stopped them before they got too carried away. "You're making it easy to believe in love again, Jenna, but I don't want to do or say anything to hurt you or the girls."

"Then don't." His words brought a dose of reality. She stepped back, bumping into the door. Lifting her foot, she kicked, hoping Michelle was on the other side.

"But I'm trying."

She kicked one more time then reached for him. "Keep trying," she whispered, ready to kiss him again, not worrying about the cost to her heart. She glimpsed the fire in his eyes, felt a soaring rush of heat and moved closer, just as the freezer door jerked open.

"Jenna?"

The vinyl curtain parted. Michelle popped her head inside. "What're you guys doing in here?"

Jenna jumped away from Wyatt, her face

hot as she faced Michelle. Nothing like nearly getting caught making out by your employee. "We were moving the new shelving units inside. The door locked behind us."

Michelle grinned as her gaze settled on Jenna's red face before moving to Wyatt. "Good thing I heard noises and decided to check it out, otherwise who knows how long you two would have been stuck in here." She paused a beat. "Alone."

"Right. Thank you."

Michelle sidestepped as Jenna bolted out of the freezer. Once in the kitchen, she jumped up and down to warm herself up.

Wyatt closed the door. "I'll get the safety release looked at. In the meantime, if you have to go inside the freezer, prop something in front of the door to hold it open. Wouldn't want anyone getting stuck inside again." He winked at Michelle.

She laughed. "Yeah. That would be horrible."

He glanced at Jenna. "I'm going to take off. Tell the girls hi for me."

Jenna stopped jumping. "Right. I was going to pick them up." She scrambled to find her cell phone on the counter. "Thanks," she called out to his exiting back, grabbing her purse to leave.

"Hey, do we need a system here?" Michelle asked. "You know, if you get locked in the freezer with Mr. Hottie, leave a dishtowel on the door latch?"

Jenna felt so embarrassed. "That will never happen again," she said to Michelle. "I'll see you tomorrow. We'll go over the inventory then."

"Whatever you say, boss."

LATER THAT NIGHT, after the open house at school, Jenna stood in the pain reliever aisle at the drug store, the bright fluorescent light adding to the pounding in her head.

The girls had come home from school very subdued, barely touching dinner. With no one to watch the twins, Jenna's only option was to take them along with her to the first parent/teacher open house. She was tempted to stay home to nurse the headache that had started earlier, but the girls wanted Jenna to see their special art projects displayed in the classroom.

The twins were still much too quiet during the school visit, and their behavior screamed a warning. By the time they got in the car to head home, their unhappy faces were pale.

When Abby complained about not feeling very well, Jenna felt her forehead. Warm to the touch. They must have come down with a bug.

They'd trouped to the pharmacy section, where Jenna had a conversation with the pharmacist on which brand of fever remedy to buy for the girls. Now, five minutes until closing, she scoured the shelf for the right box.

"Jenna, can we go home?" Bridget asked, hanging listlessly from her arm.

"Sure, honey." Jenna grabbed the recommended medication and herded the girls to the checkout.

"I want to go to bed," Abby whined.

"Soon." Jenna paid for the purchases. As they walked through the door, she nearly collided with Wyatt.

"Hey." He grinned at Jenna, then the girls. At their less than energetic greeting, Wyatt looked at Jenna questioningly.

"The girls have a slight fever," she explained.

"I feel icky," Bridget complained.

"And Jenna has a headache too," Abby volunteered.

His concerned gaze pinned hers. "Can I do anything?"

"We're headed home. The girls need to get into bed."

"I'll follow you."

"What?"

"You don't feel good and the girls are out of it. I'm coming to help you."

"Wyatt, there's no—"

"No complaints, Jenna."

Too tired to argue and secretly glad he insisted, Jenna nodded. Ten minutes later they were in the house. Jenna steered the girls to the kitchen for a spoonful of medicine.

"I'll make you some tea," Wyatt said. "Go get the girls ready for bed."

As she passed him, Jenna touched his arm. "Thank you, Wyatt."

He shrugged and got to work.

By the time she had the girls in bed, Wyatt and a steaming cup of tea were waiting in the living room. He handed her two capsules of pain reliever and she chased them down with a long drink from a glass of water. Switching to the tea, she took a sip and sank into the soft couch, rubbing her temples.

"Don't tell me those few minutes in the freezer today did you in."

She managed a small smile. "It's a combination of little sleep and whatever the girls were exposed to."

He took a seat beside her, his weight on the

cushion rolling her into his side. When she tried to move away, he threw his arm around her shoulder and tucked her close. "Relax," he whispered against her hair.

She should move, she told herself, but she was tired, her head hurt and his warmth lulled her into tranquil contentment.

"Will you keep the girls home from school tomorrow?" he asked, stroking her hair.

"Yes. They need to rest."

"How about you?"

She stirred, pushing herself to sit up as reality intruded on her serene mood. "I'll have to figure out how to watch them and get some work done. Maybe Michelle can bring some supplies here so I can start cooking."

Wyatt gently tugged her back against him. "How about you all take a break?"

"I can't. I have to get ready for Friday night. And the engagement party Saturday."

"Michelle is competent. I'm sure she can handle one day without you."

"She is."

"But?"

Jenna grinned against his chest. "But I'm one of those people who like to be right in the middle of business."

"Or, you could take a day off, trust your employee and feel better for Friday night."

"There is that option."

"The smart option."

She snuggled closer, her lids growing heavy. She hadn't felt this safe, this protected in... well, she couldn't remember when. The past few months had been a whirlwind of emotional ups and downs, from moving cross-country to getting settled here in their new home. Now with a new business to run, Jenna realized Wyatt was right. She needed a day to recharge her batteries before the busy weekend ahead.

"You win. I'll take tomorrow off and trust Michelle to get started on the food prep."

"That's my girl."

A warm rush of affection filled Jenna at Wyatt's words. She could almost envision cuddling with him on a regular basis. Almost, being the key word, because he still hadn't gotten to a place where he wanted a serious relationship. For now, in the dim shadows of her living room, curled up beside the man who held her heartstrings, she'd enjoy the illusion of them as a couple. In the bright light of day, she'd be more sensible.

"I can watch the girls on Friday if they still

need to stay home from school," he told her. "I don't have a charter scheduled."

"Wyatt, I can't ask you to do that."

"Sure you could. Besides, I'm offering. I'm pretty sure I remember how to take care of a sick kid."

"They'll be cranky."

"I can handle it."

Her lids drooped again.

"Okay?"

"Yes." She paused and then shifted to get more comfortable. "It's so odd. With you, Nealy and Dane and the rest of the wonderful people I've met here in Cypress Pointe, I have more of a support system then I ever did in LA"

"And how does that make you feel?"

"Like I'm being questioned by a psychiatrist." She giggled. "Seriously, I can't tell you how relieved I am to have all of you."

"Sounds to me like you're finally willing to let people lend a hand."

"It hasn't been easy. My entire life I've never given anyone a glimpse of the real me. I've always been guarded, probably to keep from being disappointed again and again. But here, it's different." She turned her face to him. "I'm different."

"It's not so bad, is it? Asking for help?"

"Not that I asked, since you insisted on coming over, but yeah, it sure takes the burden from my shoulders."

"As long as you're in Cypress Pointe, you aren't alone."

At his quiet statement, tears rushed into her eyes. Wasn't this what she'd longed for her entire life? To belong? To be loved? While Wyatt promised to figure out where he stood in the love department, she had most definitely fallen in love with him. How could she not? She'd seen him overcome great pain and sorrow, becoming a stronger man in the process. A man whose broad shoulders carried heavy burdens, but who didn't succumb to the weight. A man she could easily share her life with.

A tear slipped from her eye, dropping onto his shirt. He must have noticed, because he shifted.

"What's wrong?"

She couldn't reveal her overflowing heart to him. Not right now. Even though her feelings had been building, the revelation was too new. She didn't want to ruin the fragile bond by blurting out the truth when he might not feel the same. Yes, he was the real deal for her, but there were things she still hadn't shared with him. Things he needed to know if they were to have any kind of relationship.

One thing she hadn't told him about was Rod because she hadn't wanted the ugliness to drive Wyatt away. Since he had no love for the entertainment industry due to his wife's betrayal and dream to make it big in LA, how could she admit to the terrible side of fame? Maybe once this busy weekend came to a close she'd sit down with him. Reveal her concerns. See where they went from there.

He nudged her. "You asleep?"

"Close. I should probably let you leave so I can go to bed."

"How about I hang around? Once you're settled, I'll let myself out."

"You're too good to me."

He chuckled. "Trust me, it's not a hardship."

She blinked away the tears that welled in her eyes. "And while I appreciate it, I should see you out now."

At the door, he ran his thumb over her cheek. "Call me if you need anything. Anytime, it doesn't matter."

"We'll be fine."

He gave her one last lingering look. "Talk to you tomorrow."

She lifted a heavy arm to salute him.
His laughter carried on the breeze as she closed the door.

CHAPTER THIRTEEN

AFTER A GOOD NIGHT'S SLEEP, Jenna was raring to go. The girls were a bit more run down and took another day to get back to normal. Just to be on the safe side, Jenna kept them home from school. She wanted them to stay put the night of the soft opening, but the girls were heartbroken they'd miss the party. Wyatt suggested she ask his parents to bring the girls to the event. That way, if they became tired, his folks could take them home while Jenna finished up for the night. His parents' readily agreed, thrilled to spend time with the girls.

Jenna's cooking marathon turned out far better than she'd hoped, if the guests' positive response was an indicator. People mingled, admiring the transformation of the old restaurant. Jenna answered questions all night long, booking a few events and having a great time getting to know the people of Cypress Pointe better. When her dry throat made it tough to talk, she stepped aside for a much-needed break and watched the crowd.

People were enjoying a night out, laughing and chatting. At the food-sampling table, the delicious aroma of savory bacon-wrapped beef, sweet and sour meatballs, spicy chicken wings, and tangy queso dip tantalized guests. The mayor stuck to the table most of the night, waxing on about how fortunate they were to have a famous chef living in their small town.

The twins played a starring role as well. Who could resist their bright smiles and endless chatter? And who knew they would be such talented salesgirls? For Jenna, they proved to be the biggest delight of the night.

She drained the rest of her lemon-flavored water, ready to get back to work, when the front door opened and, with a flourish, in waltzed her agent.

"Surprise!"

Jenna made her way through the guests to greet Barbara with a hug. "You're here."

"Did you think I'd miss your special night? Besides, it wouldn't have been a surprise if I told you."

"When I didn't hear from you I assumed you weren't coming. If you'd called, I could have picked you up at the airport."

Barbara waved her off. "Nonsense. You've been busy."

"Where are you staying? I have room at my house if you need a place to crash."

"I booked a room at the B and B in town."

"How long will you be here?"

Barbara sent her a sheepish look. "I must be totally honest with you, Jenna. This is a combo trip. I'm here for you, but it's also a business trip for a new client. I'm meeting up with a location scout who's checking out the area for a new sports reality show to be filmed in Tampa."

"A new client?" When Jenna saw the twinkle in Barbara's eye, she laughed. "Stop playing coy with me. Tell me who it is."

"If I must." With her flare for the dramatic, Barbara should have been an actress. "Pamela Fontaine."

"Why does that name…" Jenna froze. "Wait. Isn't that the actress Rod's been tailing?"

Barbara looked momentarily chagrined. "He was. Now that I'm working with Pamela on this new show and a network sitcom, she's super busy. He's dropped out of the picture."

Jenna tried to ignore the tingle at the base of her neck. "What do you mean?"

"He's out on bail, awaiting his court date,"

Barbara explained. "Didn't the police department inform you?"

She'd been so busy lately, had she missed a call or a voice mail message?

"I don't like this."

"Don't worry. It's not like he's going to follow you to Florida. Not with his legal problems."

Jenna disagreed. She didn't trust Rod and the fact that Barbara's new client had ties to Rod made her uneasy.

"Why would you—"

"Jenna, don't worry about a thing. I have everything in hand. Tonight is about you." She glanced around the room. "What an excellent turnout."

"What. Oh, yes."

Barbara studied Jenna with a critical eye. "Hmm. I don't think I'm on board with the uniform, catchy as it is, but we'll talk later." Taking her arm, Barbara said, "Introduce me to your guests. And I want to have a conversation with this friend of yours who stole you away from LA."

Jenna showed Barbara around, making small talk even though she couldn't ignore the nagging sense that something was wrong.

When Barbara and Nealy began to talk, Jenna stepped aside, lost in her thoughts.

"What happened to the smile?" Wyatt asked as he sidled up beside her, a glass in his hand.

She hadn't seen him yet this evening and now was especially glad of his company. He had shaved recently, she could smell the masculine scent. He looked way too good in a button-down shirt and casual slacks. "Just getting tired."

"You? You have enough energy for three people."

"Don't forget, I've been working around the clock to get ready for tonight. I guess it finally hit me."

He watched her, the concern in his eyes telling her he doubted her story. "You know, if you ever need to talk, I'm here. It's about time I return the favor."

"I'm fine."

"I thought you were working on reducing that independent streak."

She shrugged. "Old habits…"

"Can be changed," he finished.

Should she confide her worries to Wyatt? If her concerns were unfounded, how paranoid would she look?

"It's probably nothing, but—"

"Excuse me, Miss Monroe. Do you have a minute?"

Jenna turned to find a young woman standing beside her, holding a small recorder. Instantly her stomach clenched.

"Mandy Rose, Cypress Pointe Weekly. I wanted to get a few comments about tonight's success."

"I really don't have the time right now. I have to attend to my guests."

"It'll only take a minute."

Jenna's voice grew more firm. "Not now."

Wyatt's brow rose at her curt tone.

"I'm sure the readers would love your insight into the food world. Hear about your new business endeavor."

"Please, if you would, talk to Nealy Grainger. She can answer all your questions."

"But I—"

Not waiting for the reporter's response, Jenna strode away, beelining for the kitchen, her sanctuary. When she nearly collided with Michelle, who was carrying a fresh tray of hors d'oeuvres to the sampling area, she opted for escaping out the back door instead.

SURPRISED BY JENNA'S abrupt reaction to the reporter, Wyatt followed her to the alley, where she was pacing along the pavement. "What was that all about?"

Jenna's head shot up. "Wyatt, I don't want to talk right now."

Instead of taking her hint, he walked closer. "This is more than you being tired, which I don't believe by the way."

"Did you not understand? I don't want to talk."

"Okay. Then I'll wait out here with you while you pace." He leaned against the side of the building, crossing his arms over his chest.

"Wyatt, go back inside."

He kept quiet.

"You are maddening, you know that?"

"Maybe, but something is going on with you. It's not like you to be so cross with anyone, let alone a reporter." He uncrossed his arms and pushed away from the wall. "Jenna, you've listened to me. You've helped me get a handle on my grief. I only want to return the favor." He stepped closer to her. "I'm a good listener."

Jenna ran her hands over her face. "I'm just overwhelmed by tonight."

"I don't believe you."

"Wyatt," she started in a quiet tone. Tentatively met his gaze. Had he finally worn her down? "This may or may not be anything to be concerned about."

"Try me."

"Where do I start?" Jenna began pacing again. "It goes back to why the girls and I left LA"

"And why was that?"

She stopped, her eyes pleading. For what, he had no clue. He only hoped she'd trust him enough to enlighten him. She opened her mouth when suddenly a loud clang echoed from the kitchen.

"What...?" Jenna sprinted toward the kitchen.

He tailed Jenna to find Michelle crouched down by the prep table, two empty trays on the floor beside her. She looked up as they entered.

"I misjudged the end of the table," she explained.

Jenna's hand flew to her chest. "You startled me."

Michelle rose, trays in hand. "Sorry. I'm not usually this clumsy."

Jenna glanced at Wyatt. He didn't miss her furtive look. "Um, I need to talk to Nealy." With that she rushed out of the room, intentionally he presumed, without finishing her story.

Wyatt made his way back into the midst of the party. When he spotted Dane, he went over to his friend.

"Great turnout," Dane commented.

"Yeah, it is, but I need to ask you something."

Dane's brow rose. "Shoot."

"Why did Jenna move the girls here? I want the truth."

Surprise flashed in Dane's eyes. "Why do you ask?"

"I just witnessed Jenna ream out a reporter. She reacted totally out of character, especially given her experience dealing with the media."

Dane's gaze darted to Jenna and Nealy. "Jenna should tell you."

"That would be nice, except she's tight-lipped about the details."

After a few tense moments when he seemed to be deciding what to do, Dane finally said, "Ask Jenna."

JENNA HAD MADE sure she'd avoided Wyatt before he had a chance to ask any more questions. Flattered that he was concerned about her, she still couldn't bring herself to think about Rod, and decided that she wouldn't tell Wyatt about him after all. Superstitious as it sounded, she didn't want to say his name out loud. Besides, what if she was blowing Barbara's news out of proportion? So Rod was out of jail. It didn't mean he'd bother Jenna again.

After a sleepless night, she had an early breakfast scheduled with Barbara. They discussed the cooking show and endorsement deals Barbara had lined up for Jenna. Her agent quipped that if another of her clients took a job in Florida, she might have to move. Glad that Barbara had a new client to focus on, Jenna smiled, barely eating the scrambled eggs she'd ordered. She'd awoken with her stomach in a knot and it hadn't eased yet.

Barbara left for her appointment and Jenna headed to work. But as she cooked for Max and Lilli's engagement party, her sense of dread increased. Because she knew she'd have to face Wyatt later? Tell him the truth?

What would Wyatt think of her when she told him about Rod? That she was too much drama to handle?

She hoped not. For better or worse, Wyatt had touched her heart. The man who had lost so much in his life had become more than a friend to her. And the gentle way he treated the girls? How could she not fall for him? Because she had. Fallen for him. Big-time. And that meant facing up to the fact that Wyatt might never return her affections. Where would that leave her?

By early evening, Jenna, Michelle and the girls had the van loaded with the food and supplies they needed to take to the beach pavilion. Colorful streamers fluttered in the breeze. Festive lanterns were placed around the perimeter of the party space, waiting to be lit.

They'd opened a full-sized canopy and set out extra tables and chairs for the overflow of guests. Small flower arrangements and matching linens completed the romantic setting. Jenna couldn't wait for the sun to set, so the white lights they'd draped around the canopy would twinkle in the dusk, creating exactly the right ambiance. They had plenty of time to get everything else into place before the lovebirds arrived for their engagement party.

Instead of wearing the new uniform, Jenna chose to dress casually. Technically, this might be considered a job, but she and Nealy were treating the event as a party for good friends. Even though the intense heat had started to abate with the arrival of autumn, she donned a simple jade-colored sundress paired with sparkly sandals. A soft breeze flitted by, finally making a dent in the lingering humidity.

"Remind me again why Max wanted an outdoor party?"

"It has to do with the first time he and Lilli met when they were teenagers." Nealy pointed to a spot a few yards away. "We were hanging out over there. The cops showed up when we set off firecrackers around an illegal bonfire." She sighed, a sappy smile on her lips. "Those were the days."

Jenna laughed at her friend's dreamy expression. "It should cool off once the sun sets. What do you say to re-creating that night? I have plenty of blankets to spread around the bonfire pit if you want to go that way."

"Awseome idea, partner. They'll love it."

Soon the guests began to turn up, including Wyatt. He was dressed casually in a short-sleeved madras shirt with tan cargo shorts and flip-flops. His blue eyes were full of questions as he approached. She hoped he'd wait until they had some quiet time later to talk.

"I'm glad you're here. Would you mind carrying the ice cooler from the van?"

"Hey, I just got here and you're putting me to work?"

Jenna made her eyes wide and plastered on a helpless expression.

Wyatt chuckled. "Got it."

When he returned, Nealy hushed the group. "Look, I see Max and Lilli coming toward us. Everyone pipe down."

Wyatt came up behind Jenna, his breath warm on her shoulder. "Everything okay?"

She turned her head. "Between us?" she guessed.

He took her hand in his. Nodded.

The small gesture meant so much, like he was willing to consider this bond between them might grow into something wonderful. Something permanent.

"It is now."

The newly engaged couple strolled closer and on Nealy's signal, the crowd yelled, "Surprise" and "Congratulations." Lilli was clearly surprised, then she looked up at Max's smiling face and threw her arms around his neck. Her friends clapped at her response.

When the couple joined them, the food and beverages began to flow. The party mood lasted well into the night. Dane started a bonfire and laughter filled the air as Max told everyone the story about the night he and Lilli met. The photographer hired for the party snapped pictures of the happy couple, and Jenna kept busy replenishing the food trays. In her element, she savored every moment.

Whenever she caught Wyatt looking her way, she waved. Her heart did a happy little jig and she relaxed for the first time in days.

As the party began to wind down, Jenna toted her supplies to the van. On her third trip, she noticed a flash off to one side. At first, she didn't pay attention because the photographer had been taking pictures all night, but on her way back to the pavilion, the flash came again. Close by. This time in the opposite direction from the photographer, who was speaking to Nealy in the pavilion.

Dread pooled in her stomach. Before she reached the safety of the group, a familiar figure emerged from the shadows. In the moonlight, Jenna's worst fear materialized.

"Nice party. I'm a little peeved I didn't get an invite."

"Rod, what are you doing here?"

"I owed you a visit after you called the cops on me. Not a smart move." He held up his camera and the flash went off again, momentarily blinding her. "You're still as photogenic as ever."

She blinked until her vision returned. "I told you in LA we were finished. How did you find me?"

"Wasn't that hard. It's not like you completely dropped off the grid. Sitting in a jail cell gave me some time to think. I've been biding my time until we met again. You didn't really think I'd stay away forever." He moved a few paces closer. The predatory gleam in his eyes made Jenna shudder. "You can thank your agent for this meet up."

"What does Barbara have to do with you being here?"

"She hasn't said much to the press about your new life, but she did tell a certain friend of mine she was coming to visit. And since my friend has been busy, thanks to your agent, I thought I'd tag along."

His source had to be Barbara's new client, Pamela Fontaine. Who else would have tipped him off?

"Rod, for the last time, I'm asking you to leave me alone. Go away now."

"Sorry. Not gonna happen." He glanced at Jenna's daughters. Her new friends. Friends who had accepted her. Made her feel welcome. She finally belonged. "Think I'll hang out. See what's going on in the local scene."

"Stay away," she warned, even as her voice trembled.

He slinked closer, his words hushed. "That's not gonna happen either."

Wyatt stepped forward to join them. "Problem?"

Before she could answer, Rod swaggered to her side. "Jenna's getting reacquainted with an old friend."

Wyatt moved closer, his eyes narrowed. "Really? Because she doesn't look happy to see you."

"Wyatt, he was just leaving."

"Planning on causing a scene?" Rod taunted.

Wyatt stood taller, fists clenched at his side. "If necessary."

"He's no friend." Jenna tugged Wyatt's arm to steer him away. "He's here to cause trouble."

"Then maybe I should do something to stop him."

"Please, let's go." Jenna dragged Wyatt with her, Rod's chuckle sounding behind them.

Wyatt glanced over his shoulder, his expression tight. "Who is that guy?"

"My nightmare."

Once they were back among friends, Jenna found Nealy. "Rod is here," she said.

Nealy grimaced. "How is that possible?"

"He found out Barbara was coming to visit. He followed her."

Nealy called Dane over and explained the situation. "We have to do something."

He pulled his cell from his pocket. "Already dialing the chief."

"Will somebody tell me what's going on," Wyatt said.

"That guy is a reporter from LA," Dane began before switching his attention when the police chief answered.

Jenna looked beyond the pavilion but Rod had either crawled back into the darkness or left. "I have to find the girls." Jenna's voice was tinged with panic. "Did they leave yet?"

Liz Hamilton, hand in hand with the twins, came toward her. "Right here. They're safe, Jenna."

Jenna pulled them into her embrace.

"He's here?" Abby whispered.

Jenna nodded.

Bridget stepped away and looked up at Wyatt, who stood by their side. "Mr. Wyatt will protect us."

Wishing she had Bridget's childlike faith, Jenna met Wyatt's perceptive gaze. "So he's the problem you didn't want to talk about."

"Yes. I'm sorry. I didn't want to drag you into my drama."

"I think I've earned the right to decide if I want to be involved or not."

"You have, but Wyatt, this guy isn't playing games. I thought we'd left him behind."

"He's here now, so we work together to solve this problem."

Her heart pounded, with gratitude and love. One of the reasons she hadn't wanted to confide in Wyatt was that she knew his protective instincts would kick in. She admired that about him, but knew that the same quality she was drawn to could also be Wyatt's undoing, if anything happened to her or the girls.

"Thank you, but—"

"No buts. Whatever you need, I'm here."

Bridget came up beside him and took hold of Wyatt's hand. "See. He'll help us, Jenna. We aren't alone."

Is that what Bridget thought? That they were alone? "Oh, honey. I know we aren't alone. We have good friends here."

The crowd began to dwindle when the police chief joined them.

"You okay?" were Bob Gardener's first words.

"Yes. Rod didn't do anything, other than catch me off guard."

"Did he harass you? Threaten you?"

"I'd call it that. He'd call it a conversation."

The chief frowned. "He violated the original restraining order by talking to you."

"This isn't the first time. The police arrested him when I was in LA on business."

"And you didn't think to mention that fact?"

"I thought that was the end of things, but I was wrong. He's good at this, Chief. He already took off so you can't get him." She looked again in the direction where Rod had been waiting for her. "Thanks for having my back."

"Have since you first showed up." He patted her shoulder. "I'll file a report. Get this in the system. In the meantime, get yourself a lawyer. If you haven't enforced the out-of-state restraining order here in Florida, do it now."

Nealy took her hand. "Call my sister Juliet in the morning. Her law firm will take care of you."

Jenna's chest swelled. She couldn't remember having so many people rally around her when she needed them most.

"Why don't you head on home," the chief suggested. "I'll have a patrol car swing by your house on a regular rotation. If the reporter comes near you, or the girls, let me know. I'll pay him a visit."

Michelle gave Jenna a hug. "Don't worry,

I'll clean up and take the supplies back to the kitchen."

Jenna smiled. "Thanks. I really appreciate it."

"I'm coming with you," Wyatt said as she collected the girls. Before she had a chance to protest, he added, "Don't try to stop me."

She didn't.

The girls hovered around Jenna. "He won't try to run me over again, will he?" Abby asked softly.

Jenna cringed, afraid to see Wyatt's response. A few beats passed and she met his gaze, not surprised to see anger burning in the blue depths. "Meet me at the house. I'll tell you everything."

BEATING JENNA BACK to her house, Wyatt paced until she pulled the van into the driveway. He ran his hand through his hair, torn between anger and fear. How could Jenna have kept this from him? Even though Dane had quickly filled him in on the short version, Wyatt thought he and Jenna had grown close over the past weeks. Could he be so wrong?

Bridget jumped from the car, rushing to his side. "You're here."

He hunkered down before her. "You bet."

She threw herself into his arms and whispered in his ear, "Good. Jenna needs you."

Jenna's and Abby's footsteps sounded as they walked to the front door. He took Bridget's hand and led her inside. Once in the foyer, the girls scrambled to their room. Jenna headed to the kitchen, switching on the overhead light as she entered.

Wyatt leaned against the counter. "Care to explain?"

Jenna stood on the opposite side of the room. "Where do I start?"

"How about from the beginning?"

And so she did, back to the day she'd first run into Rod. How his attention, at first flattering, steamrolled into the situation she found herself in today.

"Why didn't you tell me?"

"I was embarrassed. And when he stayed in California, I thought maybe he'd lost interest. And then the cops had him for violating the restraining order."

"Guys like him don't lose interest." He frowned. "Didn't you think he'd eventually find you?"

"Of course I did," she snapped. "When we left and he never showed up, I hoped..."

"What? That he'd stay away for good?"

She curled her fingers around the chair, holding on to it for support. "Dumb, I know. More like wishful thinking."

His heart softened at her dejected expression. Jenna may have been misguided thinking this guy would leave her alone, but she'd done her best. Made major decisions all on her own. He couldn't fault her.

"I'll talk to Nealy's sister tomorrow. Have her check into enforcing the restraining order here."

"If he's as slick as you say he is, what makes you think he won't slip through the cracks? Find a way to outmaneuver the law?" He almost couldn't say the last question out loud. "What if he hurts you?"

She rubbed her fingers along her temples. "I'll figure it out."

"So you keep saying."

She bristled at his doubtful tone. "I've held him off this long. I can do it again."

"And again we go back to the fact that you can't do it alone. You have a responsibility to protect the girls."

"You think I'm not doing that? We moved to Florida to make a new life."

"But the old life caught up to you."

She grimaced. "Safety's an illusion."

He knew that for a fact.

Wyatt pushed away from the counter. "We shouldn't be arguing. We should be working to fix this."

"It's late. I'm tired. Let's revisit this in the morning."

"This isn't going away."

"I'm well aware." She turned and walked to the foyer.

"Let me stay tonight."

"Rod may be a creep, but he's a smart creep. Now that he's made his presence known, he won't do anything to draw the attention of the police." She sagged against the door. "Not tonight, anyway."

He stepped close, his arms circling her. She tensed at first, slowly melting against him. "You know I care about you, right?"

She nodded against his chest.

He brought his hands to her cheeks and tilted her head. "I won't let anything happen to you."

She blinked against a sheen of tears.

He lowered his lips to hers, brushing until she returned the gesture. They stood for a long moment, lingering in each other's arms, kissing as if there was no danger beyond the walls of this house.

Jenna was right. Safety was an illusion. But no way would Wyatt make it easy on the opposition.

THE NEXT MORNING the doorbell rang just as Jenna was pouring her second cup of coffee. She'd been up since dawn after catching a few snatches of sleep through a restless night. She shuffled to the door, peering through the side window before opening it.

"Jenna, I don't know how this happened."

Barbara swept inside, her face pale, sans makeup.

Jenna quickly closed and locked the door behind her. "Coffee?"

"Please."

By the time Jenna had the mug filled, Barbara sat at the table, her hands splayed against the wood surface. "I swear to you, I had no idea Rod would come here."

"Yeah, we all keep saying that, but he showed up anyway."

"You don't think I had anything to do with this?"

Jenna sank down in a chair opposite her agent. "Not intentionally."

"What do you mean?" Barbara's eyes narrowed.

Jenna clarified. "You did take Rod's last pet project as a client."

Barbara had the grace to look guilty. She opened her purse and dug around until she produced a roll of antacids. She peeled one off and placed it in her mouth.

"Well?"

"Pamela swore to me she was finished with him."

Jenna shot her a skeptical look.

"Okay, that was naive, even for me."

"You told her about your trip?"

"Yes. It affects her career."

Jenna sipped her coffee. An uncomfortable silence blanketed the room.

"I had to make decisions to keep the agency afloat." Barbara's voice took on a defensive edge. "When you decided to start a catering business, I panicked. Then the network started making noises about replacing your cooking show. You were far from being helpful so I did what I had to do. You certainly didn't give me much choice."

"So we're going to play the blame game?"

"What about your commitments to me? For years I put all my energies into making your career successful, if you ended our business relationship, then where would I be? I needed to take on more clients. It wasn't an easy decision signing Pamela, but I had to get the word out that I was interested in representing new talent."

Barbara frowned. "I'm sorry, Jenna. I probably should have reconsidered taking Pamela on as a client, especially in light of her relationship with Rod, but how could I say no?"

"You couldn't."

Barbara wrapped both hands around her mug. "I trusted Pamela when she said she was through with Rod. He was starting the same nonsense he pulled with you. She was getting scared, wanted to break free from him. I never thought booking a few jobs for her would cause Rod to head straight to you."

"It's not like he couldn't find out where I was."

"You shouldn't have had to try to hide it."

"In a perfect world."

Barbara met her gaze. "What will you do?"

"Depends on Rod's next move. If he violates the restraining order, Police Chief Gardener will throw him behind bars and it'll give us more ammunition to use against him in court."

"Can I do anything?"

"No. I have people…friends here to help me."

Barbara pushed back the chair and rose. "I don't know what to say. I put you in danger. I'm sorry."

"You didn't do it on purpose."

"So where do we go from here?"

"Honestly, Barbara, I'm not sure."

The older woman blinked. "Are you firing me?"

Jenna shook her head. "No. I just need some time. You understand."

"Yes. I…" Barbara clutched her purse and took a step away from the table. "I have a plane to catch."

"Then you don't want to be late."

They walked to the door.

"Text me when you get back," Jenna said.

"I will. And I promise to make this up to you."

Jenna didn't think she could, but knew Barbara needed to try.

"Why don't you make sure things are still good with the network. I don't need any more surprises."

Barbara's shoulders straightened. "I can handle that assignment."

When she moved in for a hug, Jenna backed up.

"Okay then. I'll be in touch."

After her agent left, Jenna leaned back against the door. Logically she knew Barbara hadn't brought Rod with her. But taking on a client associated with Rod? She hadn't been looking out for Jenna's best interests, only her own. She didn't know what the future held for them professionally, but right now she had more pressing matters to worry about.

CHAPTER FOURTEEN

AFTER ROD'S UNEXPECTED visit at the engagement party, Wyatt stuck close to Jenna and the girls, which Jenna admired. And he did make her feel safe, but he had to have a life. One that didn't include babysitting her family. If he wasn't at the house, then the girls were at his cottage when Jenna worked. Although she was grateful for all the support, she'd grown testy over her every move being monitored.

Through the grapevine, Jenna learned that Rod had unleashed his slimy sort of charm on the townsfolk while managing to keep out of sight of the police. Thankfully, the entire town rallied around Jenna and wouldn't give the reporter one iota of information.

She wasn't sleeping well. Every time she looked in the mirror, she cringed. Dark circles lined her eyes. Her complexion had turned pasty, despite being in and out of the Florida sun. On top of that, she became short-tempered with the girls at home and Michelle at work. The twins noticed her stress, but had their own anxiety over Rod's arrival to deal with. They stayed out of Jenna's way, spending more and more time with Wyatt. Once again circumstances out of her control infringed on her relationship with the twins. She hated seeing their haunted faces, and her reassurances didn't offer much relief.

On the following Monday, she got the girls ready for school. Jenna had stuck with their normal routine for all their sakes. Dressed for work in her chef uniform, she rushed into the kitchen to pour coffee in her travel cup when she bumped into Wyatt, who'd come over early to make pancakes. He stood at the sink, rinsing off the breakfast dishes.

"Excuse me." The words whooshed out of her as she made to walk around him.

"Are the girls ready to leave?"

"Wyatt, I can drop them off at school."

"It's on my route to the marina. I need to stop by and handle a problem with the boat."

"Why don't you go ahead? We're going in a few minutes."

"I don't want to leave you alone."

The tension between her and Wyatt had grown steadily all week. Jenna knew it wouldn't be pretty when it erupted.

"We'll be fine."

"I can't take the chance."

"*You* can't—" She closed her eyes, counted to ten, then met his gaze. "Wyatt, please go work on your boat."

"It'll only take a few minutes to drop the girls off."

"Did you think that maybe I want some time with them? All week you've spirited them off somewhere safe. I've hardly seen them."

"You have a problem with my methods?"

"I don't think smothering us is—"

"Right, because you've managed the Rod problem so well yourself."

Ouch. A direct blow to her self-confidence.

Wyatt ran a hand over his bristly chin. "Sorry, I didn't mean to say that."

"Sure you did. I bet you've been waiting for the chance to tell me I blew it as a parent."

"No, it's just…I didn't protect Jamie. I don't want to see you wrestle with the same guilt if something happens."

"I've talked to the police. They're looking out for us."

"It's not enough."

"Wyatt, you can't be with us 24/7. Stop hovering."

"Not as long as that loser is in town. I wouldn't feel right not watching out for you."

Did his stubbornness know no bounds? "I get how you feel about protecting us, but we aren't yours to worry about."

His face went slack and his eyes turned dark.

Jenna immediately felt contrite. "Now it's my turn to apologize."

"No, you've made your point. I'm not your family."

She waited, hoping he'd say, *but I want you to be.*

When he did speak, his words were tight. "I guess I overstepped."

"This situation is bringing out the worst in all of us."

"Is the chief making any strides in finding the guy?"

"No. I told you, Rod knows how to skirt the law."

An uncomfortable silence settled around them. Finally, Wyatt grabbed his keys from the counter. "Call me if you want me to come by later."

She knew Wyatt took protecting them seriously, but without a solid commitment from him, she had to wonder if he was merely acting out of a sense of duty. The knowledge hurt her in a deep place.

When she didn't answer, he quietly left the house, which made her feel ten times more ungrateful. Rubbing the nearly constant ache in her temple, she filled her mug with coffee and switched off the machine.

"Hop to it, girls. We're running late."

Abby strolled into the kitchen as Jenna was disconnecting her phone from the charger.

"I'm ready. Bridget is brushing her teeth."

Jenna set her phone on the counter, bending down to kiss the top of Abby's head. "Have I told you lately how awesome you are?"

Abby giggled, her first positive reaction in a week. "You're just saying that because you have to."

"I don't have to."

"Yes you do. Moms say that kind of stuff all the time."

Jenna smiled at Abby, blinking back tears that were forming way too easily lately. "Maybe, but I mean every word."

Abby hugged her. "Don't worry about us."

Jenna hugged her back. "Definitely part of my job."

"I love you."

Jenna swallowed hard. "Love you too."

By this time, Bridget shuffled into the kitchen, dragging her backpack behind her. She frowned at Jenna. "You aren't crying again, are you?"

Jenna laughed, swiping her eyes. "Me? Of course not."

Bridget glanced at Abby. "Yeah, right."

Jenna started to laugh. Soon the girls joined in.

"Oh my, that felt good."

"We'd better leave," Abby reminded her.

"Okay, let me get—"

The doorbell rang, cutting off Jenna's thought.

"Maybe Mr. Wyatt forgot something." Bridget raced to the door.

"Bridget, wait. Don't open—"

Too late. The door swung open, revealing Rod, leaning against the porch post, his ever-present camera draped over his chest, a camera bag in his hand. "Good morning, ladies."

Bridget took a second too long to respond. By the time she tried to slam the door, Rod already had a palm out to stop it. She turned and ran to the kitchen as he stepped inside, closing the door behind him.

Jenna reached for her cell to call 911, but

Rod dropped his bag, and snatched the phone away from her.

Having lost her advantage, Jenna raised her chin, though she felt anything but confident. The girls huddled behind her.

"At last. A few minutes alone with my favorite family."

"Rod, leave. Right now."

"And miss having a conversation with you?" His eyes went dark. "I don't think so."

"What do you want?"

"What I always want. An exclusive."

"Fine. Get your story and leave."

He shook his head and tsked. "Not so fast." He crouched down to observe the girls. "You're both getting bigger. Have you missed me?"

Poking her head around Jenna's hip, Bridget hissed, "No!"

"Shame. I'd hoped I could make up for the last time we saw each other."

"I don't want you here," Abby told him, her voice shaky.

He glanced at Jenna as he rose. "I see the girls haven't forgiven me."

"Why would they? You brought it on yourself when you nearly ran over Abby."

He waved her off. "C'mon. You know I

didn't mean to hurt anyone. Getting that re-straining order was uncalled for."

Jenna shook her head. "You're delusional."

A spark flared in Rod's eyes. "We'll see how delusional I am after I get my exclusive."

"Not from us."

He picked up his camera bag, and drew out a pistol. "That's where you're wrong. I've arranged a nice roomy car for our trip back to LA."

A gun? What were they going to do now? Jenna kept up the false bravado. "We aren't going anywhere with you."

"See, that's your problem. Always trying to ruin my plans."

Jenna pushed the girls more securely be-hind her.

"Rod. We aren't leaving. We live here now."

"No. You don't."

How did she reason with him? She had to think of a way to stop him.

"Rod, take a few pictures. Tell readers we're fine. Living the good life in sunny Florida."

"Not good enough." He motioned to the door. "Get in the car."

What should she do? If she were alone, she could bolt, take a risk, but she had to protect the girls.

Bridget poked her head out again. "We have school. We can't go with you."

Rod chuckled. "So conscientious."

"Let the girls go to school. It's not like we're ready for a long trip. I have to…pack. Close up the house."

He waved the gun. "Clever, but no. Move."

As one unit, Jenna and the girls inched to the door. Once there, Jenna said, "Wait. You came all this distance and you're leaving without part of the story."

"What part?"

"The most important part. My new business. Let the girls go to school. I'll give you a tour of my new catering office. You know readers will eat it up."

Jenna watched as he stopped to consider her request. A slow smile curved his lips. "You may be on to something. Chronicling each location of our trip, starting here. Brilliant." The smile disappeared. "But the girls aren't going anywhere. You think I'll let them around anyone they can tattle to? No, they can stay here."

"Rod, they've never stayed home alone. I don't think—"

"Shut up, Jenna."

He gazed around the hallway, focusing on the closet. He gestured to Bridget. "Get in."

Jenna gave her a small push to get her to move. Abby tried to follow, but Rod stopped her.

"No way you two are staying together."

Once Bridget stepped inside, Rod closed the door. He stormed into the kitchen, grabbed hold of a kitchen chair and came back to jam it under the knob to make sure Bridget couldn't escape.

Rod grabbed hold of Abby's collar and dragged her down the hallway. Jenna tried to stop him, but he forcefully pushed her away. She lost her balance, giving Rod time to presumably imprison Abby in Jenna's bedroom closet.

Taking advantage of the moment, Jenna ran to the living room for the cordless phone. The neighborhood was quiet, most people at work and the kids at school, so she desperately dialed 911.

She had just started punching numbers when Rod caught hold of her shoulder and viciously yanked her backward. Stumbling, Jenna fell against him, dropping the phone. "Rod, stop. This is crazy."

"Not as crazy as what's going to happen later."

She tried to shake him off as he dragged

her outside to his car. He rounded to the driver side, pushing her in and then climbing in after her.

"What about the girls? You locked the girls up in the house."

"They'll be fine. Someone will find them eventually."

An icy chill ran through her. "What does that mean?"

"I'm going to get my tour. Then we're leaving town."

"But what about the twins?"

He scowled at her. "Too much trouble."

At the lack of emotion in his voice, Jenna's heart sank. *Think. Think.* She could only pray the girls would be okay until she figured out a way to get back to them. Her mind raced with ideas as Rod drove.

He pulled into the back alley and parked. After yanking Jenna from the car, he jabbed the gun into her side as he opened the door to the catering kitchen.

"Wait. Why is the door unlocked?"

"I stopped here first. Checked the place out. You don't think this is my first rodeo."

Jenna closed her eyes. Here she thought she'd been so smart but he already had his agenda in play.

"Move it."

She tripped over the step, nearly falling face-first into the kitchen. In her mind, she kept hearing, *play along. Pretend to do what he wants.* Okay, she could do that.

She took a deep breath, willing herself to remain calm. "This is the commercial kitchen."

Rod nodded. "Nice." He brought up his camera and began snapping shots. "I can see your stamp all over the space."

"Um…" She waved him into the next part of the building. "An area for clients, my office and sample tasting room."

Rod took shot after shot. Jenna thought about running off more than once, but the threat of the gun kept her from trying. She didn't want to make Rod angry enough to shoot.

After a few more minutes, he lowered the camera. They moved back into the kitchen. "I think I have enough. Anything else for me to see?"

She desperately tried to think of some way to stall. Her gaze fell on the freezer. "You know, there is. I remember you loved my recipe for chicken and dumplings. I made some for a party this weekend. The tray is in the freezer."

A smug grin curved his lips. "Lead on."

Jenna's heart raced. She pulled the screwdriver from the latch and placed it on the nearby shelf. Opening the door, she asked, "Can you help me? The tray is pretty big."

"Sure." He loosened the camera strap, laid his priceless possession on the prep table, but kept the gun in his hand.

Jenna pushed aside the vinyl curtain to lead him inside. "Over there."

When Rod came to her side, she pointed to the tray. "That's the one."

"Doesn't look heavy. You pick it up."

Jenna bit her lip and bent over to lift the tray, but at the last minute, she grabbed the side of the shelf and tugged. The whole unit toppled, hitting Rod in the shoulder, causing him to stagger and drop the gun. Before he could right himself and pick up the weapon, Jenna raced to the door and jumped outside, slamming it shut. Grabbing the screwdriver, she jammed it in the lock. Rod banged on the door from the inside, bellowing to be let out. She fell back against the cold steel, heart pounding as she tried to steady her jagged breathing.

WYATT JUMPED FROM the bow onto the dock when his cell rang. He glanced at the screen, frowning when he saw Jenna's number.

"Everyone okay?"

At first he heard rapid breathing, then a small voice. "Mr. Wyatt?"

His chest seized. "Bridget?"

"You gotta save Jenna."

"Bridget, what happened?"

"That mean guy with the camera came here. To our house. Took Jenna."

"Do you know where he took her?"

He heard soft voices speaking. "We think to the catering kitchen."

"Are you two okay?"

"Yes. Just scared."

"I'll call my mom to come over and stay with you, okay? Lock the doors until she gets there. Right now I'm going for Jenna."

"Hurry," she whispered.

Wyatt ran down the pier to the parking lot. His chest tight and his mind racing, he hit the button to speed dial his mother.

"Wyatt. Calling on a workday? I—"

"Mom. I need your help." He explained the situation.

"I'll drop everything and head straight to Jenna's."

"Thanks, Mom."

He tossed the phone on the passenger seat as he jumped into the truck, peeling out of the marina at top speed. He didn't have far to go, but it seemed to take an eternity.

He'd known in his bones this morning that something wasn't right. Couldn't put his finger on it, so he brushed off the feeling. He never should have let Jenna insist he leave without making sure she and the girls got off safely first. If anything happened… He wouldn't fall into worst-case-scenario mode. Jenna was smart. Had dealt with this guy before. She could take care of herself.

But if he lost her? He couldn't begin to fathom what that would be like. She'd given him a reason to tackle his grief and move forward to a tentative peace. Why hadn't he told her how much she meant to him instead of arguing with her? He'd never wanted to live through this kind of fear again, yet here he was, tightly holding the dread at bay.

As he raced down Main Street, he slammed on the brakes to avoid the police car angled at the curb in front of the catering office. Double parking, he jumped from the car just as Jenna burst through the door to the catering business, the chief fast on her heels with Rod in handcuffs. Once she saw Wyatt, she ran to him, falling into his arms.

"Take me to the girls. They're alone. I have to make sure—"

"Jenna, listen. I called my mother. She's almost there now."

"But, how did you know?"

"Bridget called."

She sagged against him.

"Are you okay?" he said against her soft hair.

Her breath came in short bursts, but she nodded.

He held her away from him, searching for signs of injury. When he couldn't spot any, he framed her pale face in his hands. "What happened?"

In stops and starts, Jenna related what had transpired. Wyatt listened, shocked at the lengths the reporter had gone to get Jenna alone, appalled that she had to live through the experience. The fear that had taken hold since Bridget's call intensified with each word.

"But you aren't hurt?"

"Shook up, but not hurt."

He rested his forehead against hers, thankful for her safety. When he could finally speak, he said, "I can't believe I left you this morning."

"I didn't give you much choice."

"I take off and you get yourself into all kinds of trouble."

She hiccupped a laugh.

He pulled back. Searched her face. "I wasn't there for you."

"No, but you came up with the idea of the screwdriver to lock the freezer door. Once I lured Rod inside, I escaped and trapped him in."

He blinked. "You're amazing.'

"So are you."

He couldn't wait any longer. He kissed her hard, mainly to assure himself she was really here, really okay. She returned the kiss, wrapping her arms around him as if she'd never let go. But with the kiss came reality.

He could have lost her.

He broke the kiss and took a step back. The fear dissipated, followed by wanting. He'd let her down big-time, which he'd have to live with. What he didn't know was if he could live with the worry that came from loving another person again. He'd gone through the agony of losing Jamie. His world had collapsed when his son died. How could he give himself to Jenna when there was a chance he could lose her? Or the girls?

"I have to get to the twins," she whispered, her eyes moist. "They need me."

In his haste to hold Jenna, he'd almost forgotten about the girls. "Of course. C'mon. My truck is parked by the curb."

Doing everything he could to keep to the speed limit, Wyatt got her home quickly. He remained silent as he drove, his mind working overtime. The wall that had begun to crumble around his heart in the past weeks reassembled. He allowed the welcome shell of numbness to surround him as the reality of their situation struck home. He couldn't do this again. No matter how much he'd come to love Jenna. It had taken him this long to figure it out, but the honest truth was before him.

CHAPTER FIFTEEN

IN THE DAYS that followed, all of Jenna's friends, now her extended family, stopped by to visit, bringing food and comfort. The chief had arrested Rod, charging him with multiple felony offenses that would keep him out of the picture for a long time. While she should have been relieved that the nightmare was over, Wyatt's glaring absence didn't go unnoticed.

She had sensed his withdrawal as soon as he'd dropped her at the end of the driveway after the fateful morning with Rod. Wyatt had given her the excuse that she needed time alone with the girls, to reassure them everything would be fine now.

She would have welcomed him by her side as she explained to Bridget and Abby what had happened with Rod and listened as Bridget told her how she kept pushing against the closet door until the chair locking her in fell over and she got free. He'd been with them when they needed him most, so why wouldn't he want to be here now?

Bridget asked for him, crestfallen when Jenna didn't know his whereabouts or why he hadn't come to see them. She needed to know what was going on with him as much as the girls.

Unable to take the suspense any longer, she arranged for Nealy to watch the girls for a few hours while she went in search of answers. If Wyatt wouldn't come to her, she'd go to him. She'd learned he had a charter today and planned on meeting him when he got back. They were overdue for this conversation.

By the time she got to the marina, the sun hung high in the sky, the temperatures hovering in the high eighties. She'd dressed in a simple yellow tank top with denim shorts, sunglasses protecting her eyes, her flip-flops slapping the wooden dock as she strode to his boat. She passed a group of laughing, sunburned men, probably Wyatt's clients. Good, it meant Wyatt was free to talk to her.

He'd just jumped from the bow to the pier when Jenna approached. His ball cap cast shadows over his face, but she savored the sight of him in his work T-shirt and cargo shorts. When he saw her, he visibly tensed.

Wonderful. She stopped before him, trying for a relaxed pose, though she felt anything but. "So, the girls and I were wondering where you've been. Last week we couldn't get rid of you. Now you're like the invisible man."

"I had some catching up to do."

"Really. All day and night? You couldn't fit us in?"

He took the cap from his head and slapped it against his thigh. Gazed out over the water. Long moments passed. "I haven't been by on purpose."

"I figured."

"Look, I think it's best if we take a breather. Not spend time together."

Her stomach knotted. She'd secretly expected this, but the reality hurt. "And why would that be?"

"After all the drama the other day, it was like the accident with Jamie all over again. I knew I never should have agreed to leave you that morning. I knew you were in danger from the reporter and I walked away. It was reckless and—"

"Wyatt, it wasn't your fault."

"Just like Jamie's death wasn't my fault? His death shattered my illusion that I could control anything. Protect anyone. Life is fragile,

Jenna. I don't know if I can risk my heart by loving someone again. When Bridget called and told me Rod had you…" He stopped. Gathered himself before continuing. "I flashed to the same scared, helpless feeling I experienced when Jamie was swept off the boat. I don't want to live like that again."

"But we're safe now."

"Until something else happens."

"Yes, stuff happens, Wyatt, but we can weather anything. Together." She stepped forward, taking a bracing breath. She either told him her feelings now or walked away forever with the words unsaid. "I love you."

He recoiled. She tried not to let his response wound her, but it did.

"The girls love you, too. I think we have the start of something good here."

He went still. Closed his eyes. "I'm sorry, Jenna. I can't do this. I can't take the chance."

Jenna's heart shattered. She'd hoped Wyatt could love her, hoped he could overcome the hold his son's death had over him. But she was wrong. Oh so very wrong.

Without any further words, Jenna turned to walk back to her car. Wyatt had made up his mind. The past had too tight a grip on him. Didn't matter that Jenna loved him.

He wasn't willing to fight for them and she couldn't compel him to do otherwise. He'd chosen to live with the fear instead of living with her love.

Once she got to the parking lot, she decided she couldn't go home yet. How was she going to explain to the girls that Wyatt no longer wanted to be a part of their family? How would Bridget react to another person she loved disappearing from her life?

Knowing she didn't have the answers, and pretty broken up herself, she went toward the beach. Head spinning, she kicked off her flip-flops and ambled through the warm surf, aimlessly tromping along the water's edge. The hot sun baked her shoulders. A fine sheen of perspiration bathed her face. When a seagull dive-bombed for a piece of food near her, she didn't jump away.

No, all she focused on was the fact Wyatt didn't want her. Would it have been different if they'd met under other circumstances? If he'd been further along in his grief process? Or did he simply not love Jenna? It made sense, really. He'd come so far, yet her troubles had set him back. How could he love her?

In her short time in Cypress Pointe, she'd almost gotten the life she'd longed for. A fam-

ily made up of good friends, if not blood rela-
tives. Raising the girls in a happy environment.
She'd fallen heart and soul for a good man.
And still, the dream was just out of her reach.
At this rate, she'd probably never attain it.
Now, she wouldn't bother trying.

"Oh, Carrie," she whispered, missing her
late friend so much it increased the ache surrounding her heart. "What do I do now? How
do I get through this?"

She needed answers, but received silence
instead. Carrie would have had the right advice, would probably tell Jenna to cut her
losses. Find a different man, start a new relationship.

But in her heart, Jenna knew there was no
better guy for her than Wyatt.

Okay, so he didn't love her. She'd make do.
She always did. She'd throw herself into work
and loving the girls. They needed her and she
certainly needed them. Carrie had entrusted
the girls with her. From now on, they had her
full and total attention. If Wyatt didn't want to
be a part of their life, it was his loss.

THREE WEEKS. THREE long weeks without seeing them.

Wyatt missed the girls. All of them.

He missed Jenna's sunny smile and sense of humor. Her kisses made him come alive. He missed the way she looked at him, a combination of empathy and kindness. Missed their conversations as well as their arguments. Mostly, Wyatt missed her strength and her quiet conviction that he was indeed a whole man.

He missed Bridget hanging on to his every word, as well as her small, trusting hand in his. He missed Abby's shy insistence that he join them in whatever adventure they embarked on, sure he'd watch their backs.

If he'd been able to tackle his fears, he wouldn't be missing the family they'd almost become. But that hadn't happened, and he'd now lost something very dear to him. Hope for the future.

Trudging from the marina, he felt a weariness dogging his steps. Lately, all he did was work on the boat, barely slept or ate. Loss gnawed at him every waking hour. Was this what he had in store for the remainder of his years? Nothing but sorrow? Always asking what if?

While his decision to stay away from Jenna had been a needed separation at first, lately he wondered if his stubbornness was ruining his life. Could he take a chance? Start again with Jenna? Bridget? Abby? Just when he thought maybe he could handle a future with them, the ever-present grief would come rushing in like a mighty wave, the emotional undertow dragging away all his good intentions.

He unlocked the door to the cottage, dodging an antsy Cruiser as he entered. He took the dog out for a brief run then returned, heading straight to the bathroom. A long, hot shower would remove the sticky saltwater residue and sweat on his skin, along with any emotion he had left. He'd made his decision, now he had to live with the consequences.

Fifteen minutes later, he donned a clean T-shirt and shorts. He got a glass of cold water and wandered into the den. Froze at the sight before him.

Scattered about the couch and table were tangible reminders of what he'd closed the door on. Jenna's favorite sweater, the one she insisted on wearing when they went out to eat because the restaurant air-conditioning was too cold. She'd left it here the last time they were together. He picked it up to run his fingers over the cotton, stirring up the scent of her floral perfume.

Bridget's notebook, open to a page of neatly

lined numbers. On closer inspection, he remembered the day she'd needed help with multiplication tables. He'd taught her a neat trick to remember the order of the numbers.

His gaze moved from the notebook to settle on Abby's favorite princess doll. She'd perched right on this couch, making up a fanciful story about a prince's honor when it came to his lady love. He'd laughed at the time, only now realizing Abby had meant for him to be the prince, Jenna his lady love. He'd sure destroyed that fairy tale.

He needed to get these things back to them. As he gathered up the belongings, he noticed a small blanket folded neatly on the back of the couch. Jamie's blanket.

His eyes began to water. How had this happened? His past and his future, mixed up together. He brought the blanket to his face, inhaling. The little boy scent he always associated with Jamie was gone. Just like his hopes and dreams of a future raising his son.

Cruiser lay at his feet, softly whining. Wyatt crouched down, absently rubbing his head. "What am I gonna do, boy?"

When Cruiser remained silent, Wyatt finally set the blanket down with the rest of the treasures he'd collected. He stared for a long time, until slowly, the heaviness lifted from his chest. He imagined his son, smiling at him, telling him to let go. *I'm fine, dad*, he would have said. And for the first time, Wyatt believed.

AFTER DINNER, JENNA and the girls had just finished rearranging the living room furniture when the doorbell rang. "Are we expecting anyone?"

"Nope," Abby answered.

Bridget shrugged.

Tousling Bridget's hair as she passed by, Jenna couldn't help but consider the girls' well-being again.

The past few weeks had been tough emotionally. She'd been incredibly relieved to have Nealy's friendship. Their late-night girl talk had never been more necessary.

With additional catering events booked, and Max and Lilli's upcoming wedding, she kept her mind busy. In a surprising move, the cable network had come up with the idea of filming her catering business as a limited-run reality show. Barbara was in negotiations now. Her career was in full swing again.

Too bad her personal life stunk.

She opened the door, her smile slipping when she glimpsed Wyatt standing on the porch.

"Wyatt, what are you doing here?"

From the living room, she heard Bridget. "Mr. Wyatt's here?"

Bridget joined her, hugging her waist as she looked up at Wyatt before noticing the dog. "Cruiser!"

"Bridget." He grinned when Abby came around the corner. "Abby."

"Jenna said you didn't want to see us," Bridget said.

He met Jenna's gaze. "I told Jenna a lot of things."

"So then why are you here?"

He held up a plastic bag. Cruiser barked. "You left some of your things at my cottage. I came to return them."

The small hope flickering in Jenna's heart fizzled out. He didn't want any reminder of them at his place. She held out her hand. "Thanks. You could have had Dane bring these things back to us."

"I could have, but I wanted to talk to you."

She passed the bag to Abby. "Would you take this into the house?"

"Sure." Abby took the bag and silently

turned away. Bridget glared at Wyatt before turning on her heel.

When Cruiser whimpered, Jenna pointed in the direction of the hallway. The dog took off after the girls.

Jenna crossed her arms over her chest. "Now, what is it you wanted to say?"

"Can I come in?"

"Why bother?"

He chuckled. The unforgettable sound made her chest ache. "Please."

After silently debating the idea, she stepped back to let him enter. He strode into the living room. "Redecorating?"

She shrugged.

He ran a hand over his chin, a familiar gesture when Wyatt was stressed. "You aren't going to make this easy."

"No. I'm not."

He blew out a breath. "Fair enough."

She waited.

"I was picking up around the cottage when it occurred to me I have a problem."

She arched her brow.

"You see, I had all these things from you and the girls scattered around. I realized I liked having your belongings with me. And when

I found Jamie's blanket among your stuff, it made me realize something important."

Jenna dropped her arms. She might be angry at how he'd broken her heart, but she understood how hard mingling the past and present could be.

"I panicked, Jenna. Thought I wasn't strong enough to have you in my life."

"And now?"

"Now I can't imagine a life without you." He cleared his throat, got down on one knee.

Her hands flew to her mouth.

"It might be too soon. You might tell me to hit the road, but I have to ask. Will you allow me to be a part of your life? Can we be a family, or did I blow it for good?"

Was this really happening? Wyatt down on one knee? Out of the corner of her eye she saw the arrangement of fresh honeysuckle she'd picked that morning. Gathering the flowers in her hands, just as a bride would, she sank down on her knees before him. If they were going to be a family, she was meeting him halfway.

He ran a finger over her cheek. "I love you."

She trembled at his touch, as well as his words. "I love you, too."

He leaned over, brushing a gentle kiss over

her lips. She melted into him, overcome by his change of heart. His whole heart.

She slipped her arms around his neck and dropped the bouquet, scattering the fragrant blossoms around them. She fell into his embrace, returning his kiss with all the love she had inside her. He must have understood her fervent response, because he held her like she was the only thing keeping him alive. She could relate. She'd felt like a shell of her former self when he'd said goodbye.

Before she had a chance to say yes to his proposal about spending a life together, footsteps racing down the hallway sounded behind her. Wyatt broke the kiss, a question in his eyes.

The girls, and Cruiser, skidded into the room, coming to a halt when they saw Jenna in Wyatt's embrace. The adults rose and only then did Jenna notice the package in Bridget's hands.

"Oreos?"

Wyatt nodded. "A peace offering."

"You brought us cookies?"

"Not just any cookies," Bridget blurted. "He doesn't share his Oreos with just anyone."

Jenna grinned. "Wyatt, you're saying we're special?"

"I'm saying I want to spend the rest of my life sharing cookies with all of you."

She twined her fingers in his. "It's a date."

* * * * *

LARGER-PRINT BOOKS!

GET 2 FREE
LARGER-PRINT NOVELS
PLUS 2 FREE
MYSTERY GIFTS

Love Inspired

Larger-print novels are now available...

YES! Please send me 2 FREE LARGER-PRINT Love Inspired® novels and my 2 FREE mystery gifts (gifts are worth about $10). After receiving them, if I don't wish to receive any more books, I can return the shipping statement marked "cancel." If I don't cancel, I will receive 6 brand-new novels every month and be billed just $5.24 per book in the U.S. or $5.74 per book in Canada. That's a savings of at least 23% off the cover price. It's quite a bargain! Shipping and handling is just 50¢ per book in the U.S. and 75¢ per book in Canada.* I understand that accepting the 2 free books and gifts places me under no obligation to buy anything. I can always return a shipment and cancel at any time. Even if I never buy another book, the two free books and gifts are mine to keep forever.

122/322 IDN F49Y

Name _____ (PLEASE PRINT) _____

Address _____ Apt. # _____

City _____ State/Prov. _____ Zip/Postal Code _____

Signature (if under 18, a parent or guardian must sign) _____

Mail to the Harlequin® Reader Service:
IN U.S.A.: P.O. Box 1867, Buffalo, NY 14240-1867
IN CANADA: P.O. Box 609, Fort Erie, Ontario L2A 5X3

**Are you a current subscriber to Love Inspired books
and want to receive the larger-print edition?
Call 1-800-873-8635 or visit www.ReaderService.com.**

* Terms and prices subject to change without notice. Prices do not include applicable taxes. Sales tax applicable in N.Y. Canadian residents will be charged applicable taxes. Offer not valid in Quebec. This offer is limited to one order per household. Not valid for current subscribers to Love Inspired Larger-Print books. All orders subject to credit approval. Credit or debit balances in a customer's account(s) may be offset by any other outstanding balance owed by or to the customer. Please allow 4 to 6 weeks for delivery. Offer available while quantities last.

Your Privacy—The Harlequin® Reader Service is committed to protecting your privacy. Our Privacy Policy is available online at www.ReaderService.com or upon request from the Harlequin Reader Service.

We make a portion of our mailing list available to reputable third parties that offer products we believe may interest you. If you prefer that we not exchange your name with third parties, or if you wish to clarify or modify your communication preferences, please visit us at www.ReaderService.com/consumerchoice or write to us at Harlequin Reader Service Preference Service, P.O. Box 9062, Buffalo, NY 14269. Include your complete name and address.

LILPDIR13R

ReaderService.com

Manage your account online!

- Review your order history
- Manage your payments
- Update your address

We've designed the Harlequin® Reader Service website just for you.

Enjoy all the features!

- Reader excerpts from any series
- Respond to mailings and special monthly offers
- Discover new series available to you
- Browse the Bonus Bucks catalog
- Share your feedback

Visit us at:
ReaderService.com

RS13